Upcoming Titles in the Warrior Prophets series:

Ehud: Assassin
Ruth: Ancestress

Other books by Ben-Tzion Spitz

Biblical Fiction:

Destiny's Call: Book One – Genesis
Destiny's Call: Book Two – Exodus

Non-fiction:

Jewish Adventure in Modern China:
Amusing Insights on a Serious Story

For a complete collection of the author's articles and stories, visit his website at http://ben-tzion.com

Warrior Prophets
Joshua: Conqueror

Book One of the Boaz Trilogy

Ben-Tzion Spitz

Valiant Publishing

Warrior Prophets

Joshua: Conqueror

Book One of the Boaz Trilogy

Valiant Publishing, 123 Grove Avenue, Suite 208
Cedarhurst, New York 11516-2033, USA

info@valiantpublishing.com

Website: valiantpublishing.com
Author's blog: ben-tzion.com
For schools or bulk orders, contact the author directly at:
bentzispitz@gmail.com
First Edition

1 3 5 7 9 10 8 6 4 2

ISBN 978-1-937623-20-3

Map illustration: Rachel Nachmani

To Eitan, Akiva, Elchanan, Netanel, Yehoshua, Yehuda and Tiferet.

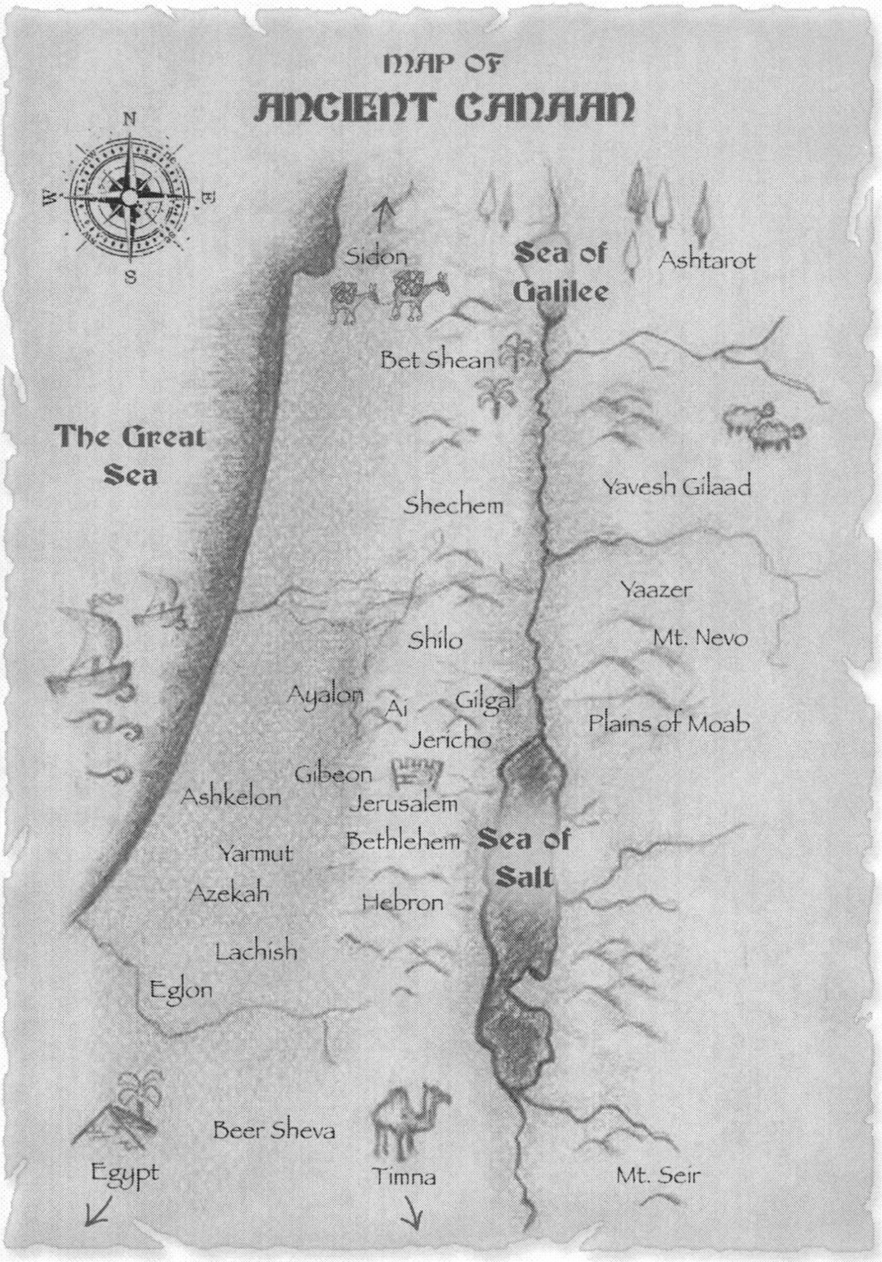

MAP OF

ANCIENT CANAAN

Sidon

Sea of Galilee

Ashtarot

Bet Shean

The Great Sea

Shechem

Yavesh Gilaad

Yaazer

Shilo

Mt. Nevo

Ayalon

Ai

Gilgal

Jericho

Plains of Moab

Gibeon

Ashkelon

Jerusalem

Bethlehem

Sea of Salt

Yarmut

Azekah

Hebron

Lachish

Eglon

Beer Sheva

Egypt

Timna

Mt. Seir

Genealogical Chart: Leadership Clans of Israel

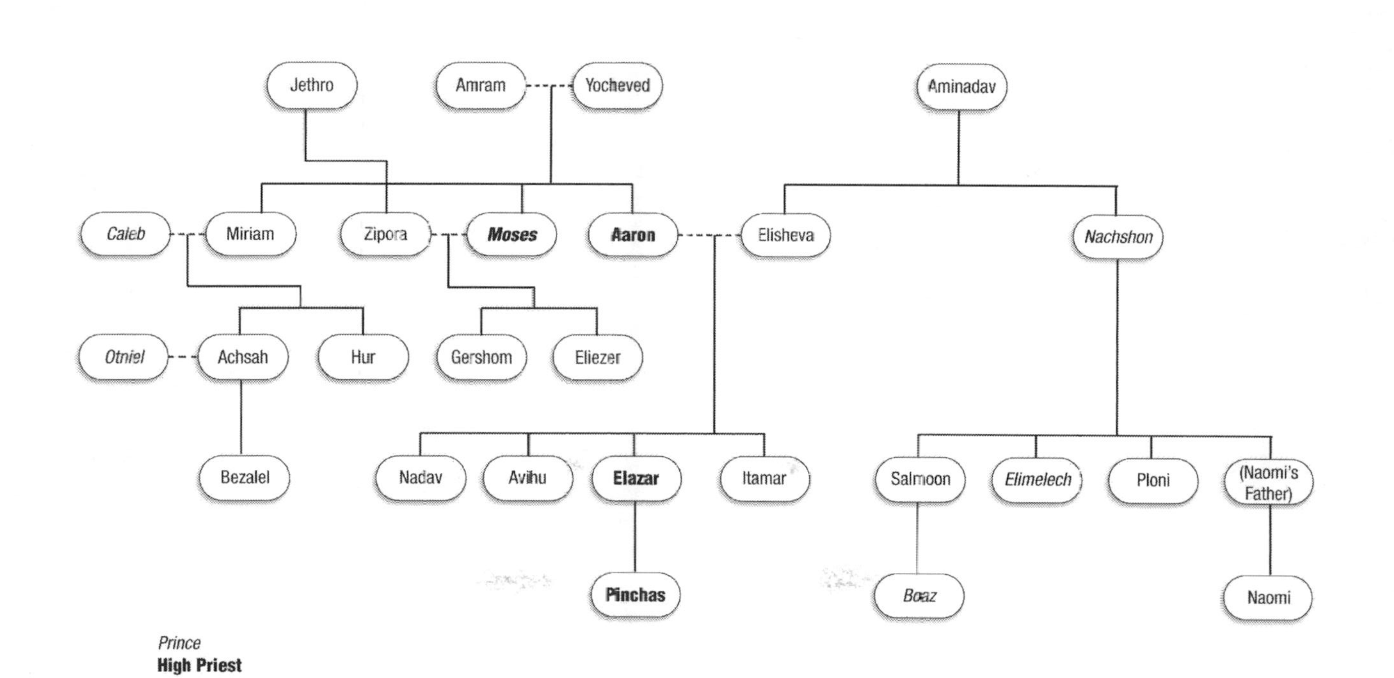

Table of Contents

Introduction

The mighty Egyptian Empire lay in ruins. Its produce and livestock had been wiped out by the plagues. Its army, with its hundreds of chariots, lay at the bottom of the Reed Sea. Only the scarred pyramids and the burnt temples remained to hint at the glory that was once Egypt.

All blamed the Israelites and their warrior God. That slave nation, millions strong, had gathered from every corner of Egypt. Israelite brick-makers, harvesters, bakers, blacksmiths, architects and shepherds took whatever possessions they could carry and left. A sea of slaves, fifty men wide and miles long, marched out of the once-great city of Ramses. They went through the desert. They went on dry land within the Sea of Reeds to the astonishment of all who beheld the waters part.

They received the Law of their God at the Mount of Sinai. Under the leadership of Moses, they trekked through the harsh desert on their way to conquer the Land of Canaan, the land promised to their forefathers.

But that generation was a generation of slaves. They were fearful. They were frightened. They were of weak faith. And so, their harsh God punished them. He cursed them to wander the desert for forty years, until a new generation of Israelites arose. A generation that was strong, a generation filled with faith, a generation that would have the stomach to fight the Canaanites in their walled cities.

And so Moses prepared to hand the reins of leadership to Joshua, his disciple. The Canaanites would fall to the disciple of Moses, together with his army of six hundred thousand soldiers. But the Israelites were not the only invaders of Canaan. While the Children of Israel attacked Canaan from the east, a new threat rose from the west.

Fleeing from the chaos of the Aegean, sea-faring peoples traversed the Great Sea and raided the coast of Canaan. City after Canaanite city would fall to these invaders. They brought strong weapons and new gods to the sandy shores of Canaan. These fearsome warriors were called Philistines. And so, these two peoples, Philistine and Israelite, though they had never heard of each other before, would one day clash, for they had only one goal in common: Conquest.

1. Saga of the Beard

From the diary of Boaz the Bethlehemite, Elder of the Tribe of Judah. The sixty-eighth year since the Tribes of Israel crossed the River Jordan into Canaan.

My first memories are of the dun colors of the desert and of a sea of tents. Hundreds of thousands of tents organized in neat rows in the craggy, dusky landscape. I remember the golden earth-brown of the sand, peppered with dark flecks, the reddish color of the boulders and stones, silent as soldiers. I remember the knotted, scratchy burlap clothing and the furry brown animal hides stretched tight over poles. The tents were grouped by tribes. Twelve large, proud tribes surrounded the inner encampment of the Levites and the grand, portable Sanctuary nestled in the midst of our camp. This was the camp of the tribes of Israel; the escaped slaves of Egypt and their children, under the leadership of Moses, our redeemer. And everywhere, the dusty hues of the desert.

As I grew up, I discovered other colors. The white and blue of the fringes all the men wore on the four corners of their garments. The red liquid that gushed out of the necks of the animal sacrifices that the Priests and Levites offered daily in the Tabernacle – the center of our camp and the center of our worship. I learned about the colors of gold and silver and copper, and the madness it engendered in certain people. I was too young to appreciate the lust for money.

I noticed the different colors of men's beards. Almost every man of the tribes of Israel was bearded. Most Israelites were dark-haired and dark-bearded, with notable exceptions. My fellow tribesmen, the descendants of Judah were often redheads, with flaming red beards. The descendants of Joseph, the tribes of Menashe and Ephraim had many blonds. Joshua, the most famous descendant of Ephraim, sported a soft blond beard. And then there were the elders. Long, thick flowing white beards were the order of the day, with Moses having the most radiant white beard.

Once a month, Moses would check in on our study group. Joshua, ever at his side, accompanied him. We were perhaps twenty children, under the tutelage of Timmel, an old judge from our tribe. Timmel told us stories of our ancestors; of the journeys of Abraham, of the trials of Jacob, of the sacrifice of Isaac. He would tell us about the twelve tribes and how we came to be. Most of all he would tell us about the Exodus from Egypt. He loved recounting the plagues, which he had witnessed thirty-five years before. Inevitably, he would point at me and say:

"Boaz, it was your grandfather, Nachshon, who jumped into the turbulent sea. We all thought he was mad. He would drown. He had never swum in his life. But he just yelled: 'God is with us!' and marched into the sea with his fist raised to the sky. When we all thought he would disappear under the waves, I saw a sight I shall not forget for the rest of my life. The howling wind cut a passage right in front of Nachshon. Walls of water extended to his left and his right. The ground in front of him was dry and flat, and Nachshon, grinning wildly, strolled forward, as if he were taking a leisurely walk on the banks of the Nile by Pharaoh's palace. The tribes of Israel rushed into the dry seabed after Nachshon. Moses followed behind, staff in hand, nodding sagely at the parted waters as if telling them, 'hold just a bit longer.'"

Timmel also taught us laws. The laws of observing the Sabbath. The laws of the many sacrifices. When do you bring a lamb or a calf or a turtledove? The laws of working the land of Canaan – the land promised to our forefathers.

It was a highly social childhood. To live in constant proximity to hundreds of thousands of my people, all in tents, within a few square miles, is something that I still miss. Neighbors would hold long conversations outside their tents.

One prank we used to play – I was already seven or even eight at the time – was to stand silently behind the talking adult men, with their long beards and loose fringes. Very quietly, behind their backs, on our hands and knees, we would tie the fringe of one man to that of his friend. Making sure the tied fringes were secure and unnoticed, we'd scamper behind a nearby tent. When the men would finish their conversation, each one walked in a different direction, only to suddenly halt and discover they were tied together. At that point we would roar our laughter and hunt for our next unsuspecting victims. The greatest pleasure ensued when we would tie the fringe of a particularly large man to that of his much smaller fellow. The force of the larger man suddenly pulling on the smaller one would throw the small man off balance, causing him to trip and fall over, inevitably bringing the large man toppling down on top of him. We achieved such wild success perhaps once or twice in our delinquent career, but cherished it for the rest of our lives. It was even worth Father's punishment. I will not forget that day either.

"Boaz!" Father bellowed as I entered our small tent. Mother was out. I did not have her usual protectiveness to ease the coming blow.

"I've been told you caused Ralmel of Simeon to fall on Elitran, his cousin." Father stood up from his papyrus scrolls and looked at me with violence in his eyes. His face was almost as red as his fiery beard.

"What? Me? I wasn't near the camp of Simeon." I looked away, guilt and fear struggling for supremacy in my suddenly sensitive stomach.

"You lie to me? You compound your sin by sullying your mouth with filthy lies?"

"No. Someone told me about it. It may have been other kids." I compounded my lie.

"Kanitol saw you and Amitai behind Ralmel and Elitran shortly before they fell. He saw you wait nearby until they fell and then laugh hysterically at their misfortune of which you were the creator. This is wrong. This is evil. I have heard of other children doing so, but never to such a hurtful effect. This is an embarrassment to me and to my name. Must I hear that Boaz son of Salmoon is a ruffian? At such a young age already? You further insult me and degrade yourself by lying about it."

"I'm sorry," I said through tears. "I'll never do it again."

"You are fickle, Boaz, and I shall beat it out of you."

Father grabbed my arm with a hand as strong as steel. He took a wooden brush, the one Mother used on the wool. With the flat of the brush he slammed it savagely on my buttocks. I yelped in pain and shock.

"I'm sorry, Father!" I cried. "I won't do it again!"

He slammed the brush again, on the same spot. Fire burned from my buttocks. "I'm sorry," I repeated, with much less strength.

Again, he slammed the brush on my burning buttocks. "I'm sorry," I gasped, almost fainting from the pain.

He raised the brush one more time and hesitated. I looked up at the outstretched hand in our small tent. He looked at me with strange eyes, perhaps trying to gauge how much more I could take.

"Never. Embarrass. Me. Again," he said through gritted teeth and let one last final blow fall on my tortured buttocks. I thought they would fall off from the pain. I thought I would die from the piercing agony that radiated to every part of my body. My father released my arm and I collapsed to the hard ground, whimpering uncontrollably, my tunic soaked by my tears. I looked at my father towering over me and for the first time noticed the tears in his eyes. His face was a mask of emotions that I had no insight to decipher. I have never forgotten that day, or his stern temperament. I ever after looked upon the fringes with mixed feelings and rarely pulled a prank from that day forth.

Life in the dry desert was idyllic and filled with miracles that we took for granted. The manna appeared every day with the heavy morning mist. It was a shock for me to learn, after crossing the Jordan, that it was not a natural phenomenon. In the desert, I never seemed to outgrow or wear out my clothing. My light woolen tunic grew as I grew. Small rips and tears in the garment disappeared the next day. My leather sandals stretched as my foot got longer. Born into this reality, we were both annoyed and excited about having to work the land of Canaan, to buy and mend clothing in the natural world. Now, in my old age, I miss the convenience of the miraculous.

In that miraculous wondering, we moved camp with little warning. The great pillar of smoke, and on the rare nighttime relocations, the pillar of fire, would stir, leading us to our next encampment. The trumpets would sound, followed by a mad scramble to pack up our belongings, fold up our tent and march in the order of the tribes. Our tribe was always first and that put the greatest pressure on our family. Father would always grumble "Why can't Moses do us the courtesy of a day's notice?" Mother would answer sagely: "He most likely didn't know himself."

Moses. He is like a dimly remembered vision now. To say that we worshiped him would be an exaggeration. We revered him. We were in awe of him. We even loved him from a distance. But we were too stubborn and querulous a people to worship any one man. To worship the false gods or the work of our very own hands was natural enough, but to put our complete faith in a mere mortal of flesh and blood would always be a challenge.

Nonetheless, Moses was a constant presence in the desert. He would routinely traverse through the regimented tents of the tribes. He would join for a few minutes one of the multiple lessons being given throughout the camp. He would sit on the ground next to the sage giving the lesson and often add: "Yes, God told me this," or "God mentioned such a case," as if he were talking about a friend he had conversed casually with just moments before.

On one such occasion, on that memorable day when I was four or five, he sat between Timmel, our teacher, and me. Moses added to Timmel's description of the plagues that it was really Aaron who had facilitated the first three plagues: blood, frogs and lice. I wasn't paying attention. I was mesmerized by his pristine white beard and the faint glow that surrounded Moses. Not able to control myself, I deliberately pushed my hand through Moses' beard as he droned on. Sudden silence pervaded our circle. I felt a slight tingle as my hand passed through his beard.

"What is it you seek, son of Salmoon?" Moses asked gently.

"Um, I'm sorry, Moses. I just wanted to see if your beard was solid or not. I thought maybe it was like a cloud, though I've never touched a cloud before."

"You would no doubt jump into the sea to determine if it would part." Moses smiled. "Now that you've ascertained the texture of my beard, would you please retrieve your hand? I have no intention to encourage it becoming a nesting place for other little hands."

I removed my hand, embarrassed that it had bothered him, though pleased with the tingling sensation and his kind attention. Moses caressed my cheek.

"Children, it is virtuous to be curious, but it must be balanced with respect. Respect of our laws, respect of our traditions and respect of others."

That is my fondest memory as a child. That and the day God commanded Moses to die.

2. Stopping Moses

Boaz and five of his friends hid behind the gooseberry bushes on the sweeping desert plain. Heart-sized red fruit adorned the bright green bushes. Boaz's back was to the flowing Jordan River, with the walled city of Jericho sitting lonely in the distance. The hundreds of thousands of tents of the tribes of Israel were camped on the Moabite plain. It had been forty years since the Israelites had escaped Egypt and now they stood upon the threshold to the Promised Land of Canaan.

The normally calm encampment of the Israelites was astir with movement. Women clutching their young children to their bosoms scurried from tent to tent. Men argued loudly in large clusters. Work and the normal day-to-day activities of the camp had ceased. There was only one topic on everyone's mind: Moses was going to die. People debated if it was possible. They wondered how they could manage without him. Suddenly, the prospect of conquering the Land of Canaan seemed daunting. The Children of Israel were filled with fear, trepidation and sadness. As one, they concluded that the news was true. Their leader, their shepherd of the last forty years would be no more. A cry of anguish rose from amidst the Children of Israel. The cry was taken up by every man, woman and child. The wailing spread like wildfire through the Israelite encampment. The nation of Israel cried out as one. Boaz's friends cried as well.

"Moses is really going to die," whimpered Amitai, a chubby nine-year old. "He is leaving us. We will be alone."

"Quiet," Boaz hissed to Amitai and the other children. At ten years old, Boaz was the oldest and the natural leader. His mop of bright red hair refused to grow in one direction and freckles spread out on his pale face. "Moses is almost here. Wait until I stop him and then follow the plan."

"I'm scared," Amitai sniffled. "What if he gets angry? We'll die."

"Don't worry," Boaz waved his hand. "Moses will not hurt us. And even if he does, it's worth the risk."

"I'm not sure," Amitai implored.

Boaz peaked through the bushes and spotted Moses approaching, escorted by Joshua.

"Look, Joshua," Boaz overheard Moses. "Wild gooseberries. I love these. God is gracing my last moments." Moses plucked several of the ripe fruits, careful to avoid the thorns of the bush. He placed them in the folds of his robe. "I will save these for the climb up the mountain."

"Stop!" Boaz jumped out from the bushes and blocked Moses, who towered above him. Moses' thick beard was pure white and flowed gently over his cotton robe. Though he leaned lightly on his large staff, he looked as strong and vibrant as ever. Joshua at his side sported a pale blond beard and still wore light leather armor, with a sword hanging from his belt.

"Hello, Boaz son of Salmoon," Moses said, a white bushy eyebrow raised high. "What can I do for you?"

"I'm not going to let you die." Boaz's voice trembled.

Moses smiled. "It is God's command. I have always followed God's command."

Boaz waved at the bushes. Amitai led a row of four other children from behind the bushes. They walked between Moses and Joshua and grabbed onto Moses' robe from behind. They closed their eyes.

"Oho!" Moses gasped. "What trickery have you hatched, Boaz?"

Boaz stepped forward and grasped the hem of Moses' robe.

"We will not let you go. If you can't go up to Mount Nevo, you can't die. We will hold on to you for the rest of our lives. We are much younger than you and can hold on as long as we need." Boaz looked up at Joshua. "No disrespect to you sir, but we want Moses to stay with us and take us into Canaan." Joshua nodded silently.

Moses looked down and around at the children surrounding him.

"The blood of Nachshon the Daring runs true in your veins, Boaz. Your grandfather would have been pleased by your audacity. Children, we might as well make ourselves comfortable," Moses said as he sat down on the ground.

The children sat down, still holding on to his robe.

"I have an important meeting to attend," Moses said to the children. "My last one in this incarnation. God has requested my presence and you are delaying my mission."

"There is one more mission we want you to do. Take us into Canaan." Boaz demanded.

Moses sighed. "I wish to with all my heart, my dear Boaz. I would like nothing better than to feel the earth of the Promised Land beneath my feet. To breathe the air of its mountains. To taste its fruit. Its grapes. Its figs. To sit in the shade of its trees. To drink the sight of its sunrises and sunsets. But it is not to be."

"Come with us. I don't always listen to my parents," Boaz whispered. "You have argued with God before. It's right here across the river. Please."

"I have often argued with God, and I argued much on this point, but I always listen in the end and so must you. My mission with the Children of Israel is complete. It has been long and difficult. God has assigned the conquest of Canaan to Joshua. You must let me go."

The other children looked nervously at Boaz.

"No," Boaz pouted. "We need you. How will we manage without you?"

"That is why I must leave. You need to learn to manage without me. You have Joshua, you will have other leaders." Moses tussled Boaz's unruly hair and closed his eyes for a moment. "You, Boaz, will be a leader one day as well. And you have the Torah. Never forget the Torah. Never let its words leave your mouth. That will guard you better than anything. It is God's word and we must follow it."

The children continued to hold his robe.

"Have you heard how I killed Og the giant?" Moses asked.

The children nodded.

"I jumped to a very great height. Would you like to see that?"

The children looked at each other in confusion.

"But first I want to give you each a gift."

Moses stood up and out of the folds of his robe he removed the ripe gooseberries. He raised his hands like a magician, showing one fruit in-between each of his spread out fingers. He flung one fruit at each of the children and one at Joshua, and then put the last one back in his robe. Boaz let the fruit bounce off his chest as he held tight to Moses' robe. Joshua caught his fruit. The rest of the children caught the fruit, letting go of the robe.

Moses crouched for a second and then leapt a dozen feet into the air. Boaz, still clutching the robe, was pulled along, screaming. Moses caught Boaz in midair and they both fell back to the ground, with Boaz in Moses' arms.

Moses put Boaz back on his feet. Boaz's whole body shook. He had let go of Moses' robe.

"I need to go now, Boaz," Moses said.

"I don't understand."

"You will one day."

"We will miss you."

"I know. I will miss all of you too."

Moses began to walk up the mountain, never to be seen by mortal man again. As he ascended, he drew the remaining gooseberry out of his robe and took a hearty bite. Joshua and the children watched Moses ascend Mount Nevo until he was out of sight.

Joshua addressed Boaz and his friends. "Go back to your families, children. Be saddened by the loss of our teacher, our leader, but do not be upset. I felt as you do, wishing to stop him, but we need to learn when to let go." Joshua's bright green eyes looked at nothingness as he uttered the last line.

"You will lead us?" Boaz asked.

"Yes, young Boaz."

"Moses told you what to do?"

"Indeed he did."

"It will be good then?"

"You see the city in the distance?" Joshua pointed at Jericho.

"It looks very strong."

"It is Jericho. It controls the entire west bank of the Jordan River. Its walls are impregnable and its gate is made of iron. It is the key to conquering the land of Canaan. Do you think we can take it, my young warrior?"

"I d-don't know." Boaz stuttered.

"God has promised that we shall."

"Th-then I guess we will."

"How should we do it? Should we just wait for God to deliver it to us or should we attack and hope God helps us out in time?"

"Why are you asking me? I'm just a kid. Don't you know what to do?"

"I know exactly what to do," Joshua smiled briefly. "But now is not the time. My master has just left us and the void is still too terrible to think of. We shall mourn his passing. Then we shall cross the Jordan to enter Canaan. And then, young Boaz, you shall see the hand of God. The Canaanites shall rue the day we left Egypt. Jericho shall be the first to fall and the land will tremble in fear."

"I would like to see that."

"Would you now?" Joshua patted Boaz on the head. He stopped suddenly. "Curious," Joshua whispered.

"What?" Boaz asked.

"I sense. I sense that you will have an important role to play. How unusual, in one so young," Joshua said vaguely. "The grandson of Prince Nachshon the Daring."

"What are you saying?"

Joshua looked into Boaz's bright blue eyes. "The shadow of death is upon you."

"What do you mean? What should I do?"

"Why, go into battle, of course."

3. Shadow of the Father

Boaz was hiding quietly behind his family's tent. He was insanely curious as to what Joshua would say to his father. Boaz had learned that the upcoming attack upon Jericho and Joshua had hinted at some dark future for Boaz. He ached to find out more. Joshua had approached their tent in the camp of Judah to talk with his father. With his typical gruff voice, his father had ordered Boaz out of the tent. Joshua, the new leader of Israel, had smiled at the departing Boaz and sat down on the simple woolen rug in the small canvas tent. Boaz had scampered away loudly, only to quickly turn around and silently return. He placed his ear close to the wall of the tent without touching it.

"With all due respect, Joshua," Salmoon father of Boaz looked down, "you go too far."

"I felt it, I tell you," Joshua pressed. "Boaz has your father's blood."

"His blood? As opposed to mine? Forty years later, and you still don't let me forget. Must I always carry the shame?"

"You are a great man in your own right, Salmoon. But you must admit that your father, Prince Nachshon, was unique. He was a hero, a natural warrior and an inspiration for our people. He was the right man at the right time. His jumping into the sea was an act of the highest faith. He led the way. God parted the waters right then because of him. We witnessed the end of Egyptian superiority and he was the spark. You can't hope to duplicate such history. No one can."

"I have not reached even a fraction of his accomplishments. I am known merely as Salmoon, the failed son of Nachshon the Daring. My own life, my own accomplishments in battle are not even worthy of mention.

Now you wish to push my son into the arena at such a tender age. Will I be shamed by the glory of both my preceding and my following generations? I will have no part in such a travesty."

"What do you fear, Salmoon?" Joshua asked. "Is the shadow of your dead father so long that you cannot escape his reputation? You are a great man, revered and admired by your tribe. You are the captain of a thousand. I saw you as you smote the Midianites, and the Amorites before them. You are a natural leader of men."

"Perhaps, but not great enough. It is Caleb, Prince Caleb, my brother-in-law, who has inherited my father's mantle. He is the leader of Judah. He is the one that receives all the acclaim. Is it not he, together with Pinhas the Priest, that you have sent on a secret mission?"

"How did you know?" Joshua asked, surprised. A light breeze from the Jordan River ruffled the sides of the tent on the Moabite plain. He saw a distinct shadow by the edge of the tent floor.

"Though my sister is quiet, I can perceive when her husband is not in their tent. Her face has an anxiousness, a worry, that is transparent. Pinhas' absence from his duties in the Tabernacle has been more obvious."

"Who else knows?"

"I have not discussed it with a soul, though anyone with eyes in their head must have noticed the unexplained absence of two such prominent men."

"I don't know that all are as perceptive as you, Salmoon. I preferred to send Caleb as, besides me, he is the only survivor of the disaster of the Twelve Spies and the only other person that knows the land of Canaan first-hand. I sent Pinhas with him as he can be quite useful when there is trouble, given his special ability. But it doesn't matter. My main intention was to send them discreetly, unlike the committee my Master sent four decades ago. However, you are not the only one in your family with perceptive skills."

Joshua pounced suddenly to the side of the tent. His arm shot outside the tent and pulled back a squirming Boaz by the scruff of the neck.

"Boaz!" Salmoon yelled sternly. "What is the meaning of this? You eavesdrop on the conversation of your elders? Is this how I raised you?"

"You were talking about me and Uncle Caleb. I couldn't help it."

"Don't talk back, child."

"You did ask him a question, Salmoon," Joshua added as he released his grip on Boaz.

"I am embarrassed by this behavior, Joshua. Please don't encourage him."

"Does he not have the right to hear discussion of his own fate?"

"There is nothing to discuss." Salmoon stood up, straightening his woolen tunic. "Joshua, I am honored by your attention, but there is nothing further for you to seek from our family."

"Would it be acceptable for me to converse on this matter with Boaz?"

"I cannot stop you from speaking to whomever you wish. But he is a willful child, with little regard for authority, of which you've just seen a small example. If you seek a warrior from him, you shall have to wait many years. Good day."

Salmoon bowed to the still-seated Joshua, signaling he wished to end the conversation. Joshua stood up and bowed back.

"Thank you, Salmoon, for your time and hospitality."

Joshua exited the tent and smiled at Boaz for the second time that day.

*

Boaz tiptoed quietly through the sleeping camp. He waited three tents away from Joshua's tent in the camp of Ephraim. Joshua's tent was the closest tent to the central Levite camp surrounding the Tabernacle.

For the third night, Joshua waited until two hours after nightfall and walked quietly and purposefully outside the camp towards the Jordan River. Boaz's small shadow followed the Israelite leader.

It took Joshua half an hour to cross the remainder of the Moabite plain and reach a gentle slope on the eastern bank of the Jordan River. The spring night air was pleasant, with a cool breeze blowing from the river. Boaz realized he was downwind from Joshua and recalled that to be downwind was a good thing when tracking someone or something, though he had never tracked anything before in his ten years of existence. Boaz kept his distance, making sure Joshua was in sight, yet not close enough that he would be noticed. He thanked the darkness of the night and the intermittent clouds that blocked the sliver of moon. His young eyes had adjusted well to the darkness. Boaz saw Joshua stop under a large willow tree, its sad leaves still lush from the winter rains. Joshua paced under the tree, constantly looking across the Jordan to the sleeping city of Jericho in the distance. Joshua finally stopped his pacing and sat down on a large rock. Boaz crawled on all four to reach Joshua's willow. He felt as if it was taking an excruciatingly long time to reach the large willow, but he dared not risk Joshua noticing him.

Two robed men ascended from the Jordan River and approached Joshua in the dark. Boaz recognized them. He could make out the large bearded figures of his uncle Caleb and Pinhas the Priest.

"Are you well?" Joshua asked them.

"We are well. We were delayed," Caleb answered. "The Canaanites have patrols up and down the river. One of them must have spotted our crossing and alerted the city. They sent troops after us as soon as we entered Jericho."

"You were not caught," Joshua stated.

"We were not. Rahav saved us," Pinhas added. "Your information was accurate. Her house is built into the wall of the city. She was most helpful. She hid us in her house and misled the troops. She bid us wait three days in the mountains, until the search party would give up, and that then it would be safe to cross the river. It was as she said. She is fully committed to our side."

"An amazing woman," Caleb continued. "What a bright aura! It is incredible that such a beacon lives in the spiritual darkness of Jericho."

"She pressed us to make a pact with her," Pinhas interjected.

"What pact?" Joshua asked.

"She sued for the safety of her entire extended family. Parents, siblings, all her father's home. We agreed. But only if they remain within the walls of her house. We bid her place a scarlet cord outside her window. It can be seen from outside the city."

Joshua placed his hand on his flowing beard and paced again. Boaz stirred restlessly on the ground behind the tree. The three men looked at each other wordlessly.

"Curious. Committed to our side and her family. Intelligent. Faithful. Her aura, you say?"

"Yes," Caleb said. "Almost blinding."

"Very well. You were correct to trust her and make a pact with her. Her house shall stand, though all around her shall fall. Rahav and her family will not be able to stay in Jericho, but I presume she understands that."

"She does," Pinhas answered. "She knows we come to destroy the city and conquer Canaan."

"What of their army?"

"Numerous, but fearful," Caleb stated. "News of our rapid destruction of Og and Sichon has shocked them. They have heard of our vengeance against the Midianites and the execution of Bilaam the Sorcerer." Caleb looked at Pinhas meaningfully, recalling the priest's magical airborne duel with the sorcerer, the tales of which had spread throughout Canaan.

"They also remember the stories of the Exodus," Pinhas added. "The plagues of Egypt. The splitting of the Sea. They tremble in fear and should we just step across the river they will scurry as mice."

Leaves rustled as Boaz tried to get comfortable on the rock-strewn ground.

The three men froze for a moment. Joshua smiled. Caleb and Pinhas looked to him for guidance.

"You may come out now, Boaz," Joshua declared.

Boaz, confused, did not move. *How did he discover me, again!* Boaz thought. *I was so quiet.*

"It seems your father's admonition has not curtailed your eavesdropping. Come out now and spare me the effort of having to drag you out."

"I'm sorry, Joshua," Boaz got up from behind the tree and brushed the pebbles and dust off his simple woolen tunic. "Hello, Uncle Caleb, Priest Pinhas." Boaz nodded at the men. "I was curious as to where Joshua was going every night. I suspected it would be important and connected to the secret mission."

"It is exciting for you?" Joshua asked.

"Yes! It is very exciting. I can't wait to see the Canaanites defeated."

"Do you wish to join us?" Joshua asked.

"Join what? Me? You're joking. I'm just a kid. My father would never allow anything of the sort anyway. I can help perhaps with the supplies, but what do you mean, to join you?"

"Your curiosity may yet get you into trouble, young Boaz. Stay in your father's tent. It is safer. We shall wait and see if there is a role for you. Go back to the camp now. There are things I would like to discuss in private."

"Yes, sir," Boaz bowed and ran off. *Thank God they were not upset,* Boaz thought. *If I'm lucky, they won't even mention it to my father.*

Boaz imagined what it would be like to fight in the battles; to fight like his father, a captain of thousands. Like his grandfather, Prince Nachshon the Daring, who had jumped into the sea and fought side by side with Joshua against the hordes of Amalek all those years ago. Lost in his thoughts, Boaz stubbed his toe against a small rock in the dark.

"Ow!" he called out to the night.

I'm just going to slip back into my tent. Time enough for battle when I grow up, he thought mistakenly.

4. Uncanny Sense

Boaz trotted lightly ahead of the column of millions of Israelites, his lithe, wiry figure running easily over the uneven plain. The sun shone hot upon his shoulders and in the distance, mirages danced. Suddenly, Boaz shot away from the crowd, as he raced towards the bank of the Jordan River.

"Kid! You can't leave the procession," a Judean officer yelled at Boaz.

"Come and catch me." Boaz laughed the laugh of a ten-year old as he scampered westward to the Jordan River. The curse of the officer was blown by the wind to the Moabite mountain range behind him.

The excitement of the spies' report the night before and the fright of Joshua's offer to fight were forgotten in the bright morning.

Boaz's mop of red hair bounced as he skipped over stones and crevices. He passed the families and armies of his tribe, the Tribe of Judah, first of the tribes. For forty dusty years, his tribe led the Israelite march. But now soldiers of the Reubenites, Gadites and Menashites led the invasion. Those tribes left their families and defensive troops on the east side of the Jordan, in the former lands of Bashan and Emor. Boaz could still not believe how swiftly and decisively Moses had conquered the kingdoms of Bashan and Emor. Moses then grudgingly bequeathed the land to the three tribes. And now Moses was gone.

"Boaz! Wait up!" a young panting voice called from behind as he ran parallel to the Reubenite head of the column.

"Amitai, what are you doing here?" Boaz turned around and scolded his younger cousin.

"Why should you have all the fun?" the chubby boy wheezed.

"Fine. Let's keep moving. We're almost at the river. Can you hear it?"

"That roaring is the river?"

"What else can it be?" Boaz replied. "It should be in sight any moment now. Come on you slowpoke. Keep up." Boaz sprinted ahead followed closely by Amitai.

Boaz stopped short. Instinctively his right hand shot out blocking Amitai from running off the cliff in front of them. The cliff was twenty feet above the bank of the roaring river.

"Whew," Amitai breathed. "Thanks. That was close."

"We're not with the camp anymore. We have to watch our step. Let's climb down. I want to get a good view of things when the crossing starts."

Boaz and Amitai followed a goat path down the cliff and reached the bank of the river. Short, thick bushes, interspersed with large willows peppered the shoreline. Through the dark green vegetation they saw the white turbulent waves of the Jordan River cascade southward. They were now half a mile north, yet parallel to the long column marching to the mighty river. They could see Joshua at the very front of the procession, together with four priests carrying the golden Ark. The morning sun bounced off the Ark. The priests and the nearby soldiers were bathed in a glowing yellow light.

Boaz heard a twang. Without thinking, he pounced at Amitai and they both fell to the ground. A long arrow buried itself into the willow behind where Amitai's heart had been moments before.

"Boaz! Get behind the bushes," an elderly voice hissed.

Boaz heard another, closer twang and then a moment later a meaty 'thwack' as the arrow buried itself into the chest of an archer across the river.

"Uncle Caleb!" Boaz whispered. "What's going on?"

A stocky man with a flaming red and white beard stepped from behind a willow.

"I've been tracking that Canaanite archer since dawn. He won't be bothering us anymore. What are you doing here? Why aren't you with our tribe?"

"I can't see anything from back there, Uncle. I want to see the priests enter the Jordan. I want to see the water stop flowing. All I see back there is the dust of other people's sandals."

"And what about you, Amitai?" Caleb gave the boy a dark look. "If it weren't for Boaz's quick reflexes, I would have to explain to your mother why you died on the very day the great promise is fulfilled."

"I'm sorry, Uncle," Amitai cringed. "I was just following Boaz."

Caleb looked at Boaz with a pensive expression. "Boaz, did you see that arrow coming?"

"No. I just heard a noise and next thing I knew Amitai and I were on the ground."

"Interesting. I will have to keep an eye on you. Now go back, both of you. You'll be much safer with the main body."

"Can't we stay with you?" Boaz pleaded. "Look! Joshua is about to speak."

From half a mile away, they could see Joshua climbing a tall rock on the bank of the river to address the people.

"Very well, let's get closer," Caleb ordered. The three of them jogged south along the shore towards Joshua. Caleb kept looking to his right across the river for enemy archers.

Joshua reached the top of the boulder. He stood tall, his tanned features contrasting with his flowing, pale blond beard. Boaz could hear him clearly even as he closed the distance between them.

Joshua was now just a few hundred yards away from them.

"Hereby you shall know that the living God is among you," Joshua's voice boomed and was heard for miles above the roar of the river, "and that He will, without fail, drive out from before you the Canaanite, and the Hittite, and the Hivite, and the Perizzite, and the Girgashite, and the Amorite, and the Jebusite." He then pointed at the four priests. "Behold, the Ark of the Covenant of the Lord of all the Earth passes on before you over the Jordan."

"There is something wrong," Boaz said to Caleb. "Joshua is in trouble."

"What?! What do you mean?" Caleb asked. "Joshua is just fine and can very well take care of himself. Don't get any strange ideas."

"I can't help myself," Boaz bolted at a breakneck pace towards Joshua.

Caleb then noticed dozens of heads peeking from behind bushes on the other side of the Jordan.

Joshua continued his speech:

"Now therefore take you twelve men out of the tribes of Israel, for every tribe a man. And it shall come to pass, when the soles of the feet of the priests that bear the Ark of the Lord, the Lord of all the Earth, shall rest in the waters of the Jordan, that the waters of the Jordan shall be cut off, even the waters that come down from above; and they shall stand in one heap."

He's going to be attacked, Boaz sensed. *Now!* Without thinking, Boaz launched himself up to intercept Joshua on the boulder. He was shocked at how high he was able to jump. Joshua, having sensed danger across the river, quickly jumped off the boulder. Boaz missed him and sailed over the top of the boulder, rolling to a rough landing on the other side. A rain of arrows from across the river filled the space where Joshua had stood.

The sky darkened as Reubenite archers sent a rain of arrows in response. Screams of agony as men were hit, merged with shouted orders and the hissing sound of arrows being released into the sky. "Archers! Keep firing!" Joshua commanded the troops. "Priests! Enter the Jordan. Now!"

The four priests carried the Ark towards the water of the Jordan as arrows rained upwards towards the Canaanite side. The priests entered the turbulent waters. Water splashed up to their knees, soaking their white ceremonial garments. Suddenly the water stopped flowing. A line of dry land formed across the entire width of the river. The priests kept walking. A wall of water formed north of the priests. The wall continued to move northward against the flow of the river. The south-flowing water continued on its course leaving dry land in its wake. By the time the priests reached the middle of the river, there was no water to be seen for miles either north or south on the Jordan.

Canaanite soldiers rose from behind their hiding places and fled in a panic. Israelite arrows mowed them down as they retreated.

A wild cheer rose from the Israelite procession. Joshua, at the head of the Reubenite troops, led the way onto the dry river bank and crossed the Jordan. Each tribe in turn crossed the river, with singing and cheering throughout the ranks. Ranks of older men prostrated themselves on the Canaanite ground of the western bank, and kissed the earth. "The promise is fulfilled," they said with tears flowing onto the dry river bank. "At long last, the promise is fulfilled."

On the eastern bank, Caleb approached Boaz at the side of the large boulder.

"How did you know Joshua was in danger?" Caleb asked.

"I don't know. I just knew. And I knew I had to do something."

"Boaz, you have an amazing talent. A talent that must be strengthened and developed."

"What are you talking about?"

"You will find out." Caleb put his arm around the young boy. "And I shall help in your training, while I can."

5. Inside the Walls of Jericho

Boaz watched as the invading Israelite army surrounded the walled city of Jericho. Its soldiers were camped beyond arrow range, in a complete circle that would not allow anyone to enter or leave the Canaanite city. Joshua and his troops had successfully crossed the Jordan River and had finally, after a forty-year delay, entered the land of Canaan. There was an eerie silence from the men surrounding the city. No one spoke. There was the rustling of cloaks in the cool spring wind of the early morning. The sun rose above the Moabite mountains on the other side of the Jordan River, brightening the shields and spearheads of the silent attackers and the anxious defenders alike. The muted sounds of footsteps and weapons being moved were the only sign that the invaders were humans. Mirroring the silent Israelites, the Canaanites of Jericho kept their voices low, their conversations hushed. The defenders of Jericho often kissed the small idols hanging around their neck, praying to their gods to defend them from the unnatural enemy.

A few hundred feet beyond the Israelite encampment, Boaz sat cross-legged on the dusty plain of the Jordan Valley and stared intently at a grasshopper. It looked like any other grasshopper as it drank from the early morning dew. Boaz squeezed his eyes shut and concentrated. Was that a flickering light he noticed in his mind's eye? Boaz opened his eyes. The grasshopper was gone. He banged his little fist on his folded leg, muttering, "Caleb is making me do the silliest things."

From the moment Boaz had demonstrated his uncanny sense in saving Amitai and his premonitions of attack upon Joshua, Caleb had taken him under his wing to train him how to use his talent.

Boaz searched for a new target. He spotted a gray desert mole digging under the exposed roots of a dead eucalyptus tree. Boaz sighed and closed his eyes again. He perceived the typical grainy lightshow of the bright Canaanite sun playing on the inside of his eyelids. *I'm not giving up,* Boaz thought. *Caleb said with practice I would develop the Sight. Isaac's Sight.*

He repeated to himself all the words with which Caleb had instructed him. *Breathe deeply. There are different levels of reality. Imagine God underlying everything. Calmly. What we see with our eyes is only the most superficial level.*

With his eyes still closed, Boaz perceived a muted, warm orange glow. It was the mole! He could see it, see its life force. He could tell the mole was hungry. It was a mother digging out a new cave for its young. Its old cave had been trampled by the Israelite army surrounding Jericho. Somehow Boaz knew this just by Sighting it. Boaz fumbled for a small stone, not wanting to lose Sight of the mole. He clutched a smooth rock and tossed it in the creature's direction. The mole hid under the tree roots. Boaz was able to follow the movements of the mole with his eyes closed.

A small red glow swooped towards the mole. *A falcon,* Boaz thought. The falcon just missed catching the mole as it shivered under the tree root.

Boaz expanded his Sight and saw a multitude of small, pale colors with his eyes still closed; reds and yellows of birds flying overhead, oranges and browns of rodents, a green aura in the distance that must have been a fast, clever fox. Small grays and blacks of ants, spiders and grasshoppers.

A large, white light approached him from behind. *Caleb. I am seeing Caleb's spirit. It is so bright!* Boaz opened his eyes as the Sight of Caleb's spirit hurt his inner vision. Boaz stood up, turned around and bowed to his approaching Master.

"Now you See?" Caleb asked.

"Yes! It's amazing. But why do you call it Isaac's Sight? I thought he was blind and couldn't even tell the difference between his sons."

"Isaac did become blind later in his life and he was confused between Jacob and Esau. We are often confused by things or people we are close to. But even in his blindness, Isaac could often discern the truth and essence of those around him."

"Fine, what's next?" Boaz asked.

"The siege will end today. I kept us away from the front so you could focus on your training. The entire army has been completely silent for the past week and I knew there was no way you could stand it." Caleb smiled.

"Not a word?" Boaz asked.

"Not a sound. I think the entire camp is ready to explode."

"It hurt my Sight to look at you. What will happen when I see the whole camp?"

Caleb smiled again. "You will see different people in different shades and colors; some brighter than others. You will get used to it. Very strong emotions may affect you, though."

"How do you know the siege will end today?"

"Joshua has informed us and he has assigned me a mission in the city. I would like you to accompany me."

"Me? Into the battle zone? I'm just a kid."

"You are no ordinary child, Boaz. I suspect that your instincts may be helpful."

"You keep talking about these instincts. How did I get them? Am I the only one?"

"Let's walk back to the camp as I explain."

They both turned back to the camp which encircled the walled city of Jericho. Hundreds of thousands of Israelite soldiers surrounded the large stone walls of the city.

"Everyone is born with natural instincts which develop as they get older," Caleb explained. "As a descendant of Judah you have been blessed with an inordinate amount of instinct. We call it simply Judah's Instinct. Of all the sons of Jacob, amongst all twelve brothers, Judah had the most developed instinct. He somehow just *knew* what to do and did it. How you have more than most people, I don't know. I expect you will play an important role in things to come. You are not unique in having a powerful attribute. Amongst each of the tribes there are people who have strongly inherited a trait of their Tribal ancestor. There is Naftali's Speed, Simeon's Courage, Yissachar's Stamina. Each of the twelve tribes has a special aspect that exhibits itself in each generation."

"Can I get the other traits as well? How about Isaac's Sight?" Boaz asked.

"Traits from other tribes are possible to develop, but much harder. Traits of the Patriarchs, Abraham, Isaac and Jacob are more easily learned by every Israelite, but we only train those that have an underlying skill."

"What are Abraham's and Jacob's traits?"

"Abraham is Generosity and Jacob is Astuteness."

"Will you teach me?"

"One thing at a time. We have a city to conquer and a maiden to protect. We are almost at the camp. From now until we hear the signal, not a word, not a murmur, not a sound. It is critical for the operation that the whole camp remains completely silent. Use Isaac's Sight to understand what is going on. I will not be able to explain anything until later. Is that clear?"

Wordlessly, Boaz nodded his head in understanding.

Boaz and Caleb reached a perimeter of Judean soldiers facing them with spears and shields in hand. Every ten steps around the camp stood a soldier with his back to Jericho. All the other soldiers concentrated their attention towards the city. The sentries nodded at Caleb as he approached. Eyebrows went up as they noted Boaz approaching, but nobody stopped his entry into the camp.

Boaz closed his eyes lightly and tried to use Isaac's Sight on the soldiers. He saw many colors. Each soldier was composed of a different hue. Some were vivid and others were subdued. Many of the auras swirled with a yellow or an orange or a blue becoming more dominant. A few had contrasting shades fighting for supremacy. There were many soldiers with bright spirits that outshone their neighbors. A small number of people appeared dark and foreboding.

Boaz opened his eyes again and tried to match the colors with the soldiers he was seeing. He recognized angry Beria, a bright red. His cousin Ruchem, a playful blue. As Boaz walked with Caleb through the troops he tried to use the Sight with his eyes open. He found he could still get a sense of the person's personality and mood, though not as strongly as with his eyes closed.

They reached the front of the siege. The front line of the camp was positioned beyond arrow range of the defenders of Jericho. Boaz had never seen a walled city before. It was constructed of massive stones; each was as long as his ten-year old height and was as high as his chest. The entire wall was as high as five grown men standing one on top of the other. It looked impregnable to him.

Then he noticed the priests. Four of them carried the Ark. Aaron's sons, Elazar and Itamar; and two other priests whose names he didn't remember, bore the poles of the Ark on their shoulders as they marched right below the walls of Jericho. Boaz was about to point out the danger to Caleb, but then he realized something. It was totally silent. There was nothing but the sound of the wind over the stones of the fortified city.

Everyone was staring intently at the Ark, completely wordless. In front of the Ark, walked seven other priests, each holding a long ram's horn and blowing on it. The trumpeting was the only sound cutting through the early morning silence. Thousands of armed troops of Israelites marched in front of and behind the priests. Rows of archers were interspersed amongst foot soldiers carrying long spears and wooden shields. All the soldiers had swords at their sides.

From the ramparts of the walls, soldiers of Jericho looked down apprehensively. Neither side attacked or made a threatening move.

Boaz looked at the soldiers on the wall with his Sight. He was overwhelmed by their fear. A sickly yellow aura pervaded their bodies. He looked back down at the Israelite troops. The priests were radiating white light. The soldiers displayed an array of colors and emotions. A steely blue resolve. A light red confidence. A darker red bloodlust.

The priests and their military entourage marched a full circuit around the city, blasting the ram's horns as they reached each of the four compass points of Jericho. They repeated the process again and again as the sun grew hotter in the spring morning of the Jordan Valley.

More than he could ever recall, Boaz wanted to speak. He had so many questions to ask of Caleb at his side. The oppressive silence of the camp and the soldiers held his tongue. Boaz had never been amongst so many people without hearing conversation. He could hear pebbles rolling with the gusts of wind. He thought he heard some whimpering from the walls of Jericho.

Caleb's attention kept shifting from the priests, to the city walls, and to one particular window high in the wall. Boaz followed Caleb's gaze. A thin red strand of silk hung from the window. Boaz closed his eyes and tried his Sight on the occupants in the wall-bound house. He sensed dozens of people crammed into a small house. They were all family. There was a strong sense of fear, like that of the soldiers on the ramparts, but it was mixed with hope, a healthy blue, like that of a bubbling spring. There were some shades of red anger, and one blinding beacon of white hope, confidence and faith. *That must be the harlot Rahav,* Boaz thought.

The priests finished their seventh circuit of the city and stood still. All eyes, Israelite and Canaanite alike, focused on the priests. They trumpeted on the ram's horns for the last time, a thunderous sound that seemed to pierce the heavens. Boaz was startled as a booming voice broke the human silence. The voice was so loud and reached so far, that it took a moment for Boaz to realize that it was the voice of their leader Joshua.

"Shout! For the Lord has given you the city!" Joshua's voice echoed and reverberated throughout the valley and against the city walls.

As one, the children of Israel shouted. It was a roar that shook the very earth. The pent up sounds of seven whole days came out in a rush of power and energy. Boaz saw the energy as a blazing inferno. The walls of Jericho shook. Soldiers on the ramparts wobbled as a wave of force washed over them. Massive stones from the tops of the walls came loose and crashed down in front of the Israelite army. The Israelites took a step back from the tumbling stones. Jagged tears streaked across the foundation stones accompanied by sharp crackling sounds. Spindly tendrils of black raced across the wall with a staccato of popping noises like the sound of a million angry crickets. The tendrils grew ferociously up, down and around all the walls of Jericho until there were more cracks than stone. The foundation stones were the first to crumble completely. The large stones turned to dust and disappeared. The upper stones of the walls fell down before they fragmented into smaller pieces.

Suddenly, there was an explosion of sound and movement. It sounded like the end of the world ten times over. Boaz stood in amazement, almost unable to take it all in.

The entire city wall imploded and fell in on itself. A gigantic cloud of dust and dirt filled the air. What had just moments before been proud Jericho was no more.

Soldiers on the ramparts fell to their death with the stones and were in turn crushed by large fragments. Shields, spears and swords flew into the air like a tidal wave. Cries from the dead and the dying reverberated throughout the city. Soldiers and civilians on the ground ran in panic, seeking loved ones and rushing for escape. What seemed like a million years was only moments. When the dust began to clear, Boaz could see that most of the Jericho army was destroyed along with their wall. Only one part of the wall still stood whole with not even a crack in its stones. The one with the red string hanging from its window.

"The city shall be consecrated!" Joshua called out again in a voice that filled the valley and traveled over the remains of Jericho. "It, and everything in it shall be the Lord's. Only Rahav the harlot shall live. She and whoever is with her in her house, for she hid the messengers we sent."

The Israelite soldiers that had accompanied the Ark were the first to enter the city, climbing over rubble and the remains of the city's defenders. The rest of the troops rushed to the fallen city in the wake of the initial wave. The priests, their job done, moved away from the cursed city with a stately, dignified march, carrying the Ark somberly.

"Follow me," Caleb said and ran towards Rahav's house, sword drawn, with a wooden shield on his left arm. He looked fearsome with his blazing red and white beard.

"But I don't have a weapon," Boaz fought down his panic.

"Pick up a stick," Caleb said without looking back. "You are sure to find many a broken spear in the ruins of the wall. Hurry up. I know how fast you can move."

Boaz climbed over the broken stones and broken bodies. He saw Canaanite soldiers with their bodies in impossible positions; broken legs and crushed skulls. The dead were mostly soldiers, but he also noticed women, children, and babies. They had been crushed to death in their own homes. A heavy layer of dust had settled upon the corpses, giving them an unnatural pallor, as if they had been dead for many days. Some of the bodies groaned and the Israelite soldiers quickly silenced them with a spear or a sword to the gut. The Israelites did not discriminate. They killed any Canaanite that lived, no matter what their age or gender. One Canaanite boy, no older than Boaz, scuttled between the rubble, tear-streaks staining his dusty face. The boy kissed the idol around his neck as Caleb bore down on him.

"Curse you, Israelites," the boy said as Caleb ran him through with his sword. The boy crumpled to the ground still clutching his idol.

Boaz looked at the face of the boy and wondered exactly what the Canaanite had done wrong. Boaz could tell little about the dead boy. He closed his eyes and tried to use his sight, but no aura emanated from the Canaanite. He wondered if they might have been friends, or played together.

Fighting back tears, Boaz followed Caleb, wondering again why a ten-year old was allowed on a battlefield.

Boaz caught up with Caleb's long strides. He nimbly climbed over the broken wall. He almost retched as he saw bodies of entire families amongst the dead soldiers of Jericho. Then he saw the Israelite army decimating the rest of the Jericho population. This is not a battle, Boaz thought, this is a massacre. Some residents resisted and fought back, but most just fell to the merciless onslaught of attacking swords. Old, young, women, children; all succumbed equally to the sharp metal of the Children of Israel.

Caleb made way towards the entrance to Rahav's house. Next to a dead Canaanite, Boaz found the lower half of a broken spear and grabbed it. Its broken end was still wet with blood. Boaz wondered whose blood it was.

A crowd of two dozen defenders stood on a stone ramp leading to the door to Rahav's house. A tall, swarthy man was banging loudly on the heavy oak door.

"You betrayed us, Rahav. I will break down this door and kill you and the rest of your family."

"This is what Joshua was afraid of," Caleb whispered to Boaz. "Watch my back."

Caleb dived into the crowd on the ramp. He landed low and spun around, quickly slicing all the men in arm's reach. Half a dozen defenders fell dead in one turn. Caleb walked to the door and dispatched one Canaanite after another. He seemed to know their moves before they did, and efficiently stabbed, sliced and hacked at each man. Boaz watched the whole battle from a few steps behind Caleb, walking up the ramp as yet another man fell.

The tall, swarthy one turned to face Caleb with a heavy broadsword. He looked in fear at the bodies all around Caleb. Caleb was unscratched. The man snarled at Caleb and attacked with a furious wave of blows. Caleb blocked each blow and parried. Their sword skills were evenly matched. The Canaanite battered at Caleb with his heavy sword, hoping to either break Caleb's thinner sword or wear him down.

Boaz felt a tingling on the back of his neck. He turned around quickly but did not see anyone. He closed his eyes and saw him. A swirling mass of yellow fear and red anger; an archer hiding behind the rubble. Boaz instinctively raised his stick. The stick intercepted an arrow aimed at Caleb's back. Boaz looked at his stick and the arrow with his mouth ajar. An Israelite swordsman spotted the hidden archer and cut him down. Boaz recognized the swordsman as Pinhas the priest. Pinhas tied a golden headband around his forehead, closed his eyes, muttered a few words and levitated to the sky. Boaz looked wide-eyed at the floating priest scanning the ruins of the city for other defenders.

"I knew you would be handy to have around," Caleb said to the shocked Boaz. "Yes, that's Pinhas' unique ability. Time to end this fracas."

Caleb jumped into the air. He somersaulted and landed behind the swarthy fellow, facing the door. Without looking, Caleb stabbed backwards, piercing his opponent in the back. The tall, swarthy Canaanite fell to his knees and then on his face. Caleb knocked politely on Rahav's door.

"Rahav! It's me, Caleb. It's safe to come out now. Hurry, before other neighbors show up!"

Boaz stood behind Caleb and looked through the door. There was the bright essence that he knew to be Rahav. Next to her was a dark red glow, mixed with a crazed yellow. The door opened.

Boaz was shocked by two contrasting sights. The beauty of Rahav was indescribable. He had never seen a woman as beautiful as her. Even at his young age he understood that men the world over would die or even kill for her. The other sight was the burly man grabbing her hair and holding a sword to her neck.

"Make way, Israelite," the man demanded of Caleb.

"I am not going anywhere without Rahav safely in our hands," Caleb stated calmly.

"She has betrayed us all. Betrayed her city, betrayed her family, betrayed her people. Give me free passage, or I shall slay her right here."

"Rahav has saved your life by protecting you in her house. All of your family has been saved through her efforts. You all would have been doomed otherwise. You are free to go now, but without her."

"No! I will escape this city you have destroyed and then I will kill this traitor." The burly man pulled Rahav's hair tighter. Rahav looked at Boaz with a silent plea in her eyes.

Boaz felt the spirit of Judah fill him. He dived underneath the burly man's legs, rolled on the ground, turned around and with all his might slammed the tip of his stick into the man's back. The man dropped his sword and released Rahav's hair. Caleb grabbed the man by the neck.

"Stop!" Rahav yelled. "Don't kill him, Caleb. He is angry and confused. My sister's husband is a decent man. The fall of Jericho was a big blow to him."

"As you wish, my lady." Caleb bowed to Rahav, stepped on the fallen sword and pushed the brother-in-law back into the house.

"And you my young hero," Rahav smiled and tousled Boaz's mop of red hair. "Thank you for saving me. I shall ever be in your debt, Boaz."

Boaz thought his heart would break. Rahav was so beautiful, he wasn't sure where her physical beauty stopped and where her shining essence began.

"How, how do you know my name?" Boaz stuttered.

"Why, you have been in my dreams, Boaz. I have also seen the young man that wants you dead."

6. The Capture of Ashkelon

As the Israelites were destroying the spoils of Jericho and invading the land of Canaan from the east, a new enemy approached the land from the distant islands of the Great Sea to land on the western edge of the ancient land. Tens of miles directly west of the Israelites, off the coast of the Great Sea, the *Aegus,* together with the rest of their armada approached the unsuspecting Canaanite cities.

Young Akavish walked casually on the shifting deck of the *Aegus* and looked pensively into the dark sea. At twelve years old he longed to prove himself, to prove that he was a man despite his small size.

The *Aegus* glided ahead of the rest of the fleet. The sleek wooden war boat rode the western wind, leaving behind its dozen sister ships, their sails wrapped up tightly for the night. The sailors on the sister ships drank and danced loudly around their fires. Big Larus, the Philistine chieftain, had given the orders for revelry. In contrast, the *Aegus* cut through the water, dark and silent.

Akavish, son of Larus, blessed the moonless sky. He combed back his dark, slick hair with his hands. Risto, his spider monkey, clutched Akavish's shoulder as always. Risto's fur was a patchwork of black contrasted with bright white that glowed softly in the night sky. The light mist over the Mediterranean concealed their approach to the coast of the city of Ashkelon. Ashkelon, the rich Canaanite city on the coast was to be their prize. The Philistines under the command of Big Larus intended to make it their new home. Akavish had seen the Ashkelon walls miles from the boat. He was impressed. In his twelve years of life, he had never seen a city so fortified. Risto nodded his agreement, reading Akavish's thoughts. The fortifications were thirty feet high, ten feet thick at the top and twenty feet thick at the bottom. It was impenetrable by conventional means. Constant torchlight patrols paced the top of the ramparts.

The *Aegus* steered towards a cove south of the city. A hill blocked the view of the cove from the Ashkelon sentries. The first mate quietly slithered the anchor down, where it nestled in the sandy bottom. Larus ordered the crew to sleep for a few hours, before the planned attack.

"You will stay on the ship, my son," Larus whispered to Akavish.

"I am ready to fight," Akavish whispered back. His voice pitched higher than he liked.

Larus punched Akavish in the stomach with a beefy fist. Risto hissed, feeling the pain. "The fighting will be short and brutal. If we succeed, it will save us a long and hard siege. Argue with me again and I'll punch your pretty face next."

Larus turned around without another word and headed fore, towards the first mate.

Akavish limped aft and found a secluded spot on the long wooden deck.

"I will not be left behind," Akavish told Risto. "I'm always left behind. Every raid, every ship, every council, father always leaves me behind. We have finally come to a new land, a new beginning and I will not be treated as a mere child. I will show him. I have not trained with Krafus for nothing."

Akavish looked around. Nearby crew were snoring gently. His father was busy talking heatedly with the first mate, gesturing with thick fingers towards Ashkelon behind the hill.

"Hold on tight," Akavish needlessly told Risto still on his shoulder. Akavish climbed over the side of the ship. He thought of using a rope, but that might alert someone as to his departure. His small fingers found impossible cracks on the side of the ship. He slowly climbed down the sloping side, his body upside down as he neared the bottom, until he reached the dark waters. He quietly sloshed into the cold waves. He looked up. Silence. No one had noticed his exit. His father would not think to look for him. Akavish swam thirty feet to shore. Risto dug his nails into Akavish's skin. Risto despised getting wet.

At shore, Risto jumped off Akavish's shoulder and shook violently, spraying water over the soft sand. His small teeth chattered. A crab, disturbed by the intruders, scrambled across the sand and dug a new hole, out of sight of Akavish and Risto.

"I know. The water is cold. But if we're dead it won't matter. Come on," Akavish beckoned, "let's take the city."

In one jump, Risto latched himself back on Akavish's right shoulder. The monkey's head rested against the back of Akavish's neck and his black and white tail curved around Akavish's right arm.

Akavish trotted lightly on the dark sand. His young eyes adjusted to the night as he traveled silently to the walls of Ashkelon. The only sound in the night was the waves of the Great Sea sloshing gently against the shore.

He knew other tribes had conquered Canaanite cities to the north. The tribes were like his. From the Aegean Islands, seeking a new home, leaving the growing anarchy of their crumbling empire. He heard the Canaanites called his people Philistines. City after city had fallen to Philistine war boats. Few could compete with their weapons or tactics. The Canaanites were mere farmers and merchants, mostly vassals to the Egyptian Pharaoh far south.

Canaanite sentries stood at the top of the wall looking nervously to the west at the firelight of the Philistine ships. They held their spears tightly and kept their round wooden shields close to their bodies. Akavish could hear the revelry that carried across the miles of waves from his father's ships. Akavish hiked to the eastern side of the city fortifications. He noticed fewer sentries as their attention was to the west.

Akavish picked up several smooth stones and put them in a satchel on his left side. He patted his jagged knife on his side. He used it to gut and clean fish. Now he wondered about using it on humans. He gritted his teeth and started climbing the wall of Ashkelon. His thin frame moved easily up the rocks, finding hand and foot holds where most adults would not manage. He held himself lightly at awkward angles, his wiry muscles supporting the little mass he had. Risto hung on to the young Philistine as if grafted to him.

"I'm more concerned about the Israelites." A nearby voice rumbled. Akavish held tightly to the wall. Risto held back a small squeal.

"I don't believe those stories." A second, higher voice answered. "Just by yelling the walls of Jericho fell down? Supernatural powers? I think the stories grew by the telling."

"My brother-in-law heard from his cousin, I tell you. He was one of the few that were allowed to leave Jericho. He was related to some Israelite spy. They massacred everyone; women, children. They leveled the city. He spoke about men with superhuman speed. He fled to Egypt. He said they aim to capture all of Canaan and they will."

"Well the Philistines are at our doorstep and they're taking over the coast. Mark my words. They will yet challenge the Egyptians."

"But it was the Israelites who trounced the Egyptians forty years ago. They have never recovered from that blow. The old slaves are strong, crafty and merciless. They are not interested in being in charge. They want to kill everyone. Did you hear what they did to Ai?"

"Another tale?"

"No. This was less magical, but equally vicious. They baited the troops to chase them and abandon the city. The Israelites then sent a second force and burned the defenseless town to the ground, killing everyone in it. They don't want our wealth or our cities. They don't even want us as slaves. They want us dead. Dead, dead, dead. At least the Philistines are reasonable. They kill the leaders, some of the troops, take over the palaces, and then it's back to business as usual. I can live with that."

"You forget that *we* are some of the troops."

Akavish had heard enough. Enough to know these Israelites were also invading Canaan and were fighting for the same land. He grabbed a stone and gave it to Risto. Risto, understanding, dashed silently across the wall and tossed the stone down into the city. It rattled as it landed on an empty cart. A nearby donkey brayed loudly at the noise. The sentries left their post to check the disturbance. Risto joined Akavish and together climbed over the wall and down the inside of the fortification. Akavish landed lightly on his feet next to an animal shed.

Akavish stroked Risto's fur. Risto was a part of him. His father had captured the baby monkey together with the plunder of some fat merchant years ago. The merchant had claimed the monkey came from south of Egypt and was extremely valuable. Larus was more interested in the gold and weapons and tossed the little monkey to Akavish. Since then, the two of them had been inseparable. Risto ate what he ate, slept when he slept, saw what he saw.

The city gate must be north, Akavish thought to Risto. *That is the only side of the city I haven't seen.* Akavish skulked like a wraith deep in the Ashkelon night. The only light were the torches of the sentries on the wall. They were all looking outward. Akavish passed squat stone houses with thick thatched roofs. Sheds held goats, cows and mules all sleeping. Large stones paved the narrow paths in-between homes.

Akavish reached a plaza in front of the gate. There were two dozen archers at various states of alertness on an inner wall around the perimeter of the plaza. *A killing ground,* Akavish thought. *If the Philistine raiders should somehow breach the gate, they will be easy pickings once they reach the plaza*. From the shadows Akavish examined the gate.

It's open, Akavish thought in excitement, seeing torchlight blazing from the opening in the thick outer wall. Then he realized it was a tunnel. The tunnel was at least twenty feet long, eight feet wide and sloped downwards with a torch in the wall every four feet. The tunnel ended with two solid oak doors reinforced with bronze brackets, and three bronze beams across the doors. *This needs to be an inside job. How did father expect to capture this city?*

Still in the shadows Akavish crawled closer to the gate.

"This Joshua is fearsome." Two sentries passed inches in front of Akavish. He held his breath.

"I hear that Caleb is an unbelievable swordsman." His companion replied.

"And they say that Pinhas can fly in the air like a bird. How can anyone stand up to them?"

"They are all ancient though. Perhaps they'll die before they get here."

"No. I heard there is a kid also. A ten-year-old who can predict an opponent's move before he makes it."

"If the Philistines don't get us first, the Israelites certainly will. What's the kid's name?"

"Boaz. A redhead firebrand that will kill you just by looking at you. If you meet a Boaz, run the other way."

"I think it's time to move to Egypt. I'd rather be a slave in Egypt than butchered here."

The sentries moved out of Akavish's earshot. He let out the breath he forgot he was holding. *So the enemy has a name,* Akavish thought. *Boaz.*

Akavish noticed metal pulleys at the entrance to the tunnel. There were chains that ran from the pulley the length of the tunnel and were connected to the doors. The doors could only be opened from the entrance to the tunnel. *Smart,* Akavish thought. *It removed any defender from outside danger.* The pulleys were on either side of the tunnel entrance. It would take two people to open the gate. The left pulley raised the bronze beams, and the right pulley opened the heavy oak doors. Risto was not strong enough to pull either lever, so Akavish couldn't count on him.

Akavish reached the corner of a house on the outskirt of the plaza. He peered down the dark narrow alley. There was no one in sight. He crossed the alley and was suddenly grabbed across his chest. A hand clamped his mouth and dragged him into the alley. Risto jumped to the roof of the house.

"Tell your little monkey to come back," an ancient voice whispered and let go of his mouth.

"Grandpa!" Akavish whispered at the thin, muscular man. "What are you doing here?"

"I've told you repeatedly, stop calling me grandpa. I was amorous with your grandmother, but I don't know that I'm responsible for your family."

"Yes, Krafus." Akavish nodded to his grandfather. Risto jumped back to his perch on Akavish's shoulder.

"Larus will be furious that you're here. But let's do some work. We have much to accomplish and Larus will be at the gate before dawn."

"I don't understand. What is the plan?"

"Simple. Kill the guards and open the gate."

"And you were going to do this yourself?" Akavish looked incredulous.

"Their defense is better than I thought and I hadn't figured out how to pull both levers, but now that you're here, that's solved."

"What do I need to do?"

"First, send that intelligent pet of yours to fetch the torches from the tunnel. After that, follow my lead."

"Won't they shoot him?"

"Probably. They will also look for intruders and raise an alarm."

"Are you sure you're on our side?"

Krafus smiled. "We will know how to respond based on how they react. And unless they are especially gifted archers, your monkey will be too hard a target to hit."

Akavish nodded and whispered a few words to Risto, pointing at the tunnel and the torches.

Risto shot towards the tunnel, invisible in the dark.

The torchlight in the tunnel moved and guards yelled.

Risto ran out of the tunnel towards the alleyway with four torches, two in each of his thin, hairy arms. Krafus grabbed the torches from Risto and launched them at the soldiers standing on the inner wall. Three caught on fire and ran into their fellow soldiers. Two soldiers ran out of the tunnel.

"We're under attack! Sound the alarm!" a soldier yelled.

A horn blast played counterpoint to the pandemonium of the Canaanite soldiers.

"Scale the wall and take out the soldiers on the left," Krafus commanded. "I'll do the right. Meet me at the tunnel entrance in five minutes. Your father will be waiting at the gate."

"Kill them, you mean?"

"Use your knife. Cut throats. Most efficient." Krafus ran across the dark plaza.

Akavish gulped and with Risto back on his shoulder scaled the wall. Miraculously, he was still undetected. The flames on the burning soldiers had been put out and the remainder looked around wildly for the intruders.

"The lights of the ship are gone!" a sentry yelled. "I can't see the Philistine ships. Have they left?"

"You fool. They are probably approaching in the dark. Archers! Ready on the outer wall!" the Canaanite captain commanded. "Inner wall sentries, aim at the plaza and the tunnel, there are..." his windpipe was cut mid-sentence as Krafus wove his way through the soldiers.

Akavish trembled as he faced the back of a large soldier. Swallowing hard, he jumped on the large man's back. Akavish tightened his grip on his knife, not wanting to kill his adversary. The soldier spun around and tried to cut at the body on his back. With moistness in his eyes Akavish sliced the man's throat. He was off the man before the fresh corpse fell to the ground. Another soldier faced him, with sword drawn. Risto launched himself at the soldier's face forcing him to drop his sword. Akavish cut the man's throat as he tried tearing Risto off his face. Akavish grabbed Risto off the dying man and put him back on his shoulder. One by one, Akavish dodged his way through each soldier on the inner wall, until all he saw were dead bodies. Part of him wanted to retch, but another part exulted in the power. The power of life and death. The power of a child over an adult. The power of agility and dexterity over a trained soldier's strength and experience.

He scaled down the wall and ran towards the tunnel.

"They're at the shore!" a sentry shouted. "They're at the shore!"

Akavish looked up at the sky as a faint touch of pink announced the arrival of dawn.

"Hold your arrows!" a soldier yelled. "Wait until they're close enough!"

Akavish reached the tunnel. From out of the tunnel, a long hand grabbed Risto violently. A short soldier put a sword to Akavish's neck.

"What is the plan?" the short soldier demanded. "How are you taking the city?"

"I, I don't know," Akavish mumbled.

"Then you are no use to us."

The short soldier fell down with a knife in his back. Akavish stabbed the taller soldier holding Risto and stepped back. Krafus dropped from the ceiling of the tunnel, retrieved his knife from the short soldier's back and mortally stabbed the taller soldier Akavish had wounded.

"What took you so long?" Krafus asked.

"I'm new at this." Akavish replied.

"Pull the lever. Your father's timing is perfect. Having the fleet beach at dawn is the perfect distraction."

Krafus and Akavish pulled on the levers simultaneously. The chains drew the bronze bars up and opened the heavy oak doors. Two dozen men entered the dark tunnel with swords, spears and bows. In front was Big Larus, long steel sword in hand.

"Well met, Krafus," Larus bowed to the thin man.

"Well met, Larus," Krafus bowed back. "Your son was most helpful in this operation. It would have been difficult to complete it without him. Thank you for sending him."

Larus looked at Akavish strangely. "I'm glad he was helpful." Then he slapped Akavish across the face. "But I did not send him. If he implied otherwise, he is a liar and no son of mine. Come, we have a city to conquer. You," he pointed at Akavish, "back to the ship."

Larus marched into the city followed by his two dozen men. Akavish gave Krafus a pleading look, but Krafus merely shrugged his shoulders and followed Larus.

"I don't need this," Akavish grumbled to Risto as he walked down the tunnel. "I don't deserve to be treated this way. I did not lie. I gave my father the city, killed for him and this is how he treats me? I will not go back to the ship. I'm a fighter, a killer. I will go where I'm appreciated."

As he exited the tunnel, he saw the rest of his tribe's fleet on the beach. A red dawn greeted them. The raiders walked up the pristine sand uncontested. The defenders were most likely occupied with his father's force. The Philistines would rule Ashkelon.

The morning sun glinted off something in the wall. Akavish climbed the wall and found a small silver statuette of a calf nestled in a large crevice.

"This must be the Canaanite god," Akavish said. "Didn't do them any good and they won't be needing it anymore." Akavish grabbed the silver statue and climbed back down.

"This will fetch me a handsome price, I'm sure. I don't need my father anymore. I need to follow my own path, Risto. That path lies east. If I am to make my own mark, it will be against the Israelites. The Israelites and their young hero, Boaz."

7. Gibeonite Deception

"We just made camp, why do we need to leave?" Boaz complained. He looked longingly at the hundreds of thousands of neat tents on the western bank of the Jordan River. The walls of Jericho had tumbled down and the Israelites had destroyed all the inhabitants, save for Rahav and her family. Boaz had learned how to sense people's auras using Isaac's Sight and he had been instrumental in saving Rahav from her murderous relative.

The morning sun peaked over the eastern mountains of Moab. The river flowed lazily, never having recovered its strength after the miraculous Israelite crossing.

"Joshua wants us to scout ahead," Caleb answered. He glided with long strides over the mountainous terrain. "But we will put this time to good use. I think we shall continue to work on your speed. You will learn the swiftness of Naftali."

"Where are we going?" Boaz asked.

"West. There are a few cities at the top of this mountain range that may comprise our next target. Joshua has sent other scouts northwest and southwest to determine the enemy activity there. For now, from our camp in Gilgal we control the entire valley of the Jordan."

"Will the camp follow us into battle?"

"No. The women, children, elderly and a security detail will remain in Gilgal. Just the troops will travel throughout Canaan until we have taken the land."

"How long do you think it will take?"

"I don't know. Before we entered Canaan, we lived a miraculous existence. Manna from the sky. Clothing that did not wear out. Moses conquering two kingdoms in a matter of weeks. God's presence was strongly felt. However, now I suspect the plan is different. God wants us to settle into the normal order of the world. The manna has stopped falling, and I for one could benefit from some new clothing." Caleb tugged at his fraying robe. "I think we will see less and less miracles and will have to rely more on our own tactics and strength. Do not doubt that God will fulfill his promise, but it may take many years."

"Who will take over after Joshua?"

"You are filled with questions today, aren't you? Enough talk. Let's train. You see that olive tree at the top of this hill?" Caleb pointed at a lonely ancient tree in the distance. "Race me there. Now!"

Caleb sped through the craggy landscape, covering ten feet with each stride. He snatched a wild wheat stalk as he effortlessly navigated the field of rocks. A young deer, startled by Caleb's burst of speed, bolted away from the man flowing rapidly through the mountainside. Boaz moved quickly, but stumbled often over the loose rocks and stones leading up to the tree. Boaz panted his way up to the hill and found Caleb leaning casually against the tree, chewing on the wheat stalk.

"How did you get here so fast?" Boaz wheezed. "I couldn't run any faster. I had to watch out for the stones. I kept tripping."

"You know that the gazelle is the symbol of the Tribe of Naftali. How does a gazelle run? Does it look down to see where it's going?"

"No. It just runs."

"So how doesn't it trip without looking?"

"I don't know. Some animal sense?"

"Indeed. It perceives the form of the ground instinctively. Its eyes merely glance ahead, and from a distance its mind recalls the position of every rock, shrub and tree. It can then move as swift as the wind. I want you to do the same. Look down the mountain," Caleb pointed towards the valley. "Notice the placement of each stone, imagine the path you will take down the hill, etch it into your memory. Now, you will walk down blindfolded."

Caleb removed a heavy woolen cloth from the satchel at his side and tied it around Boaz's eyes. "Meet me at the bottom," Caleb announced as he strode away.

"You're kidding," Boaz muttered, but started walking gingerly. He was surprised that only twice did he bang his feet against the stones and only once tripped, landing unceremoniously on some prickly shrubs. Eventually he made it to the bottom of the valley.

"Very good," Caleb declared as he removed the blindfold. "It is much easier with your eyes open. Let's race again to the top of this next hill. We have to keep moving. We are scouting and we must hurry back."

With a smile Boaz sprinted ahead, skipping over the rocks, without looking down.

*

The elders are petrified, Shakra thought angrily as he sat in the back row of the council circle. They sat on the ground within the gate of the city of Gibeon. *They are willing to give up everything, to leave our home, our ancestral lands, rather than confront the Israelites. There must be a way.*

"They massacred Jericho and Ai unprovoked," wizened Silu stated. "Their God is more powerful than any in Canaan. There is no way we would survive a direct battle of arms."

"That's it!" Shakra stood up.

"Sit down, youngster," Silu reproved him.

"No, no. You must listen to me. You may be right that we cannot fight them directly, but we don't need to run away."

"What are you saying?"

"The Israelites have been commanded by their God to destroy all the people of Canaan, right?"

"That is why we are having this council, is it not?"

"What if we convinced these Hebrews that we are not of Canaan, but rather that we are from outside Canaan and wish to ally with them?"

"Nonsense. How could we ever accomplish such a ruse?"

"I will need the Magi's help and several industrious women," Shakra grinned, happier than he had been in weeks.

*

Boaz ran merrily over the central mountains of Canaan in the afternoon sun. He spotted a wild rabbit racing away from him. In a blur, Boaz caught up with the rabbit and overtook it. Boaz laughed as he vaulted over boulders and shrubs. He leapt to the top of a short olive tree and waited for Caleb.

"Come on, old man," Boaz laughed back at Caleb, "what's keeping you?"

Caleb merely smiled, shook his head and quickly reached Boaz's tree.

"Do you see anything interesting from up there?" Caleb asked.

Boaz looked at the rolling Canaanite mountains. Behind him, to the east, he could make out the dusty Jordan valley intersected by the ribbon of blue, the once mighty Jordan River. Near the banks of the river he could still make out their base camp at Gilgal. Ahead of him, to the west, the mountains rose higher and were more verdant than the mountain range he was on, which extended to the north and south.

"No, I don't see anything. No, wait. There is movement ahead of us."

Caleb climbed to the top of the tree and looked.

"They appear to be refugees," Caleb noted. "Tens of them. They are not carrying any weapons. There are many women and children. Must be the survivors of some internal Canaanite conflict. Let's go meet them and see what we can find out."

*

Shakra's sharp eyes spotted the odd duo far off on top of the olive tree: a sturdy man with a flaming red and white beard, and a young boy with a mop of red hair. Hebrew scouts, Shakra thought. The man was armed with a long sword on his side and a bow and a quiver full of arrows on his back. The boy merely had the bottom half of a broken spear tied to his back.

"The ruse begins," Shakra announced. "We are about to meet our first Israelites. Magi, start weaving your spell."

An ancient woman, bent in half by age, in a cloak too old to tell its color or fabric, twirled her fingers in the air. She looked at the approaching man and murmured quickly, urgently. *"Ahlakch tribelh chakna tubarl. Ahlakch tribelh chakna tubarl. Ahlakch tribelh chakna tubarl!"*

The Magi collapsed, crumpling to the ground. An assistant picked her up.

"Are you well, Magi? What happened?"

"That one," she pointed at Caleb, "has strong natural defenses, but I overcame them. The illusion shall work on him."

"Remember, everyone," Shakra whispered. "We are from a small city near Sidon far north of here. We have been walking for weeks. Our city was captured by the Philistines and now we wish to ally ourselves with the Israelites and their powerful God. Spread the word so no one forgets."

An obedient murmur worked its way towards the back of the marching Gibeonites.

*

Boaz immediately disliked the young man in the front. He was tall and very brown. Brown skin, brown eyes, brown tattered robes and thick curly brown hair. Boaz guessed he must be around twenty years old, but walked with an arrogance that belied his age. Boaz closed his eyes to examine their aura. He sensed a yellow fear in all the people, but something else as well. The young man radiated a purple triumph, though Boaz could not understand why.

Caleb and Boaz approached the front of the Gibeonites. Caleb walked with arms raised high.

"We do not wish to fight," Caleb declared.

Shakra threw himself to the ground at Caleb's feet, bowing and cried, "O merciful master, you must be of the sainted Israelites about which we have heard so much. We are your servants. Show us mercy and do not kill us."

The rest of the Gibeonites followed suit and bowed to Caleb. The Magi murmured something under her breath and weaved her hands discreetly. She stared at Caleb as her eyes shimmered.

"Who are you and where are you from?" Caleb asked slowly, feeling unusually distracted.

"From a very far country your servants have traveled," Shakra answered, still on his knees, "because of the name of the Lord your God. We have heard the fame of Him, and all that He did in Egypt, and all that He did to the two kings of the Amorites, that were beyond the Jordan, to Sihon king of Heshbon, and to Og king of Bashan, who was at Ashtaroth. And our elders and all the inhabitants of our country spoke to us, saying: 'Take provision in your hand for the journey, and go to meet them, and say unto them: We are your servants; and now make a covenant with us.' This our bread we took hot for our provision out of our houses on the day we came forth to go unto you; but now, see, it is dry, and has become crumbs." Shakra unbundled a loaf of bread. It was dry and falling apart.

"And these wine-skins, which we filled, were new and, see, they are torn. And these garments and shoes are worn because of the very long journey."

Caleb examined the clothing of Shakra and those around him. The Judean suddenly felt mildly nausous, and was not sure why. The clothing of the refugees was worn, ripped, old and tattered. The shoes were mud-caked and cracked at the soles.

Boaz pulled on Caleb's robe to get his attention.

"Caleb, there is something wrong with these people," he whispered.

Shakra gave Boaz a piercing look. The Magi looked at Caleb intently, her eyes growing brighter.

"Of course there is something wrong," Caleb said angrily, feeling suddenly defensive of the refugees. "They are hungry and tired and worn out, from a far away land. Where exactly are you from?" he asked Shakra in his friendliest tone.

"We are from outside of Canaan, a small city near Sidon on the coast of the Great Sea. A ship full of Philistines conquered our city. Since then we have sought the sanctuary of your God's protection."

"You must talk to Joshua then. Our camp is less than a day's walk due east of here," Caleb pointed. "Tell Joshua what you told me."

"You are most kind, noble master," Shakra bowed again. "Your servants shall go presently." He stood up and directed his people to keep walking.

"Caleb, they are lying," Boaz hissed.

"What are you talking about?"

"It's a sham. That bread was over-baked. They look like they purposely ruined their clothing. Those people haven't been walking for weeks. I would be surprised if they've walked more than a day or two."

"I don't see it, Boaz." Caleb shook his head, feeling troubled. "They are poor miserable refugees from outside of Canaan. They pose no threat. We should welcome them gladly and I expect Joshua will."

"It would be a mistake," Boaz said, as the tens of Gibeonites passed him, headed towards the Israelite camp. The Magi smiled as she passed Caleb, her eyes finally returning to their normal appearance.

*

"We have been outsmarted," Caleb groaned as he looked upon the half empty city in the midst of the Canaanite mountains. "The refugees' tracks originated from this city. You were right, Boaz, and I apologize. They came from here, right under our noses. They left their elders and their strongest men with all the weapons. You see that one on guard?" Caleb pointed at a brawny Gibeonite guarding a small stone hut. "That must be where the city's weapons are stored."

"Let's go back and warn Joshua," Boaz urged.

"It will be too late once we get there. The Gibeonites will have arrived by now and if Joshua and the elders fall for the story, they may indeed make a pact with them. How did I not see it? Even after you pointed it out to me."

"It was a well planned deception," Boaz consoled.

"Very well planned, but there was something more. I must analyze."

Caleb sat on the ground, cross-legged, and closed his eyes. He was motionless for several minutes with only his eyelids fluttering.

"Sorcery," Caleb stated and opened his eyes. "They used sorcery on me. I can feel the remnants of the effect on my mind. They have a powerful sorcerer amongst them. The spell was strong and subtle. If there are more such amongst the Canaanites, we shall have hard work ahead of us."

"What now?" Boaz asked.

"We head back to camp, quickly. It may be too late to stop the forging of a pact, but we have to prevent the sorcerer from further mischief. Let's run. Run like the gazelle."

"Good, but next time listen to me, Caleb."

"I will. I shall not underestimate your judgment again."

Boaz smiled, eager to confront the young Gibeonite.

8. Detour to Jerusalem

"Wake up." Caleb's voice was hushed in the darkness.

"What's going on?" Boaz whispered back groggily, "I just fell asleep."

"We're surrounded," Caleb said, his voice echoing lightly in the unlit cave. Damp moss on the stones of the wall looked grey as the moonlight shone through the cavern entrance.

Boaz sat up abruptly despite his exhaustion. After discovering the deception of the Gibeonites, he and Caleb had headed back to the Isralite camp. They needed to inform Joshua as soon as possible that the Gibeonites were lying. They had found shelter for the night in a small cave a day's journey away from their camp in Gilgal and the last thing Boaz could remember from the night before was the sweet relief of sleep. But there was much to do.

"Who is it?" Boaz asked, now fully awake.

"They're not Israelites, and they're not those treacherous Gibeonites, so that only leaves other Canaanites."

"What do they want?"

"I suspect either to interrogate us, kill us or most likely both."

"Now what?"

"There are at least fifty of them, all well armed. I think I shall have to distract them while you make for Gilgal."

"I can't leave you, Caleb."

"You must, Boaz. Joshua must be informed of the Gibeonite ruse and of the sorcerer in their midst. I will exit the cave shooting and turn west. Once there is a wide enough opening, run and don't look back. When no one can see you, circle around the mountain and head back to

Gilgal. Grab a handful of stones as well. It was an oversight not to teach you the sling."

Caleb notched three arrows to his bow and knelt by the cave opening. He spotted half a dozen men climbing the hill to their position. Boaz grabbed what stones he could find on the cavern floor.

"We know you are there, Hebrews," one of them called from forty paces away. He was a tall muscular man. That was all Caleb could make out of him in the moonlight.

"The king of Jerusalem has offered a handsome reward for a live captured Israelite," the man continued. "Three hundred silvers! Come along and we shall not hurt you. You are only worth a tenth as much dead."

Caleb's answer was an arrow through the man's throat and that of two of his companions. Before the Canaanites could return fire, Caleb notched two more arrows in rapid succession and downed two more Canaanites. Five fresh bodies lay on the approach to the cavern. The remaining Canaanites paused and then backed away from the sudden assault.

"Now!" Caleb commanded. "Run, Boaz, and don't look back!"

Boaz sped through the opening in the ring of Canaanites surrounding the cave. He heard the 'whoosh' of arrows flying through the moonlit night. He heard the sounds of arrowheads penetrating flesh and of bodies falling on the rocky mountainside.

A Canaanite appeared by a boulder ten feet in front of Boaz. Without slowing his pace, Boaz flung a smooth stone at the Canaanite's head. The man fell on the pale moonlit shrubs. As Boaz ran past a large olive tree a rock slammed into his forehead. The last thing he remembered before passing out was a Canaanite voice wishing greedily, "I hope I didn't kill him."

*

Boaz awoke to a kick in the stomach.

"Wake up, Hebrew," a grating voice commanded.

Boaz did not move. He felt the cold stone floor under his body. His head was poorly bandaged. He could feel blood dripping down his forehead. His hands were tied behind his back. He kept his eyes closed and focused on the people in the room. *I should have used my Sight before getting smashed in the head,* he thought ruefully.

Right in front of him he sensed a cruel man. His orange aura hinted at a man who sought to inflict pain on others. Beyond the orange-hued aura sat a complex personality with swirling colors. A steely blue of command, a bright red of anger and a growing yellow of fear. There were other colors and emotions that Boaz did not understand.

"I know you're awake, Hebrew," the grating voice said and kicked again. Boaz instinctively twisted. The foot sailed over Boaz's body. The man lost his balance and precariously hopped on one foot until he planted the second foot firmly back on the ground.

"The child is quick, Basten," the seated man said.

"Yes, my king." Basten grabbed Boaz by the back of the neck with beefy hands, picked him off the floor and stood him in front of his king.

"What is your name, child?" the king asked.

Boaz opened his eyes and looked around. He noticed the cold stone chamber with narrow slits for windows. The dim morning light that entered the room shone on the man sitting in front of him. The man was middle-aged with thinning brown hair, and little beady eyes that looked intently at Boaz.

"Who are you? Where am I?" Boaz asked back, thinking of Caleb, of the ambush, of the Gibeonites and the urgent need to reach Joshua. *I have to get out of here,* Boaz thought to himself.

"You don't know? I am the king of Jerusalem and you are in my palace. Now answer my question before I poke some holes in you." The king played absently with a long sword. "What is your name and what are the Hebrew plans?"

"My name is Boaz. Our plans are to conquer all of Canaan, and we shall do so." Boaz stood straight.

"Your people are doing more than conquering. You are killing everyone in your path. Is it your God fighting for you? Can Joshua draw miracles at whim? Is he such a powerful sorcerer?"

What does he want from me? Boaz thought. *He is scared. I can sense that. He wants to find some way to beat us, to survive, to stay in power. I just need to get out of here. I need to find Caleb. Now.*

"It is difficult to talk with this heavy bandage on my head and my hands tied like this."

"How inconsiderate of me. You are, of course, right. Basten, clean up the boy, give him some food and drink and bring him back for more serious discussion. Boy, I hope you will be more forthcoming upon your return." The king of Jerusalem touched Boaz's neck with the tip of his sword and then pushed the edge into his soft skin until he drew some blood. "And I hope, for your sake, that your answers will be to my liking."

Basten squeezed Boaz's neck and led him out of the chamber. They walked through a narrow corridor and down stone steps. At the bottom of the staircase they entered a large kitchen with a roaring fire in the corner. Two women were at work in the kitchen. One was kneading dough on a large wooden table and the other was stirring a pot over the fire.

"Merta, attend me," Basten ordered the plump woman by the fire.

"Shut your trap, Basten. If I overcook this stew, the king will have my head."

"Merta, if you don't attend me, I shall be the one to have your head."

"Tell it to your mother, Basten. Your tough man act doesn't impress me. When you leave your mother's skirts and make your own home you can tell me about your manliness. Until then, stop talking. I shall be with you in a moment."

Merta stirred the pot further and then removed it from over the fire, placing it on three stones adjacent to the roaring flames.

"There," Merta stated, satisfied. She approached Basten and Boaz. "Now what have we here? Another victim of your games?"

"No. It's a Hebrew we captured."

Merta stepped back and looked at Boaz as if he were a fox that had invaded her hen house.

"Is he dangerous?" she asked nervously. The second woman stopped her kneading.

"He bleeds like a man, and is as willful as any child I know. I expect he will die as normally as any other once the king is finished with him."

"What do you want me to do?" Merta asked.

"Help me clean his wound and bandage it again, and give the boy something to eat."

"Our enemy? The Hebrews that are killing every Canaanite they see? My cousin lived in Ai. They massacred her and her six young children. They are merciless." Merta looked daggers at Boaz.

"He is under our roof for now. Besides, this boy is more useful alive than dead. Come."

Basten tore the dirty bandage off Boaz's head. Boaz let out an involuntary yelp as scabbing ripped off his forehead. Fresh blood trickled down his face. Merta took a cloth and soaked it in a basin of dirty water. She quickly wiped Boaz's head and face. She found a dry cloth and tied it snugly around Boaz's head. Basten untied Boaz's hands and showed Boaz a large dagger.

"Don't try anything funny, boy, or I'll get started on those holes the king mentioned. Sit by the table."

Boaz obediently sat on a three-legged wooden stool by the table. Merta placed a cup with some liquid in front of him and scooped out some of the stew onto a plate.

Boaz picked up the cup and smelled the liquid.

"What is this?"

"Picky, aren't we?" Merta answered distastefully. "It is barley mead."

Boaz sipped at the mead and grimaced at the strong taste. He drank some more.

"Hurry up," Basten barked. "We don't have all day."

He's right, Boaz thought. *I need to get moving.* He looked at Basten, holding his dagger. *I need to get the angle just right.*

Suddenly, Boaz banged on the edge of his plate. The hot stew went flying into Basten's face. Basten roared in surprise, dropped his dagger and removed chunks of meat and carrot from his face. Boaz lunged for the dagger and sliced at Basten's hamstrings. Basten fell to his knees as Boaz bolted out of the kitchen.

A few steps down the stone corridor took Boaz outside the palace and into the plaza of the city. Looking back, he saw a large two-story stone structure built into the wall of Jerusalem. The rest of the city was made of other smaller houses built into the wall and squat one-story stone homes.

"Get him! Get the Hebrew kid!" someone yelled from the palace.

Boaz spotted the gate to Jerusalem busy with morning merchants. The gate was twenty paces deep, bursting with people. Two guards stood on either side of the exit, both with shields and swords. The guards saw him and moved determinedly to intercept. Boaz knew his dagger skills would be no match for two adult swordsmen. He found some stones on the floor. He unwrapped the bandage from his head and prepared a makeshift sling. *Caleb wanted me to learn to use the sling,* Boaz thought. *Now's my chance.*

Boaz's first throw went wide off the mark. It whizzed by one soldier and hit a wine jug on a merchant's ox-driven cart. The jug shattered, spilling wine inside the gate. The second throw also missed the soldier, hitting a hapless donkey on the rump. The donkey brayed and kicked backwards, hitting a burly blacksmith in the chest and sending him flying into a crowd of merchants entering the city.

By now, there was a large commotion in front of the gate. People were yelling, "Hebrews! We are under attack! They will kill us all!"

This isn't working, Boaz thought as the two soldiers ignored the growing panic and got closer. Boaz saw two other guards from the outside of the gate starting to close the heavy oak doors of the city. *No time,* Boaz feared.

When the soldiers were ten paces away he threw Basten's dagger, which spun in the air towards them. The soldiers ducked, and that's when Boaz ran. He sped around the soldiers and darted toward the mob at the closing gate. Boaz reached a velocity that let him run on the inside wall of the gate, parallel to the ground, and then dive through the doors before they closed with a heavy clang.

Boaz rolled to a soft landing and stood up quickly. He looked around to get his bearings. He saw the walled city of Jerusalem towering above him. It reminded Boaz of the walls of Jericho, except that Jerusalem was much more imposing, sitting as it did on a hilltop, commanding the view of the mountain roads.

A Canaanite soldier grabbed Boaz from behind, clamping steel-like arms around his chest. The soldier suddenly fell with an arrow through his neck.

Caleb called from behind a tree. "Hurry, Boaz, this way."

Boaz reached Caleb at the tree and hugged him tightly.

"Caleb! I thought you were dead! The last thing I remember was getting knocked in the head and a whole army of Canaanites archers attacking you. How did you survive? How did you find me?"

"That's a story for another time, Boaz. In the meantime, we must make haste back to Joshua. He still doesn't know about the Gibeonites and the sorcerer." Caleb pointed Boaz in a northeast direction and together started jogging back to their camp.

"How was your stay in Jerusalem?" Caleb asked as they made their way across the mountain road.

"Mostly hospitable, good drink, though I did not try the stew."

Caleb looked at Boaz quizzically. "Let us get off the road. The Jerusalemites are not the only ones preparing for war. It seems that all the cities in the area are gearing up for war and I caught mention of them allying together to fight us."

"Is that bad?"

"An alliance of all the cities, with all of their soldiers, fighting us in the open, in land that has long been theirs and that they know intimately? It will be a battle to remember."

Boaz was not sure if that was a good thing.

9. Death in Lachish

"I can't keep lugging all this silver," Akavish the young Philistine told his pet monkey, Risto, as they entered the gates of Lachish with the early morning sun. As always, Risto, the black and white spider monkey, rode atop Akavish, as if glued to his shoulder. The unusual duo entered the fortified Canaanite city together with the hustle of merchants and farmers. Rickety ox-drawn wagons carrying jugs of oil and wine ambled on the main road. Farmhands with large sacks of grain on their shoulders walked through the cobblestones of the busy city. Vendors with boxes of spices and dried fruit cried out the prices of their merchandise.

"I should have taken the gold instead," Akavish muttered. "But it looked like so much more as silver." His pockets and bags bulged with the five hundred silver coins he had traded for the stolen god of Ashkelon. Passersby eyed Akavish strangely, but the young Philistine was lost in thought. He was happy with his role in conquering the city, but was still upset about his father's harsh treatment of him. His thin wiry frame tired from the weight of the silver.

The new Canaanite city impressed Akavish. Ashkelon had been a port fortress, focused on the sea and the merchant's wares the waves would bring. Lachish was a different city. Lachish looked out over the rolling Canaanite mountains. It controlled a vast area of grain fields, vineyards and olive groves. It was much larger than Ashkelon. Akavish knew the farmers would leave their simple homes by their fields and seek the sanctuary of Lachish in times of trouble. Those times were here. Philistines from the west and Israelites from the east. Akavish was happy to be right in the middle.

The morning traffic into Lachish grew heavy with merchants and farmers bringing their wares. Donkeys were the most common beasts of burden, interspersed with some large oxen a few horses and a rare camel. They pulled carts with fruits, vegetables, and grain.

"I need to start using this money," Akavish said to Risto, as he looked at different establishments on the main cobblestoned road of Lachish. A tavern, a hostel, a brothel, a blacksmith, a temple.

He was inexorably pulled to the clanking of a hammer pounding on an anvil. He remembered fondly his own apprenticeship with a blacksmith before his father decided to leave their home by the Aegean and invade Canaan. He once dreamed of owning his own smithy when he grew up and he suddenly realized he now had the money to do so. The fire of an open hearth roared as a giant of a man banged in front of his store front. The blacksmith swore merrily, drawing passersby to watch his performance.

Akavish was pleased to see sparks coming off a long sword in the blacksmith's thick hands. The man was bulky, as were all men of his trade. Akavish was surprised to see the man's grey hair pulled back in Philistine fashion. A gaggle of children watched the blacksmith at work, while a one-eyed Canaanite soldier waited impatiently for what was surely his sword. Two teenage apprentices, not much older than Akavish, assisted the blacksmith, stoking the fire and bringing the sweating, hulking man different tools.

Akavish approached the bulky man.

"Are you Canaanite?" he asked, confused.

"Ah, a fellow seaman!" the blacksmith bellowed, recognizing the foreign accent.

"You're Philistine?" Akavish asked, incredulous. "How long have you been here?"

"Years and years. I came with a wave that conquered the northern coast. But I sought new pastures on my own. The Canaanites here are happy enough with my blacksmithing and one god is very like another to me. The priestesses are just as attractive here," the blacksmith smirked.

With sudden inspiration, Akavish blurted:

"How much would it cost to buy your smithy?"

"Hah! You jest, little boy," the blacksmith smiled patronizingly. "Go back to your father and play your little war games, my young Philistine."

Enraged, Akavish jumped onto the blacksmith's back. With his thin legs wrapped around the man's broad chest, Akavish drew a dagger to the man's thick neck. Risto chittered nervously, eyeing the frightened spectators.

"I do not jest, old man," Akavish whispered. "How much for ownership of your smithy and your services?"

"You are mad! You are a child. What will you do with a smithy? Get off of me!" The blacksmith tried to tear Akavish off his back. Akavish held on to him tightly and pressed the blade of his dagger into the blacksmith's neck.

"I was a smith's apprentice and I know very well what to do with a smithy," Akavish whispered back. "Think quickly old man. I'd rather operate a smith with an experienced man. What will it be?"

"I never thought of it before," the smith answered, as sweat poured down his face. "I don't know. This is my life's work. I will not sell it at knifepoint."

"Then you will die for it," Akavish tensed his blade arm. The sharp dagger nicked the blacksmith's neck, drawing blood.

"Wait! Think, you little blood-thirsty murderer. The smithy is worthless without me. We can make an arrangement. I can hear the clink of the silver on you. You pay my fee, I will teach you, and the smithy will be yours to do with as you wish. I will work for your money and you will be lord of the smithy. Is that what you want?"

"Yes." Akavish slid off the sweating blacksmith's back and faced him, dagger still drawn. "Name your price."

The blacksmith rubbed his neck and looked up and down at Akavish, as if seeing him for the first time. He noticed the bulge of his pockets, the weight of his bags.

"For my life's work, to be the master of my domain, to order me around and to avoid getting poked by you, I will sell you the smithy, my services and an apprenticeship for six hundred silvers."

"Six hundred? I only…no. Six hundred is too much."

"How much do you have?"

"I...It is none of your business how much I have." Akavish waved his dagger threateningly. "Are you trying to swindle me?"

The blacksmith grabbed his hammer and banged it loudly on the anvil in front of him. The curious crowd jumped back at the loud sound.

"Look here, you young pup. You threaten to kill me, you demand my smithy at knifepoint, and now you ask me if I'm swindling you? I think the Canaanite sun has addled your brain." The blacksmith lifted his hammer in the air. "Are you an Israelite that will bring doom raining down from the sky? I will not be caught off guard a second time. Approach me again and I'll swat you like a fly."

"I was wrong to threaten you. I do want to learn your craft and I do have money to use. Perhaps we can start again." Akavish raised his hands and backed away from the enraged blacksmith.

"That is better, pup. What is your name?"

"Akavish."

"Mine is Gargus. And you have wasted enough of my daylight. Come back here at dusk and we can discuss the matter rationally, like men. You, your silver and your furry friend."

*

Akavish walked by the entrance to the temple. A sweet scent invited him closer while a rhythmic thumping of drums stirred his curiosity. Risto bounced excitedly on his shoulder.

"I'm too tired for gods and their dancing priestesses, Risto," Akavish said as he walked passed the entrance. "I need some rest."

They left the temple entrance and headed to the hostel. They did not notice a one-eyed soldier following them through the crowded street.

Akavish entered the large stone structure of the hostel. Three circular wooden tables were filled with merchants enjoying a midday meal of bread and meat. Akavish found an empty table in the back of the room and planted himself on the wooden stool.

"What do you want?" a raspy woman's voice asked at his side.

"Um, some food and a bed for the night."

"Do you have money, child?"

Akavish angrily slammed a silver coin on the table. The woman's hand snatched the coin before Akavish could say another word.

"You should not make such a display, boy. Others may want your coin for no service. The second room on the right," she motioned down a dark corridor, "is empty. I will bring your food now."

The woman reappeared with a bowl of thick porridge, bread and a cup of wine. Akavish ate hungrily, all the time giving morsels and sips to Risto.

A tall figure approached their table. "May I join you?" the one-eyed soldier asked.

Akavish motioned to the seat in front of him as he tore into another piece of the heavy bread.

"I was very impressed with your display this morning by the blacksmith. I have rarely seen old Gargus taken by surprise."

Akavish continued chewing and nodding.

"The king of Lachish would appreciate your talent. He is always seeking new blood for his army."

"I'm just a kid," Akavish said through a mouthful of stew. "What does he want with me?"

"You are a born killer, fearless and very agile to say the least. You are in possession of great wealth," the soldier eyed Akavish's pockets. "The creature with you is also most interesting. I have never seen one like it before."

"Risto?" Akavish petted his companion as his eyes narrowed. "He's a monkey, from south of Egypt. What do you want, man? Speak plainly." Akavish's hand grabbed the pommel of the dagger by his side.

"You are a newcomer to this city. It can be a dangerous place to be alone. The king is known to do and take what he will. It is a time of war and all foreigners are suspect. Perhaps you are a Philistine spy, brazenly and openly walking our streets. The king may confiscate your money, take your pet, and kill you, just to be safe. I don't believe you are a danger to us, but rather a resource. I am willing to be your intermediary with the king. To represent your interests and thereby protect you and your wealth."

"And what will this service cost me?"

"Cost you? You are a shrewd boy. It will only cost you half of all your money. And the monkey."

Akavish stood up and drew his dagger on the one-eyed soldier.

"This is robbery and I shall never part with Risto."

The soldier whistled sharply and quickly. Five soldiers with drawn swords entered the hostel. Merchants at their tables sat still until the soldiers had reached the back of the room, surrounding Akavish. The merchants then quietly scampered out of the hostel, many of them with their goblets in hand, a shank bone, or both.

"I would have preferred to reach an amicable solution, boy," the one-eyed soldier smirked, as Akavish looked nervously at the large soldiers surrounding him. "I will make my offer one last time and then the nature of our services will be less to your liking. Half your money now, and the monkey, or we shall take all from your corpse."

Akavish took Risto off his shoulder and held him in his hand. Risto cackled excitedly, his black and white fur bristling.

"You want the monkey!?" he yelled. "Here!"

Akavish threw Risto at the head of the one-eyed soldier. Risto bit into the soldier's head and scratched at the good eye. Akavish furiously upended the table, spilling his drink and porridge as his remaining bread bounced on the floor. The closest soldier jumped out of the way of the table only to be stabbed by Akavish's dagger. The soldier crumpled to the ground, but not before Akavish grabbed his remaining bread and stuffed it into his mouth.

"Get it off of me! Get it off of me!" The one-eyed soldier yelled as he wrestled with the bundle of black and white fur on his head.

Two soldiers tried to dislodge Risto from the soldier's head, while two others converged on Akavish.

Akavish swallowed the bread in his mouth, somersaulted into the air above their heads and sliced the necks of both men as he landed behind them. The silver in his bag and pockets jingled musically. The soldiers clutched their necks to no avail as they fell to the floor. Akavish then stabbed the backs of the two men struggling with the violently thrashing monkey atop their commander's head. Their backs arched as they yelped a final gasp of pain and collapsed onto the crowded floor of bodies. Risto, his mission accomplished, jumped off his victim's head and landed back on Akavish's shoulder. The proud little monkey swung his tail merrily and licked his bloody paws.

The one-eyed soldier was aghast as his working but puffy eye registered the five soldiers lying dead at his feet.

"You still want to do business with me, soldier?" Akavish asked, still enraged.

"I, I…I knew you were a murderer from the moment I saw you," the one-eyed soldier took a step back.

"I need to give you something to remember me by. It should not be said that you attacked me and walked away unscathed." Akavish grinned evilly. "I know."

Akavish jumped on the one-eyed soldier, knocking him to the ground. He pinned the soldier to the floor with his knees and extended the man's right arm. With surgical precision he slashed at the soldier's arm above the elbow, sawing through the bone with his sharp dagger. The innkeeper hid behind a table at the gruesome sight. The soldier screamed and hammered at the relentless Akavish with his left arm, then fainted.

"Now you will be known as the one-eyed, one-armed soldier," Akavish laughed cruelly as he tied the stump with a dirty cloth. "I will visit your king soon enough and then we will have business to discuss."

*

At dusk, Akavish, with Risto tense on his shoulder, stood in front of the smithy.

"Get in here, pup," Gargus hissed from the door to his workshop. "The entire city heard what you did to Balhad and his men. I'm surprised the king hasn't sent his whole army after you."

Akavish walked in. Gargus closed the door behind him.

"Did you really kill them all and maim Balhad?" Gargus asked.

"They wanted my money, and Risto," Akavish stated.

"Your jingling coins are a beacon for trouble and that pet of yours is sure to fetch a princely sum from some royal brat. You are wise to want to use the money quickly."

"I will not be swindled!" Akavish pointed his dagger at Gargus.

Gargus moved with amazing speed for his massive bulk. He grabbed Akavish's wrist and pointed the dagger at Akavish's own neck.

"You ever threaten me again, pup, and I will kill you. I have no more patience for your outbursts. I don't even know why I'm helping you. You may be a talented killer, but friendless, you will be nothing but shark bait. Now put your dagger away and listen to reason."

Gargus released Akavish's wrist. Akavish sheathed his dagger.

"Sit down," Gargus commanded, pointing at a work stool.

Akavish sat, shoulders drooping.

"I am willing to help you," Gargus explained, "though Baal knows why. I must be losing my mind in my old age."

"Tell me what I should do." Akavish said quietly.

"The first thing is to safeguard your money, or every ruffian from here to Jerusalem will be seeking your head. The next thing is to make an apology to the king or he shall hound you all the way until Egypt, no matter what war he's facing. I can help with both."

"How?"

"We can bury your money here, though you should use part of it as your apology to the king. There is no apology as convincing as hard money."

"What do you want out of all of this, Gargus?"

"What do you want to give me?"

Surprised by the response, Akavish sat straight, alert again.

"I will give you fifty silvers for your saving me and the money, and another two hundred to make me apprentice and partner in your smithy."

Gargus smiled. "You are bright and generous, though still reckless, pup. I accept your offer." Gargus put out his large hand. Akavish shook it, comforted by the hand's strength and firmness.

"I would suggest, however, that you send a hundred silvers to the king with an apology and an offer of your services. That is the only thing that may appease him."

Akavish nodded.

"Now, how should we start with your apprenticeship?" Gargus asked.

"I have a new idea for a weapon, a long distance weapon that will suit me."

"What's wrong with the arrow?"

"I'm not strong enough for a bow, and they are too big and bulky for me to sneak around with. I need something small and light that I can throw for long distances."

"Can you throw knives?"

"I've tried, but they don't go far enough. I have another idea."

"Draw it for me." Gargus handed Akavish some old parchment and a piece of cold charcoal."

"This is what I imagined, and why I wanted a smithy," Akavish started by drawing a circular shape with pointy extensions all around it. "The edges of the points should be thin yet razor sharp. The middle should have a little more weight so it can fly further and faster."

Gargus looked in horror at the drawing. "This is an instrument of pure evil. You cannot even pretend it has a constructive or defensive use. It has one purpose. Murder."

"Will you make it?"

"Though all the gods will curse me, yes. I will make it. If it will help you." Gargus' hand shook as he held the parchment. "Though why such a nasty mind should enter my home I can only guess. Do you have a name for this horrific invention?"

"Yes. It is a star of death. And I'm getting closer to its ultimate victim."

10. Masters and Slaves

"We have a problem, Caleb," Joshua said. "Our soldiers will kill the Gibeonites." Joshua paced in his tent, running his hand over his long white beard. Joshua eyed Boaz in the corner guardedly. No one else was in the tent. They had just returned to the Israelite camp at Gilgal after Boaz had succeeded in escaping Jerusalem. Joshua was distressed with the news they brought of the Gibeonite deception.

"Must the boy be present? I know he shows promise, but should he be involved in our councils?" Joshua asked.

"Boaz is my pupil whom I have come to trust implicitly," Caleb answered. "He was the first to detect the Gibeonite duplicity. He noted that the Gibeonites could not have been from outside Canaan as they claimed. They knew the alternative would be to flee Canaan or face us. Boaz saw through their trickery and magic. I would have him as part of our council. He is strong in Judah's Instinct."

Joshua looked at Boaz closely. Boaz squirmed under the glare.

"Very well," Joshua concluded. "I will bow to your judgment on this. I made a grave misjudgment by making an alliance with the Gibeonites and not checking the matter thoroughly. But it cannot be rescinded. If we were to attack them, it would be a great desecration of our vow in God's name."

"They deserve to be destroyed," Caleb retorted.

"Perhaps, but our word is sacred. All of the princes swore to the Gibeonites. All except you."

"Then let *me* take troops and wipe them out."

"No, Caleb. You too are bound by our oath. All of Israel is. I need you to guide the princes and the troops and prevent bloodshed. You must create consensus. Only then will I be able to decree and dictate a peaceful alliance."

"Alliance? This whole thing is a farce. They cannot walk away unpunished. They made a laughing stock of us."

"I have thought of this too. They shall be slaves. Woodchoppers and water carriers for as long as their lines continue. That way our shame will be cleared and our word will be true. What think you of this, young Boaz?" Joshua turned to the quiet ten-year old in the corner of the tent.

"You are wise, Joshua," Boaz stated. "But I recall learning that he who takes a slave for himself, in reality takes on a master."

"This boy is precious!" Joshua grinned and clapped his hands. "You are too right, young master. I expect we shall yet have to come to their defense, as word of an alliance between us and the Gibeonites will enrage the other Canaanite cities. They may decide to attack the Gibeonites as a reprisal. But it will serve our purpose. It will concentrate the forces of the other cities in one place and make it easier to fight them, rather than laying siege to individual cities."

"Joshua," Caleb interrupted. "Perhaps one of the other princes should take the troops to Gibeon. The other princes swore the oath – they should be the ones to uphold it."

"No, Caleb. For that very reason you are the perfect choice. The men will follow you. You and I know very well you can read the sentiment of the crowd and do not fear to speak against it." Both men looked down as painful memories from forty years earlier resurfaced.

Joshua remembered how Caleb single-handedly stood against the counsel of the ten spies who placed fear in the hearts of the Israelites in the desert. The spies had warned that to attempt to conquer the superior forces of the cities of Canaan would be suicidal. The people of Israel had threatened rebellion against Moses and even cried to return to Egypt. Caleb was the lone voice arguing to conquer the land as per God's command, to which Joshua had then added his own support. In the end it didn't help and God punished the Israelites with forty years of wandering in the desert. Caleb and Joshua and the Levites were the only men over twenty years old who had survived the punishment.

"I hope we have better luck this time than we did with the spies," Caleb finally said.

Joshua reached and held Caleb's arm. "We will, old friend. We will."

*

Shakra perspired heavily in the cool morning breeze. He sat at the head of the council circle facing the large stone archway of the gate of Gibeon. *Scouts have spotted Israelite troops on their way,* Shakra thought. *More than ten thousand strong. They have surely discovered our deception. Will they honor their word? Or will they slaughter our people as they slaughtered all in Jericho and Ai? How should we react? The council now looks to me for answers.*

"Defenses will be useless," Shakra argued with the elders.

"We will not die without a fight," old Silu stated.

"Fighting will give them more cause to attack. Our only hope is in begging for mercy and imploring them to honor their word. They claim their god is the god of truth. To betray their word would be betraying their god."

"If they have a god of truth, then all the more so they should destroy us for our massive lie."

"Perhaps. But there is no other choice. We must beg for mercy. They claim their god is one of compassion as well."

"I have only heard of their god of war."

*

Boaz marched with pride beside Caleb at the front of the Israelite troops. Caleb had outfitted him with a sling, the use of which he had also taught him the rudiments. Boaz still carried his broken spear-bottom; the one that had saved Caleb from arrows in his back at Jericho. The other princes looked strangely at the young red-headed boy, but did not ask any questions.

Boaz could see the open gates of Gibeon. It had seemed like ages ago that he and Caleb had reconnoitered the area alone and figured out the deception. Now they marched at the head of twelve thousand troops. One thousand from each tribe.

"We will kill those liars," a tall, pale soldier murmured from behind.

"They will die painful deaths for making fools of us," another added.

"Enough!" Caleb turned around and with his hand held high, ordered the troops to halt.

"Enough of this talk. Rasmer!" Caleb pointed at the tall, pale soldier. "As commander of your troops, you will maintain discipline."

Caleb climbed a nearby outcropping of rock and faced the twelve thousand men behind him. He waited until the masses of spears, bows and swords quieted down.

In a booming voice he declared:

"We are not here to massacre the Gibeonites. We have made an alliance with them. Though it was made under false pretenses, our word must not be violated. Otherwise, we are no different than these idol-worshippers that God Almighty has commanded us to destroy. We will meet with them and let them know their deception has been revealed and that we are furious." The troops cheered mildly.

"But no man shall raise his hand against them," Caleb continued, "for by the power of our vows they are now our bond-brothers." Muttering broke out through the ranks.

"We go now to parley. Remember my words!" Caleb climbed down the rock and led the troops to the gates of Gibeon.

"Thank God they left the gate open," Caleb whispered to Boaz. "Someone there has some wisdom."

"Or cunning," Boaz replied.

*

Shakra stood in front of the gate with Silu and another elder at his side. He had never seen so many soldiers in his life. The Israelites looked angry, ready for blood. The troops carried their spears with the point up. Archers marched with arrow in bow, scanning the walls of the city. Shakra noted Caleb and Boaz at the front of the army. He had learned their names when he had played his deception on the Israelite camp. Caleb wore an expression of determination, though it was not directed at Gibeon. *Caleb looks like a man holding back a wave of fury threatening to consume the city,* Shakra thought. *Caleb will be our hope.*

"Hail, Prince of the Hebrews!" Shakra called out. He prostrated himself on the ground and bowed. The elders on either side bowed as well. *The troops are hesitating,* Shakra noted. *Good. I must play this role until the end.*

"Hail, masters. We are your servants." Shakra proclaimed from the ground.

Caleb approached with Boaz and eleven other men. Shakra recognized them as the princes he had deceived. They looked at him with a mixture of distaste and anger. Behind them followed another twelve purely angry men. *These must be the commanders of each tribe's troops.*

"We know of your deception," Caleb pointed at Shakra. "You should die for it." A murmur of assent flowed through the troops.

"Yes!" one soldier cried out.

"Kill them!" another shouted.

"Liars! Deceivers! Idol-worshippers!"

Shakra and the two elders stood up and stepped backwards in mortal fear of the Israelite anger.

Caleb and the princes turned to face the troops. Caleb motioned to four princes. He climbed on the shoulders of two of them, a leg on each shoulder, while the two other princes held his legs upright. Standing high, Caleb addressed the army.

"We have sworn to them by God, Lord of Israel. We cannot touch them. This we will do to them, and let them live, lest wrath come upon us, because of the oath which we swore unto them. Let them live and become hewers of wood and drawers of water for the entire nation."

"Caleb! Caleb!" a runner cut through the assembled troops and breathlessly reached the princes. "Joshua has reached the back of the army and asks that you bring the Gibeonite leaders immediately."

Caleb jumped off the princes' shoulders. He motioned to Shakra and the elders. They walked towards Caleb. The other princes formed a protective circle around Shakra and the two elders. Boaz walked next to Caleb. Together they sliced through the troops, who split apart, as the sea did for them forty years before.

Joshua met them in the middle of the troop formation.

He pointed an accusing finger at Shakra.

"Why have you lied to us? You say you are from far away, yet you live right under our noses! Therefore you are cursed!" A collective gasp echoed from the troops. Shakra and the two elders fell to their knees.

"Your people and your descendants will forever be slaves!" Tears poured from the Gibeonite eyes. Israelite soldiers shuddered at the curse, some still remembering the feel of the whips of their Egyptian masters.

"Hewers of wood and drawers of water shall you be for the House of my God," Joshua concluded.

Shakra noticed that the Israelite anger had been spent. The troops looked at him now with pity. *At least I have life,* Shakra thought. *For me and my people. The fight for liberty may come another day.*

Shakra bowed to Joshua. "We are your servants. We feared for our lives. We had heard that your God had commanded Moses to give you the entire land of Canaan, and to destroy all of its inhabitants. The deception was the only way for us to survive. We are now in your hands and you may do with us as you see fit."

"Your doom and curse have been cast. You may now return to your city and await our commands."

Shakra and the elders stood up. The princes opened the protective circle around them, making way for the Gibeonites to return to their city. Boaz looked at Shakra with a mixture of pity and apprehension. He unconsciously rapped the end of his spear against the palm of his hand. *This Boaz still does not trust me,* Shakra thought. *Never mind. We are safe for now.* The army parted again. Not one Israelite soldier touched them or blocked their way.

Shakra forced himself not to smile. *I fooled the Israelites and have secured life for my people. I wonder how the other cities will fare.*

As if in answer to his hidden thought, Shakra's sharp eyes noticed a glint to the south. *A spy!* He recognized the spear as one from Adonizedek's soldiers. Shakra could not hide the frown that darkened his face as the spy returned south to Jerusalem.

11. Alliance of Hate and Fear

Since his abrupt departure from his father's presence at the conquest of Ashkelon, Akavish had tried to find his place in the Canaanite city of Lachish. Akavish had learned that dusk was an excellent time to sneak around. The rapidly dimming light played tricks on one's eyes. Lengthening and intersecting shadows camouflaged movement. At dusk, Akavish, the young Philistine, became invisible to the untrained eye.

Climbing the stonework of Yafiya's palace up to the unmanned battlement had been easy for the wiry twelve year-old. Akavish, with Risto on his shoulder, fastened a coil of rope around the solid portion of the parapet and let himself down, head first, to the thin lancet window. He squeezed silently through the window, his bony frame sliding soundlessly over the stonework, and found himself high up in a dark corner of the throne room. His welcome to the city of Lachish had proven complex. On one hand he had befriended the Philistine blacksmith, Gargus, who had created the stars of death for him. On the other hand he had drawn the unwanted attention of Balhad and his men obliging him to kill the soldiers and maim Balhad in the process.

Akavish recognized Yafiya, the handsome King of Lachish, with his long unbraided dark locks framing his triangular face. Yafiya sat upright on his wooden throne facing his Chief of Staff, the squat, steely-faced Margun. Two torches on the wall behind the king lit the long room.

"We cannot sit still and wait for the Israelites to pick us off one at a time, my lord. We must unite!" Margun declared.

"With whom, Margun? With Eglon? They are more concerned with the Philistine encroachment. With Hebron?

They are still upset about our raid on their flocks last spring. With Adonizedek in Jerusalem? They are most likely to fall next. Let them be a buffer. I will not waste my soldiers on the Israelite forces until I absolutely have to."

"What about Gibeon? They are strong and canny."

"I would sooner strike a deal with the blasted Phoenician merchants than with a Gibeonite. They are not to be trusted."

A loud rapping on the heavy door echoed in the room.

"What is it?" Yafiya asked, annoyed.

"Urgent messenger from Jerusalem," a guard announced.

"Let him in." Yafiya raised his eyebrow at Margun.

A young man in leather armor ran breathlessly into the room.

"Your majesty," he bowed to Yafiya.

"Speak," Yafiya ordered.

"I bring word from my king, Adonizedek. The Gibeonites have allied with the Israelites."

"What!?" Yafiya jumped out of his chair, startling Akavish in the shadows.

"How is this possible?" Yafiya yelled at the messenger. "Is this some deception? Is Adonizedek so desperate that he would fabricate a story to get our support?"

"No, your majesty. I saw them myself outside of Gibeon. I swear to you by Baal, Ashtarte and all the gods, this is the truth. I saw Joshua, Caleb, the princes of Israel, the young Boaz, and more than ten thousand Israelite troops." Akavish's pulse quickened at the mention of Boaz's name.

"They made a pact with the leaders of Gibeon," the messenger continued. "The entire scene was surreal. Joshua accused the Gibeonites of deceiving them and pretending to be from outside Canaan."

"That sounds like a Gibeonite tactic," Margun interjected.

"Joshua cursed them and their descendants to be slaves for eternity, but held the Israelites back from killing them. I have never been so fearful before in my life. The Israelite anger was palpable. But the Gibeonite leaders walked back into their city, untouched by the ten thousand soldiers that wanted to kill them. The Israelites retreated back to their camp."

"This is very bad," Yafiya sat back on his throne, resting his elbow on the side of the throne and his head in his hand.

"Your majesty," the messenger pleaded. "My king begs for an alliance. I have just come from Yarmut, whose king has agreed, and my next stop is Eglon. After that I shall cross back east to Hebron and return with them north to Jerusalem. We shall together punish the Gibeonites and thereby strike at an Israelite ally that we know we can defeat."

"What value is there in striking Gibeon when the Israelites are the real danger?" Yafiya asked.

"No one has survived a direct encounter with the Israelites," the messenger explained. "Their god is powerful and Joshua is a magician of the first order. By attacking their allies we fight normal men of flesh and blood, except perhaps for that old witch of theirs. The Israelites will then be forced to help their allies. Bloodying the Gibeonites will give us a tactical advantage and then we can meet the Israelites on a battlefield that we know and control. With our five armies and some of the most powerful sorcerers in Canaan we shall prevail."

"It could work, my lord," Margun agreed.

"Or it can bring our destruction sooner," Yafiya twirled the curls of his long hair in his fingers.

They heard a swift 'whoosh' through the air and Yafiya felt a sharp tug on his hair. The curl he was holding was suddenly separated from his head. A loud thud alerted him to a small, thin, star-like device protruding from his chair.

Yafiya jumped out of his chair and Margun pivoted around, sword in hand.

"Who is there?" Yafiya called out.

"An ally," Akavish tried to deepen his young voice in the shadows.

"Show yourself," Margun commanded.

"There is no need for violence," Akavish said. "You may lower your weapon."

"You attack us and say there is no need for violence?" Yafiya asked incredulously.

"I merely wanted to demonstrate my skill and value. Had I wished, you would all be dead."

"Show yourself, coward!" Margun shouted, holding his sword in both hands.

A dark blur flew through the shadow striking Margun on the left shoulder. Margun cried out in pain, as a star of death protruded from his shoulder, yet faced the shadow with sword in his right hand. Another blur cut his right wrist, forcing Margun to drop his sword.

"I could have easily struck your eyes, throat or heart, but I merely wished to disarm you. Do you still threaten violence or am I wasting my time with fools?" Akavish asked from his shadow. Margun grasped his bleeding wrist with his left hand and then with his right hand awkwardly pulled the star of death out of his shoulder. He gave the device to Yafiya.

"Come forward 'ally,'" Yafiya called nervously, gingerly holding the bleeding star. "We are impressed by your skill and wish to understand you better. We shall not threaten you, if you show us no further harm."

Akavish exited the shadow of the room with a long dagger strapped to this back, three stars of death in each raised hand and Risto clutching his shoulder.

"You are the Philistine," Yafiya exclaimed. "The one who killed Balhad's men."

"Yes."

"How old are you?" Yafiya asked incredulously. "I did not believe Balhad when he said you were only a boy."

"Do not judge me by my age or my size, King Yafiya," Akavish answered, balancing another star in his fingers. "Judge me rather by my usefulness – and deadliness."

"What do you want, child? If I didn't have more pressing matters, I would sic my army on you and your pet."

"If I didn't need you, you would have been dead already, and your army would be headless," Akavish responded, smiling. Risto chittered in agreement.

Yafiya sat back on his throne, letting his cut curl fall from his fingers, but still clutching the star with the sticky blood.

"Pardon my manners then, young Philistine," Yafiya said. "How can we be of service? I now recall you sent us a contribution. Very noteworthy."

"It is I who is offering you services. You shall join the King of Jerusalem, you shall attack Gibeon, it will draw the Israelites in and I will fight for you."

"Why?"

"There is someone I must kill."

Yafiya's eyebrow shot up in surprise.

"Who?"

"Boaz."

"The young warrior from the tales?"

"Is there another?"

"But why?"

"To prove myself. To prove that a child of the sea can best a hero of this strange people that everyone fears, with their invisible gods. To prove to my father that he was a fool for treating me like a child. Does that answer your question?"

"Yes."

"Will you join with Jerusalem and attack Gibeon?"

"Yes, but not because I think we will win, nor because you desire it."

"Then why?"

"If we are to be defeated, I would have it at the time and place of my choosing, and at the very least we can hurt those devious Gibeonites."

"If you go with such an attitude, even I know it will affect morale."

"Do not worry, young warrior. To my troops I shall be the epitome of optimism and confidence. I have been a ruler long enough to falsify all emotions and feelings," Yafiya smiled grimly. "You may come with us, my young assassin, but we shall keep a close eye on you, and you will only go where we direct you. There may be several other targets to kill before you have a chance at your Boaz." Yafiya lightly tossed the star with the dried blood at Akavish.

"That is fine. I will enjoy the practice." Akavish licked his lips as he caught the star.

12. The Nation that Cried Wolf

It started as a trickle of soldiers. A few dozen commanders on their mounts rounded the mountain pass within view of Gibeon. The dozen horsemen were followed by hundreds of foot soldiers, carrying their spears high in the morning sun. Shakra watched in quiet fascination as the hundreds turned into a wave of thousands. His fascination turned to horror as the avalanche of soldiers did not stop. They filled the entire face of the mountain opposite the city of Gibeon. Shakra trembled violently above the ramparts of Gibeon, no longer able to hide his fear of the coming onslaught.

Where are the soldiers all from? Shakra wondered in a panic. *Jerusalem does not have so many soldiers!* Then he noticed the kings together on their horses. Five of them. Adonizedek of Jerusalem, with thinning hair and beady eyes. Hoham of Hebron, squat and dusky. Big Piram of Yarmuth. Handsome Yafiya of Lachish. And heavy Debir of Eglon.

Shakra clutched the little copper statuette of Baal hanging from his neck. *Baal save us,* he prayed. *There must be over twenty thousand soldiers! They've come prepared for siege. It's just a matter of minutes before we're encircled. I must reach Joshua. The Israelites are our only hope!* Shakra kissed the statuette, placed it back under his shirt and ran as fast as he could.

*

Shakra managed to escape the city before the Canaanites encircled it. Silu the Elder and the ancient Magi joined him on his mission to seek the Israelites.

Approaching Canaanite soldiers noted the escaping trio and launched a volley of arrows at them.

An arrow pierced Shakra's left shoulder as he made towards the woods outside of Gibeon, heading towards Gilgal. He collapsed against a young oak tree. More arrows thudded against the trees as the ancient Magi and old Silu, his advisors, joined him in the protection of the forest.

"This is better than an Israelite attack?" Silu accused the slumped Shakra.

"Silu, you ungrateful wretch," the Magi whispered in a high pitched voice. "If it weren't for Shakra's plan, we would now lie dead, killed by the Israelite hordes. At least under Israelite dominion there is still hope. Help me with the arrow. Hold the head of the arrow firmly. I don't want to cause more damage to the boy."

Silu held the shaft of the arrow that protruded from Shakra's shoulder. The Magi intoned a spell in a low voice and quickly broke off the rest of the arrow, leaving the arrowhead and a short stump of the arrow's shaft in the shoulder.

"That's better," Shakra thanked the Magi and slowly stood up.

"Should we try to take out the arrowhead?" The Magi asked Shakra.

"No. There is no time." Shakra gently felt the remaining shaft and winced at the touch. "We must reach Joshua at Gilgal before there is no Gibeon to return to. I can't believe Adonizedek attacked us! And that the others joined them. How did they overcome their differences? Now we will see if the Hebrew God is truly powerful."

"If they will believe us," Silu added.

"May Baal be with us," Shakra answered.

*

The three Gibeonites were escorted to Joshua's tent near the center of the encampment. Snickers and jeers accompanied Shakra as he limped through the Israelite camp, suffering from the arrowhead still in his shoulder.

The princes and generals of Israel assembled at Joshua's tent at word of a new Gibeonite delegation. Young red-headed Boaz was at Caleb's side, as always.

"That is the sorceress," Caleb pointed at the Magi and exclaimed, as they neared.

"Rasmer, draw your bow," Caleb commanded to the Judean general, "and kill her if she so much as makes a magical twitch."

"Shakra," Joshua addressed the injured leader, "what brings you back to our camp so soon. New tales?"

"My master," Shakra fell to his knees and bowed to Joshua. Silu and the Magi followed suit, the Magi with a wary eye on Rasmer's arrow.

"We have been attacked, my master," Shakra continued. "Adonizedek of Jerusalem has rallied at least four other kings and their armies and they are attacking Gibeon as we speak. Here is evidence of their intentions." Shakra pointed to the arrowhead in his shoulder.

"How do we know it is not self-inflicted and just a ploy to deceive us?" Joshua asked.

"You think I would have myself shot in order to bring your troops back to Gibeon?" Shakra asked back.

"Boaz," Joshua addressed the young boy. "You've been able to see through their deception before, what are your thoughts?"

Boaz stepped forward from Caleb's side and looked carefully at Shakra and then at Silu and the Magi.

"I would have been more impressed had the injury been more severe and on the right side," Boaz replied to Joshua in front of the princes and general. "This is little evidence and they have proven that their words are to be doubted."

"Well said!" Joshua delighted in Boaz's analysis. "So, Shakra," Joshua turned back to the Gibeonites. "Stand up and give me another good reason to come to your supposed assistance."

"My master, please," Shakra stayed on his knees and put his hands together. "My people are being killed by the five kings. They have over twenty thousand soldiers. This is the truth. I swear by…" Shakra hesitated.

"You swear by whom?" Joshua stood from his chair and paced. "You are proven liars on a grand scale. You and all your people, as even young Boaz knows. There is nothing you can say that can convince us. Your words have no meaning. An arrowhead in your left shoulder demonstrates nothing. Had you cut off your right hand, I would still doubt you. You don't even know who to swear by. Do you still pray to Baal? Do you still worship your idols? If that is the case and what you say is true, you deserve to be killed. We should come and aid your enemies. Is that what you wish?"

"My master," the Magi said in a trembling voice. Rasmer pulled the arrow back further on his bow. Joshua motioned for Rasmer to hold from firing.

"If I may," the Magi continued. "I have the means to show you what is occurring at Gibeon right now."

"We do not condone sorcery, woman," Joshua replied.

"Yet you are amongst the most powerful sorcerers I have ever met," the Magi said, in confusion.

"It is not sorcery. We are strong in the ways of our God and that protects us from your magic."

"What I propose is not sorcery either. It is a tradition going back from mother to daughter since the days of Naama, wife of Noah, our common ancestor. It allows one to see for far distances. I have heard that your teacher, Moses, had such power as well."

Joshua put his hand to his long, white beard. "If it will bring clarity to your claims and involves saving lives, I'm willing to consider it. But know that we are aware of your powers and shall sense if you plan any mischief. As Caleb rightly instructed, we shall kill you where you stand."

Shakra gave a meaningful look to the Magi and whispered. "Are you sure? We cannot afford to lose you."

"It is the only way. Why else did you bring me along?" she whispered back. "I will need a basin with water, my master," she addressed Joshua.

Joshua nodded at Boaz, who understood and ran off. In a few minutes he returned with a copper basin filled with water and placed it in front of the Magi.

The ancient woman pulled a jagged knife from the folds of her robe. Her wrinkled hand drew the blade across the overlapping layers of skin hanging from her arm. Rivulets of blood trickled down her arm to splash in the basin. The Magi returned the knife to her robe and clasped her arm to stem the bleeding. She closed her eyes, muttered unintelligible words under her breath, circled the basin with her hand and swayed as her muttering grew to a loud chant. She opened her eyes. Her pupils were now white.

"Behold!" she announced. "The city of Gibeon."

Joshua, together with the princes and generals surrounded the Magi and the basin. In the waters of the basin they saw the city of Gibeon. It was surrounded by thousands of soldiers. Arrows filled the air between the ramparts of the city and the troops below. Large scaling ladders approached the city. Most of the ladders were successfully toppled before attackers could reach the top. Some hardy swordsmen did make it to the top only to be rebuffed moments later and their ladder knocked down. A team of oxen slowly hauled a large battering ram towards the gate. There was an intense exchange of arrows between the defenders of the gate and the troops escorting the battering ram.

Hopping between attackers and the torrent of arrows, the onlookers noticed a young boy, no older than thirteen, with a strange furry creature on his shoulder. The boy kept flinging something towards the defenders. Whenever the boy flung his arm, a defender fell, dead. A chill went up Boaz's spine. *He is the one from Rahab's dream,* Boaz shuddered.

"You see," Shakra pointed at the images in the basin. "We are under attack. We cannot last long under such an onslaught and in such numbers. Please, I swear by..." Shakra reached for his idol but held himself. "I swear by the Almighty God of the Hebrews, that I speak the truth. Please my masters, help us."

The Magi who had been muttering the entire time, fainted and the image in the water disappeared. Silu caught her before she fell to the floor.

"Caleb," Joshua turned to his old friend. "Your thoughts."

"It may be another sophisticated ploy. Her powers are impressive, but we still do not know if we see the truth or what they wish us to see. I would ask Boaz again. He has been immune to their deception."

Joshua, Caleb and the leaders of Israel all turned to Boaz.

"I believe the vision is true. Gibeon is under attack by the combined forces of five kings. But the Gibeonites still worship their idols. Shakra here can barely hold himself from touching his idol and Baal's name is not far from his lips."

"It is true," Shakra fell to his knees again and bowed. "It has been difficult for us to abandon our old ways, our old beliefs. But we renounce them now." Shakra looked at Silu holding the Magi upright. "I speak for all my people when I say that we renounce Baal and all the other gods of Canaan. We hereby proclaim our exclusive allegiance to your God. We are your servants. Our lives are in your hands and in the hands of your God."

"Pretty speech, Shakra. Pretty words. But I am far from convinced." Joshua sat back on his chair. "It seems we are at an impasse. I may believe that you are under attack, but I do not believe that you have renounced your base idol worship. How is one to read the hearts of men? How can you prove your dedication when evidence is otherwise and we do not believe your words? I doubt there is anything that you can say that would convince us."

"Please, please, please," Shakra begged tearfully. "Don't let us die. We have joined you. We have allied with you. We are your servants, under your protection. How can you leave us to die, to be slaughtered? By your enemies?"

"I am unmoved. Does anyone here see a way to believe these liars?"

Boaz stepped forward.

"Why am I not surprised?" Joshua smiled at Boaz. "Share with us your insight."

"They are wearing idols around their necks. They may have other idols on their bodies. They should destroy them all, right in front of us, now. That would be a first step. The moment they are free of danger, all the Gibeonites need to do so, or they will again be open to attack."

"Out of the mouth of babes and sucklings you establish strength," Joshua uttered with joy.

Shakra spotted a nearby fire, removed his copper Baal, kissed it and threw it into the fire. Silu removed a silver Baal from around his neck and repeated the procedure. The revived Magi, almost in tears, took a small golden Baal off her neck and threw it into the fire.

Shakra removed a small pottery statuette of Ashtarte from his garment. He kissed the statue, placed it on the floor and with a grimace crushed it under his foot. Silu took three small statues also of clay and did the same. The Magi, openly crying, took over half a dozen tiny, pretty statues and stomped them to dust.

"All our people shall do likewise," Shakra stated.

"I am more convinced," Joshua said.

Boaz focused intently on the Magi. Joshua noticed and asked: "What is the matter, Boaz?"

"She has one left."

The Magi narrowed her eyes and peered intently at Boaz. She dug deep inside the folds of her robe and removed an exquisite colorful glass statue of Ashtarte the size of a fingernail.

"This is over a hundred years old," the Magi wailed. "It was made for the king of Damascus, of whom I am a descendant."

She threw the tiny figurine into the fire. It smashed on a stone and disintegrated into powder with a sharp popping sound.

"Boy," she pointed a gnarled finger with a long black fingernail at Boaz. "You think you are so smart, but I can see your future. Death hounds you and you shall know little joy."

"I guess that means we are going to Gibeon," Boaz replied nonchalantly.

13. The Battle of Gibeon, Part I

The sun rose slowly and engulfed the majestic hills of Canaan with the dusty golden light of dawn. The dark green Jordan rippled and glittered with the promise of a new day.

Suddenly the peaceful dawn was shattered by the violent groan of solid oak splintering with brutal force. The battering ram of the five armies smashed the wood again and again, ripping the heavy brass hinges off the sides of the Gibeonite gate with loud, metallic screeching. A flock of crows, frightened by the sound, exploded out of the nearby forest and escaped towards the mountains.

Akavish was gleeful at the opportunity to retrieve all the stars of death that lay implanted in the warm corpses of the defenders of Gibeon. As the army of the five kings rushed into the city with raised swords and engaged the Gibeonite soldiers, Akavish, with Risto on his shoulder, hopped from body to body, evading the raging battle around him and extracted his metal stars from immobile heads or necks. *I have become too dependent on these stars,* Akavish thought. *Once I run out of them, I have lost my long-range advantage. I need another weapon.*

A Gibeonite attacked Akavish. Risto jumped off Akavish's shoulder and scratched at the soldier's eyes. Akavish ran him through casually with his short sword and continued gathering his precious stars. Risto rejoined Akavish's shoulder.

Yafiya, king of Lachish, watched Akavish's dance of destruction together with the troops of his four other allies: Adonizedek, king of Jerusalem; Piram, king of Yarmut; Debir, king of Eglon and Hoham, king of Hebron. Each was the monarch of their own little fiefdom, the city-states that peppered the land of Canaan. Up until now, the five cities had been competitors, trade partner and adversaries. But now, the threat of the Israelites had made them into allies. There was desperation in the air. Yafiya knew that if they did not succeed here against Joshua's army, there was a serious threat of their being completely destroyed. This would be their one and only opportunity to stop the supernatural Israelites. Under his leadership, the armies of the five kings attacked the Gibeonites, but they knew their real enemy wouldn't be long in coming.

"The Israelites are here!" someone yelled. Akavish was not sure if it was a defender or attacker. He looked past the city gates and saw Lachish's troops ambushing the Israelites on either side. The Israelites had been expected, though perhaps not so early in the morning.

I hope Boaz is here, Akavish thought. *I want him for myself.* Akavish exited the city and trotted towards the site of the ambush two hundred paces away. Before he could take a few steps, the ambushing army of Lachish turned and began to retreat. The retreat quickly became a rout, as the troops ran into Gibeon through the gates the other troops had secured. Akavish fell back into the city.

"What is going on?" Akavish asked a Lachishan soldier.

"The Israelites fight like devils! They must have known about the ambush. Three hundred of our men fell during the ambush and not one Israelite. Not one! Find a safe boulder and crawl under it." The soldier ran off without looking back.

"Hold the gate!" Akavish recognised Margun's voice. The Lachish commander rallied his troops. "We outnumber them five to one!" Margun yelled.

Ironic that they are now defending the gate they just broke down, Akavish frowned.

Akavish climbed the ramparts over the gate to seek Boaz. The troops of the five kings that had breached the city turned from the Gibeonite defenders to prepare for the Israelite onslaught. The Gibeonite defenders disengaged and ran deeper into the city. *They will regroup,* Akavish concluded.

He looked outside the walls of Gibeon. Surrounding the city were mostly the troops of the five kings, including a high concentration of Lachishans at the gate. The five kings had raised an army of close to a hundred thousand soldiers. The Israelites, perhaps twenty thousand strong, had formed an impregnable wedge. The tip of their formation methodically cut through the troops defending the gate. Canaanite troops attacked both flanks of the Israelite army, only to be shot or sliced as they approached. Mounds of bodies slowly grew as the Israelite front inexorably penetrated the defense at the gate.

Margun joined Akavish on the ramparts with a dozen archers.

"Quick!" Margun commanded. "Kill their front! Stop them!"

The archers loosed their arrows on the front of the Israelite force. A flurry of swords and sticks knocked the arrows aside. Not one Israelite fell.

Akavish saw a large man with a flaming red and white beard at the very front of the attack. He swung his sword at a speed Akavish had never witnessed before. After each swing another Canaanite attacker fell. *That must be the legendary Caleb,* Akavish realized. To his side was a young, tall, dark Gibeonite, wielding a sword competently. *That is the Gibeonite leader who concocted the original deception, Shakra.* Akavish's heart skipped a beat when he beheld the young boy behind Caleb. *Boaz. That can only be Boaz. He is so small! He can't be more than eleven years old.* Boaz was whirling a sling and downing Canaanites left and right. He seemed to have an inexhaustible supply of stones.

The dust of the battle made Akavish choke and cough as he struggled to keep his eye on Boaz. Nearby, a Gibeonite woman wailed as she knelt over her fallen husband.

This is it! This is my chance to make history, Akavish thought as he reached for his deadly stars. He ducked as a spear thudded into a wall behind him then threw three stars one after the other, as fast as he could, at his sworn enemy, at Boaz. To Akavish's amazement, Caleb's sword intercepted each one, sparks lighting the air on impact. The stars bounced off the sword loudly and pierced three Canaanite soldiers in front of Caleb.

Incredulous, Akavish threw six additional stars as rapidly as he could. Caleb blocked four of them, with the resultant sparks. Two got past his guard. Boaz moved with supernatural speed. One star passed him harmlessly, embedding itself in the ground. The last star flew straight towards Boaz's throat. Akavish watched eagerly as the final star approached his enemy's exposed neck. Is that it? Akavish wondered. Will my nemesis fall so easily? Boaz moved his arm with blinding speed. Akavish did not realize what Boaz was doing until it was too late. Boaz caught the star in his sling, just hairbreadths away from his neck and with the momentum of Akavish's own throw, hurled it back towards Akavish. The young Philistine froze for a moment, not believing the speed with which Boaz had moved.

Finally Akavish ducked, but not before the star hit Risto's arm. The small black and white spider monkey shrieked in pain. Furious, Akavish grabbed a dozen stars. He was startled to see Boaz running towards him, leaping on the heads and shoulders of the Canaanite soldiers between them. Akavish threw a continuous stream of his deadly stars at Boaz. Boaz twirled and somersaulted in the air as the stars of death sailed around the young Judean, not a single star touching him. Finally, Boaz caught a star aimed at his head with his sling and launched it furiously at Akavish. The star hit Akavish's right hand, deadening it immediately. Akavish howled in pain and surprise and for the first time in the battle, heard the anguish of all those around him. He heard the screams of Canaanite soldiers hacked to death by the Israelites. He heard the panicked horns of the five kings directing the battle and reinforcing losing positions. He heard the thundering hooves of riderless horses seeking escape. *I never knew these stars were so painful,* Akavish held back tears as Boaz approached rapidly. *My hand is useless now. We've got to escape.*

Akavish climbed down from the rampart into the city and ran as far away from the gate as possible. He looked back to see Boaz stab Margun with a short sword, on the rampart. *The five kings are doomed,* Akavish realized. *None will survive.*

Akavish prodded the metal star out of his hand and licked the oozing blood from his wound. *I will live to fight another day.*

14. The Battle of Gibeon, Part 2

I'm going to die, was Boaz's first thought, as he saw the metal stars spin at him in a deadly blur. His body moved of its own accord. Time slowed to a crawl. Boaz, Shakra the Gibeonite and the rest of the Israelite army were attacking the Canaanite troops of the five cities that in turn had been attacking the Gibeonites, the new, unlikely allies of Israel. Boaz could see the stars approaching his head and neck. He felt the wind ruffling his hair as it carried the smell of ashes, of some Gibeonite home on fire. His body felt the reverberations of the Israelite force smashing against the Canaanite soldiers. He could see the wiry young Philistine flicking star after star at him from atop the rampart of Gibeon. Six stars now intended his death. That furry animal still clutched the boy's shoulder gleefully. Impossibly, Caleb intercepted four of the stars with his sword. One passed Boaz harmlessly. In his slow motion world, Boaz had the presence of mind to catch one of the stars in his sling. With the star's own momentum, Boaz slung the weapon back at its thrower. The Philistine boy ducked quickly, but not before the star hit the animal on the shoulder.

"Well done!" Shakra, the young Gibeonite leader, complimented Boaz.

"Shakra, quick. Lift me up. I need to stop the Philistine. We may not be so lucky next time."

Shakra, understanding Boaz's intent, threw the light ten-year old Boaz over the heads of the Canaanite troops. Boaz started running on the top of the heads and shoulders of the Canaanite army as he neared the Philistine. Impossibly, Boaz jumped lightly from helmet to armor, launching quickly from the heads and shoulders of his enemies before they had time to react to his unexpected presence. He avoided their spears and swords, dancing in the air as he rushed towards the Philistine. The Philistine flung another barrage of deadly stars at Boaz. Boaz's body once again took over. Boaz followed his Instincts and blessed his ancestor Judah for passing on such a life-saving trait to him. He twirled and somersaulted midair. The stars passed him by, buzzing as loudly as angry hornets. He watched their trail as they missed his body and embedded themselves with bloody thumps in the backs of the Canaanites below him. More purposefully with his sling, Boaz caught a star mid-flight and flung it back with violent speed at the Philistine's throwing hand.

Boaz, pleased to see the star hit his adversary's hand, saw him cry out in pain and run. Boaz reached the rampart, intending to pursue the Philistine. A large Canaanite commander intercepted Boaz and thrust a long sword at Boaz. Boaz pulled out a short sword from his side and parried the Canaanite sword.

"You are the wonder boy?" the Canaanite asked, smashing his sword on to Boaz's short weapon. "You have chosen your opponent poorly. I am Margun, commander of all the troops of Lachish."

"I did not choose my opponent and I do not care who you are," Boaz replied as he rolled under the blow and stabbed Margun under his guard. Margun fell to his knees and looked at Boaz incredulously. Boaz placed his foot on Margun's shoulder, kicking him to the floor. Margun was dead before his body hit the cold stone. Caleb reached Boaz at the rampart, clearing the swordsmen and archers with long swipes of his sword.

"Warn me next time you attempt something so foolhardy," Caleb saluted Boaz.

"There was no time. I was following the Instincts you've been telling me to listen to," Boaz answered.

"Remind me to teach you the trait of Diligence of Yissachar. Your Instinct does not make you invulnerable."

Caleb and Boaz watched as Canaanites at the gate of Gibeon fell to the Israelite onslaught. Gibeonites who had retreated rejoined the fray. Joshua and Shakra joined Caleb and Boaz on the rampart over the gate. Shakra noticed Gibeonites fighting Israelites. The Israelites killed every Gibeonite that attacked them. But no Israelite fell, whether by Gibeonite or Canaanite sword.

"You are killing my people, too!" Shakra shouted at Joshua.

"That's terrible!" Joshua exclaimed. "But there are three armies here. How do we tell foe from allies who've never met?" Joshua asked.

"Our fringes," Boaz answered.

"Of course. Instruct Shakra." Joshua patted Boaz on the shoulder and ran off the rampart to where the fighting was heaviest.

Boaz held the fringes on the side of his garment and showed them to Shakra. Seven long white strings with one deep blue one rested in Boaz's hand. He had fringes on each corner of his garment.

"Shakra, tell your people that the Israelites are all wearing fringes," Boaz urged. "And tell your people to rip the idols off their necks. That way our armies can recognize each other."

Shakra nodded, took Boaz's fringed garment off of him, and stood on the top of the rampart.

"Gibeonites! The Israelites are the soldiers with the fringes on their garments!" He waved Boaz's garment in the air, the fringes flying as a flag for all the Gibeonites to see. "Take your idols off your necks! Otherwise, the Israelites will kill you! Pass it on!"

Gibeonites wildly yanked the telltale idols from around their necks. Israelite soldiers examined their combatants' necks, while the Gibeonites focused their gaze upon their opponents' waists. The Canaanites looked at both waists and necks, wondering in morbid fascination about the nationality of who was killing them.

The Canaanites remaining within the walls of Gibeon were quickly dispatched by the joint Israelite/Gibeonite attack. The Israelite army outside the walls engaged the bulk of the Canaanite troops surrounding the city. The Canaanites fled from the unrelenting Israelite onslaught. They fell, as before a wild bull in a vegetable patch, leaving discarded husks of fringeless bodies with their cold idols still adorning their necks.

The Canaanite troops of the five kings retreated from Gibeon.

"Chase them!" Joshua ordered from the front of the Israelite force, pointing his sword towards the sky. "We must destroy their armies today. Do not let them leave unhindered." Joshua led the Israelite pursuit of the Canaanites.

Caleb, Boaz and Shakra descended from the ramparts.

Shakra, finding one of the Gibeonite commanders, called him.

"Lurus, order our troops to secure the city. There may be some Canaanites hiding about. And tend to the wounded. It looks like the Israelites can handle the Canaanites without us." Shakra looked meaningfully at Caleb.

"Yes," Caleb agreed. "Our Lord is with us and you shall see how He deals with those who cross us. You are welcome to come along Shakra, to see for yourself."

Shakra gulped and nodded. Together, they joined the Israelite army in pursuit of the Canaanites.

The Israelites hammered and hacked at the Canaanite rearguard all the way up the mountain pass eastward to the village of Beit Horon. At Beit Horon, the Canaanite commanders attempted to hold the Israelites, but to no avail. The Israelites cut through their defenses as the scythe cuts through wheat.

The Canaanites retreated southeast, down from Beit Horon towards the fortress city Azekah. The downhill terrain allowed the fleeing Canaanites to put some distance between themselves and the Israelites.

Suddenly, the clear afternoon sky darkened. An eerie silence descended over the Canaanites as ominous, dark clouds gathered above them and seemed to suck both air and sound from the army. Horses neighed and looked nervously at the sky as rabbits and foxes ran away from the Canaanite position.

A light drizzle fell on the Canaanite soldiers. Some laughed nervously as the sudden reprieve hid them from the attacking Israelites and slaked their thirst. Most of the Canaanites raised their mouths to the sky to capture some drops and wet their parched lips. The drizzle turned into a pleasant rain. Adonizedek, the Canaanite King of Jerusalem, laughed merely and proclaimed "We are saved! You see! Their god is not all powerful!"

The rain stopped as soon as it had started. A small pebble from the sky bounced off of Adonizedek's helmet, ringing loudly in the otherworldly silence. It was followed by more pebbles, falling with sound of waves against the shore.

Then a blast of thunder shattered the silence of the dark afternoon, knocking soldiers off their feet and sending panicked horses in all directions as their riders toppled from their saddles. The rain of pebbles turned into hailstones. Stones of ice, the size of human fists knocked Canaanites to the ground. Soldiers scurried in all directions to escape the deadly hail, but it did not make any difference. The hail found the Canaanites wherever they ran. Hailstones the size of human skulls rained down on them. The stones killed or maimed every Canaanite they hit. The Canaanites were immobilized under the fatal barrage. The Israelites kept their distance, allowing the divine downpour to do their killing for them. Shakra looked aghast at the carnage. Canaanites fell in waves. Hundreds and thousands of Canaanites crumpled to the ground, more than the Israelites had killed by the sword. They lay as freshly slaughtered quail, littering the mountain with their corpses.

Just as suddenly as the hail had started, it stopped. The dark clouds disappeared, revealing the setting sun and the remains of the Canaanite troops continuing towards the sanctuary of Azekah. Boaz could see the sun glinting on the walls of Gibeon and the summer moon starting to rise from the valley of Ayalon.

The Israelites closed in again on the retreating Canaanites, running over the corpses mangled by the unnatural hail. Joshua, Caleb, Boaz and Shakra were in the lead, together with the other Israelite generals and princes. The Canaanites, noting Joshua at the front, stopped their retreat and counterattacked. Archers shot their arrows at the leader of Israel, only to watch him deflect them with his sword.

"If we don't finish them soon," Boaz remarked to Joshua, "we will be forced to stop, or fight them in the dark on their territory."

"The child is right," Joshua agreed as he looked at the setting sun. "We have never been in these areas and we must destroy their troops while we retain the advantage."

Joshua climbed onto a nearby ridge.

"Caleb, protect me," Joshua requested. "I need to concentrate."

Joshua faced the Canaanites, closed his eyes tightly and raised his arms heavenward.

A volley of arrows sped towards the unmoving Joshua. Caleb slashed through the arrows, stopping them mid-flight.

A bright light enveloped Joshua as he opened his eyes, revealing a blazing fire where his eyes belonged.

"Sun!" Joshua commanded in a booming voice. His voice echoed and reverberated throughout the mountain and beyond. "Sun! Sun! Sun!" both the horrified Canaanites and astounded Israelites heard over and over. Joshua's voice seemed to bounce off the very sky. "Stand thou still over Gibeon," Joshua continued. "And thou, Moon! In the valley of Ayalon." The words "Gibeon" and "Ayalon" echoed from the rocks and the trees. All of nature screamed back Joshua's words.

Then there was utter silence. The birds stopped their chirping. The leaves stopped rustling. The wind died. No human uttered a sound. The entire world seemed to stand still at the sight of a mortal commanding the heavens. Boaz was not certain, but thought he heard a deep rumbling or groaning sound, as if the movement of some giant mass was being held in check.

Israelites and Canaanites both looked from the moon to the sun. Over the course of long moments they did not notice any movement of the celestial bodies. The world seemed brighter, the colors sharper. Time had been suspended. One leaf could not contain itself any further and finally decided to fall to the ground. It floated slowly, the only movement in a paralyzed world. All looked in awe at Joshua standing on the ridge until he commanded: "Attack!"

The Israelites attacked. Whatever fight might have been left in the Canaanites dissipated at the god-like powers Joshua had displayed.

The sun and moon did not move from their places in the sky for the length of an entire day. It was sufficient time for the Israelites to annihilate the remains of the Canaanite armies of the five kings. Very few Canaanite soldiers ever made it to the town of Azekah.

*

Far behind the Israelite troops, a lone thin figure hugged a tree. He whimpered at the raw display of power. Akavish, the young Philistine, still clutched his wounded right hand. Risto, with a makeshift bandage on his furry little arm, sat on Akavish's shoulder dejectedly. *I must go back to my people,* Akavish concluded. *I cannot fight them alone.*

15. Royal Executions

"Let them out," Joshua commanded the troops surrounding the mountain cave. An enormous circular stone the height of two grown men blocked the cave entrance where the Canaanite kings had sought refuge, after their disastrous losses to the forces of Israel. No army could have stood up to the deadly hail and the miraculous stopping of the sun that Joshua had called upon. Even in the summer heat, Boaz shivered, thinking of the fate of the cave's residents. He looked towards Shakra the Gibeonite by his side, who looked pale and worn. Boaz was not sure if Shakra was tired from all the killing, or from his burden as the youngest Gibeonite chieftain.

Half a dozen Israelite soldiers rolled the massive stone from the entrance. Silence greeted the Israelites.

"Kings of Canaan," Joshua announced. "We know you are in there. Come out and save yourselves the discomfort of a needless struggle."

"You will have to come and fetch us," a high-pitched voice called out. "We shall not willingly walk to our deaths."

Joshua nodded at Caleb. Caleb motioned to a dozen soldiers to accompany him into the dark cave, with swords drawn and bows on their back. Boaz followed on Caleb's heels. Shakra did not follow, nor was he asked to.

"They are no longer a threat," Boaz whispered to Caleb. "Why do we hunt them? We've completely destroyed their armies."

"Because they are our enemies," Caleb answered without looking back. "And not just any enemies, but the leaders of our enemies. If we let them live they would assemble a new army to fight us again. We must wipe out the snakes, both the bodies and the heads."

Caleb and Boaz walked deeper into the damp, dim cave, leaving the familiar, bright hot sunshine further and further behind them. Dank water dripped, here and there, onto their heads. Muffled cries and whispers drifted ahead of them and Boaz closed his eyes as he was met with the swirling colors that represented the cowering, defeated souls of the five kings hidden in the darkness. A dull sepia of despair, the sharp red streaks of anger, and a drifting, weak cloud of purple – was it arrogance? Or dignity? Boaz didn't understand. He noticed two dozen auras to their left, waiting in ambush.

"To the left," Boaz whispered to Caleb.

"Very good. Your senses have become sharp indeed. I've only noticed them now."

"Arrows," Caleb commanded quietly to his troops. "Stay in line with me." Caleb grabbed the hands of soldiers on either side of him and turned them to directly face their hidden adversaries. Each soldier grabbed his companion and did likewise.

"Fire!" Caleb ordered. A dozen arrows flew. Ten bodies fell to the ground.

"Fire!" Caleb repeated. A dozen more arrows flew. Six bodies fell to the ground.

"Engage!" The Israelite soldiers shouldered their bows, drew their swords and approached the surviving Canaanites in the dark.

Boaz closed his eyes again and saw the vibrant green Israelite auras slaughter the remaining Canaanite ones. The dull brown auras were extinguished one after another. Boaz thought of rats being drowned.

Caleb and his troops turned to the five quietly whimpering voices in the back of the cave. The five kings offered no resistance and let themselves be walked out of the cave. Each king had an Israelite soldier on either side, holding their arms firmly.

Both Israelite soldiers and Canaanite kings blinked in pain at the bright afternoon sun.

Joshua pointed at five of his generals and called out:

"Come near. Put your feet upon the necks of these kings."

The escorting soldiers forced the kings to lie on the ground. Each general placed his foot on the neck of a king.

"Fear not, nor be dismayed," Joshua adjured the generals as he approached them with outstretched sword. *I am fearful and dismayed,* Boaz thought. *They are defenseless. They have surrendered themselves.* He noticed Shakra turning his head away.

"Be strong and of good courage," Joshua continued, "for thus shall the Lord do to all your enemies against whom you shall fight."

Joshua methodically beheaded each king, their heads rolling down the gentle incline. The head of Yafiya, king of Lachish, with its long locks, reached Boaz, who stopped the roll with his foot.

Though Boaz had seen many dead in his short military career, he felt his insides churning. Not able to contain himself, he ran aside, hid behind a boulder and started to retch until his stomach was empty, and even then, he continued, while hot tears rolled down his face. This was a part of war that he could not yet comprehend.

He sensed Caleb approaching him.

"What is the matter, Boaz?" Caleb asked gently.

"Nothing," Boaz sniffled and wiped the tears from his face.

"I think this fighting is too much for you," Caleb commented. "Perhaps you should take a break."

"No, I'm fine," Boaz answered quickly.

"I should not have brought one so young to a bloody battlefield," Caleb continued. "I was too optimistic in thinking you could handle it. I'm sorry, Boaz. You should return east, to the camp at Gilgal."

"Gilgal!? How can I go back to camp and play with the other children after all I've been through. No. I'll stay."

"Boaz, I can see your emotions. Your heart is in turmoil. You must return to camp. Our future battles will not get any easier, nor will we stop the executions of captured monarchs. There are many more Canaanite cities left to conquer, and they will fight hard. When word spreads that we do not even spare their kings they will fight until their dying breath.

"No."

"No, what?"

"I will not go back to Gilgal. I cannot go back to the life of a simple Israelite boy. I will go elsewhere."

"Are you mad?" Caleb asked angrily. "Where else can you go? How will you live?"

"I don't know. Perhaps amongst the Canaanites that we are exterminating. I'm curious about this enemy that we are commanded to kill. Or perhaps I will go west to the Philistines. There is no command to kill them, is there? I might find out why that Philistine hates me so, and is intent on killing me."

"You might discover much more than you anticipate. This is a foolish notion. Please get it out of your head and make ready to return to Gilgal."

Boaz crossed his arms, pouted and did not move.

"If I must leave the battles," Boaz declared, "I shall not return to Gilgal, whether you like it or not."

"You will disobey me!? You will turn your back on me? On your training? On your people?"

"I understand that I can't stay here, but I can't go back either. That is what I know in my heart."

Caleb brought his hand to his bushy red and white beard and looked for long moments at Boaz. He closed his eyes briefly and then opened them again.

"I see that your mind is made up. But you should not mingle with the Canaanites. It is against all our laws. If you must, seek out the Philistines. You may learn a thing or two. They are renowned as great metal workers. But do not learn from their foreign ways, for they are idol-worshipers too and if they continue their strange worship in this land, that will make us enemies as well."

"Thank you for understanding," Boaz said.

"I understand your feelings. But I still know you're making a mistake. You are stubborn though, and you will need to discover this on your own. I just hope the damage will not be too great. Also, you should not go alone, but who to send with you?"

Caleb turned to look towards Joshua and the dead kings. Soldiers had tied the bodies to nearby trees, letting them hang and sway in the mountain breeze. He saw a morose Shakra staring sadly at the dead kings.

"Shakra!" Caleb called.

Shakra, surprised, turned, and saw Caleb and Boaz. He walked slowly, with hunched shoulders, towards them.

"Yes, Prince Caleb?" Shakra asked unenthusiastically.

"I would like to make a request of you."

"I am your servant, and at your command."

"Good. I would like you to accompany Boaz."

"And where is the young master going?"

"He is not sure. He has had too much of fighting and bloodshed but does not want to return to our camp at Gilgal. He wishes to explore the land and its inhabitants."

"But who will lead my people?" Shakra asked.

"Do you still desire to lead Gibeon?" Caleb asked back, through narrowed eyes.

Shakra's jaw dropped at the question. He stood speechless for a moment, then looking down, answered: "No."

"We can send word to your people," Caleb suggested, "that you are on a mission on our behalf and that you request someone else take on the mantle of leadership."

Shakra's face transmitted his emotions. First he frowned

in contemplation, then a wide grin lit up his face.

"That would relieve me of a burden that I felt was too heavy to carry."

"Do I have a say in any of this?" Boaz interjected. "Who said I wanted or needed a companion?"

"I say," Caleb stomped his foot on the ground. "As God is my witness. I only allow you to leave us if you are escorted. The alternative is for me to drag you in chains back to Gilgal and keep you in chains until you regain your senses. I much prefer to keep my eye on you, but I accept your need to see this enemy you've been killing. But do not get too close. You will see that they may breathe and eat and work as we do. That their wishes for their children are to grow up healthy and strong. That they mean no harm to anyone. You will come to think of them as very much like yourself. But you would be wrong. We stand for something else. Something entirely new in Canaan and most likely the world. We are descendants of Abraham, Isaac and Jacob. God, the one and only God, took us out of Egypt. I was there. I saw the plagues and the splitting of the sea and Moses bringing the Law from the mountain. I heard the voice of God and I shall never forget it. And God abhors these Canaanites. He abhors these people that worship the work of their hands. That worship lifeless husks of clay and metal. That are immersed in gross sensual gratification, and care little for the life of the spirit and of truth. Their world is one of falsehood, lies and evil. Go young Boaz, if you must, if you must examine the enemy from up close. But do not be enamored of their ways. Do not be seduced by their pleasures and exotic rituals. Do not be impressed by their powers and their magic, for it is all as nothing compared to the path of our God. I do not wish for you to go. I allow it only reluctantly as I would not yet break your spirit by forbidding you. But by God, you either go with Shakra, who I pray now has the maturity, sense and understanding to keep you from harm, or I will call for the chain-master right now and you will have an uncomfortable journey back to Gilgal."

Boaz stepped back and stared at Caleb with wide eyes. Caleb had never spoken to him so forcefully, so passionately.

"I will go with Shakra," Boaz conceded.

"Good," Caleb nodded. "And I want you to return by Passover, though you are welcome and encouraged to return earlier than that. When the rains stop, you should start your journey back, especially if you've reached the coast."

Both Boaz and Shakra nodded.

"Get provisions from the supply-master and then come take your leave from Joshua," Caleb directed.

Boaz and Shakra ran excitedly to find the supply-master. The squat middle-aged supply-master grudgingly gave them each packs with a small tent, pots, fruit and dried meats. He gave them the few copper pieces he had on hand. "Don't eat anything you haven't killed or cooked yourself," he warned their backs.

They found Joshua and Caleb by the entrance to the cave where the kings had been. With the descending sun, the kings' bodies were cut down from the tree and thrown into the cave. Israelite soldiers piled large boulders in front of the entrance until the cave was impenetrable.

"I understand you are leaving us," Joshua addressed Boaz.

"Yes, sir," Boaz replied.

"I will sorely miss your special insights and your growing skills, but Caleb thinks it may be for the best."

"I wish to see the people of the land," Boaz answered.

"That is dangerous. Be cautious and make sure you come back. And remember your lessons. Not just your training with Caleb, but the commands of our teacher, Moses."

"I will."

"And you, Shakra," Joshua turned to the Gibeonite. "Guard our Boaz well and do not revert to your old ways. We take your forsaking idol-worship as permanent and steadfast. Do not expose yourselves to unnecessary risk or danger. Forty years ago, Caleb and I spied this land and learned much of great use. You are to learn and to avoid trouble. I have heard of new Phoenician weapons and iron chariots. I would learn more, their strengths and weaknesses. But remember God, our God. Do not forget Him and do not forsake Him and He shall guard you and return you safely. Godspeed."

Boaz and Shakra both bowed to Joshua. Boaz ran to Caleb and embraced him.

"Thank you, Caleb," Boaz muttered, holding back tears.

"Keep your wits about you and come back soon."

"I will."

Boaz let go of Caleb, turned around and together with Shakra, walked westward, towards the coast and the Philistines.

16. Yered the Plooper

Boaz and Shakra ran for their lives. Three ferocious dogs chased them, after the Canaanite farmer had determined the boys were not friends, relatives or even distant kinsmen of his. Boaz, much swifter than Shakra, managed to circle around the dogs, pelt each one with a stone on the head, and watch them retreat from their prey, whimpering mournfully.

"That was close," Shakra commented, catching his breath. "I could smell the dogs' last meal, and I had no intention of joining that aroma."

"Why was that farmer so distrustful?" Boaz asked. "He barely saw us before sending his attack dogs."

"Since your invasion, the Canaanites have become suspicious of anyone they don't recognize. I don't blame them."

What were we going to do? Eat all his wheat?"

"It doesn't matter, Boaz. Thanks to the devastation that Joshua is unleashing on the land, every stranger is an enemy. Not just you Israelites, but also the survivors of the city-states you've conquered. There are now hoards of refugees seeking food and shelter. I just hope we don't meet any particularly aggressive ones."

"It's getting dark. We should find a campsite for the night."

"I can see a thick copse of trees to the side of this path. Let's check it out."

Boaz and Shakra found the campsite to their liking and set up their small tent. They chewed on the dried meat and fresh fruit the supply-master had provided them. Shakra, ravenous from his exertions, gobbled his portions quickly.

"You should take it easy with the food," Boaz commented.

"I'm just so hungry, I can't help myself," Shakra answered through mouthfuls of food.

The two finished eating and lay down in their tent for the night. Each one covered in his own blanket, just a few finger-breadths from each other. Slivers of silver moonlight radiated through the folds of their tent. They both fell fast asleep.

In the middle of the night, Boaz was woken by a strange rumbling sound coming from Shakra, tossing uncomfortably next to him.

"What's the matter?" Boaz asked, rubbing his eyes.

"My stomach. I'll be back." Shakra got up and departed the tent.

Boaz rolled over and went back to sleep.

Moments later a finger jabbed him in the ribs. Boaz ignored it and rolled over. The finger jabbed him again.

"Stop it," Boaz murmured.

The insistent finger jabbed him another time.

"Shakra! Stop it!" Boaz said angrily.

Boaz felt the finger yet again.

"What is the matter with you!?" Boaz sat up quickly and yelled to his side. He was surprised to see golden teeth shining from the reflected moonlight, on the face of an ancient-looking man sitting next to him. His skin was as wrinkled as a prune, yet somehow pulled tightly on a small skeletal frame. Boaz reached for his short sword, but before he could move, the old man jabbed Boaz's neck and arms, paralyzing his limbs.

"Greeting guests with swords?" the old man asked. "Rude."

"Who are you?" Boaz asked as he shimmied backwards on his unparalyzed buttocks. "Where is Shakra? Why did you jab me?"

"Jab you? To see if you were awake. As to your companion, we believe he is parting with his dinner sooner than expected. And we? Why, we are Yered son of Job."

"Job? As in Job from the stories?"

"What stories? What have you heard of our father?" Yered insisted.

"How he suffered horribly, lost all his family and wealth. How his friends came from far to console him, how they debated with him for ages about reward and punishment, how God Himself came to settle the debate and how he got everything back afterwards. But I thought it was just a story."

"Pfah! You reduce a lifetime to a few sentences, and not even believe?"

"Our teachers in the desert would tell us Job's story in our lessons. Moses would often chuckle when he heard it."

"Moses would. We never expected that runaway to amount to anything more than a shepherd. We remember him as a child. Always causing trouble in Pharaoh's palace. Ploop!" Yered pinched Boaz's nose at the last word.

"Stop that! Why have you come here? What do you want from me?" Boaz demanded, arms and torso still paralyzed.

"We were lonely. We left home ages ago. Boring, to deal with children and grandchildren and great-grandchildren. Embarrassing, not to remember all the names. Ploop!" Yered pinched Boaz's nose.

"Ow! Please stop that!" Boaz pleaded.

"Ah. The little Judean is finally polite."

"How? How did you know I was Israelite, let alone my tribe?"

"Your little red top is like a beacon. Your facial features are not Canaanite or Egyptian. Semitic. Strong resemblance to Nachson at the same age."

"You knew Nachson? And Moses? Are you Egyptian? Why are you in Canaan?"

"Knew, of course. Egyptian? Heaven forbid. Though my father was in Pharaoh's council. We wish to see if Joshua will succeed. Ploop!"

Boaz flinched at the last word, but Yered held his hand back with a wide grin.

"If we free you, do you promise to behave?" Yered asked.

"Yes, but why do you talk about yourself in the plural? And what's with the nose-pinching?" Boaz responded.

"We carry the thoughts and memories of many generations. How else should we refer to ourselves? And nose-pinching is good for the soul." Yered quickly jabbed Boaz's neck and arms. Boaz was able to move freely once again.

Suddenly, the tent fold opened and Shakra's sword stabbed at Yered. With blinding speed, Yered moved behind Boaz.

"He's friendly!" Boaz exclaimed. "I think."

"Friendless," Yered cackled. "Wealthy, pious, wise, but friendless – curse of long life."

"Who is he?" Shakra asked, his sword still extended.

"He's Yered son of Job. You know. From the stories."

"Job's a myth. He's just some looney old geezer. Get out old man!" Shakra waved his sword at him. "Go bother some other naive fools."

"Myth?" Yered exclaimed and before anyone could move, Yered jabbed Shakra's arms and neck. Shakra collapsed onto his blanket. Yered retrieved Shakra's sword mid-fall.

"Dangerous swords. Could hurt if fall on. Ploop!" Yered pinched Shakra's nose on the floor.

"Who are you? What did you do to me?" Shakra twisted his head to look at the golden-smiled Yered.

"Carotid artery, jugular vein, vagus nerve, and radial nerve of forearm muscle we disabled. Practice of many decades to find quickly. We are Yered son of Job."

"Huh?" Shakra groaned. "Okay, okay. Let's say you're Job's son. What do you want from us?"

"From filthy Gibeonite charlatan, nothing I want. Little Hebrew interesting."

"What do you want from me?" Boaz asked.

"Company. You are the descendant of old acquaintances. It almost reminds us of younger days. Ploop!" Another squeeze of Shakra's nose.

"Agree," Shakra begged. "Anything to stop him squeezing my nose."

"Yered, you will be welcome to travel with us, if you free Shakra and promise not to squeeze our noses anymore."

"What? Nose squeezing is the best part. Look. Ploop! Ploop! Ploop! Ploop!"

"STOP!" Shakra yelled. "By the Israelite God on heaven and earth, please stop. I believe you are Job's son. I'm sorry I called your father a myth and you a geezer. Though the stories never mentioned a nose-pinching fetish in your family."

"We know the Hebrew God. The lying Gibeonite is perhaps more sophisticated than we thought. But we shall not relinquish our freely taken right to nose-pinch until you have tried it yourself," Yered motioned to Boaz.

"I shall not." Boaz crossed his arms.

"Wonderful!" Yered exclaimed. "More for us! Ploop! Ploop! Ploop! Ploop!"

"BOAZ!" Shakra screamed frantically. "Just do it and get it over with!"

"Okay, okay," Boaz agreed. "I'll squeeze his nose, and then you'll stop?"

"Yes," Yered nodded. "But you must say 'Ploop!' while squeezing."

"I'm sorry, Shakra," Boaz told his friend and he grabbed his nose. "Ploop!"

"Delicious," Yered grinned gleefully. He jabbed Shakra in the neck and arms. Shakra's stiffened limbs revived.

"Why don't you just join the Israelite camp, if you are looking for old friends or their descendants?" Shakra asked as he massaged his neck and arms.

"Only Caleb and Joshua do we remember from those days. They would not welcome us. Our father did not stand for Hebrews in Pharaoh's council. They would chuckle, as their master Moses did, at the story of my father's tribulations. Nachshon was more understanding, always more daring, more open. Not a philosopher. Enough of philosophers. We will settle for young descendant." Yered looked down, hiding his gleaming teeth from the moon.

"Why do you have golden teeth?" Boaz asked.

Yered smiled again, lightening the tent.

"Our invention. Our own teeth rotted. Egyptians use wood in place. Doesn't last. Different metals hurt. Rich enough for gold. Best. Where are you travelling?"

"To the Philistines," Boaz and Shakra answered in unison.

"Good. Excellent taverns."

Yered immediately grabbed Shakra's blanket, lay down, and fell into a deep sleep, quietly cooing 'Ploop'.

Boaz and Shakra, their mouths hanging open, stared at their suddenly unconscious uninvited guest.

"Can you believe this guy?" Shakra finally said.

"Not really, but he's got the right idea. Let's go back to sleep. Here, I have a spare blanket." Boaz tossed the woolen fabric to Shakra, turned over and covered himself.

Shakra looked at the ancient guest, at the young Judean and then wondered to himself, *how did I get into such strange company?*

17. Philistine Homecoming

Seeing his briefly adopted city of Ashkelon again, brought Akavish pangs of pain and remorse. He remembered killing the Canaanite defenders as he assisted his grandfather, Krafus, in disabling the defenses and opening the gate to the fortified city. He remembered his father's callousness towards him. Big Larus was not only ungrateful for Akavish delivering the city to him, but had smacked him in a most demeaning fashion. Only his pet, Risto, showed Akavish love and appreciation.

The little monkey clutched Akavish's left shoulder, as always. Akavish had decided to enter the city at night, unannounced, just as he had on the night his sea-faring tribe invaded Canaan and conquered Ashkelon.

Akavish scaled the eastern wall this time. The Philistines had no fear from that direction and left no guards upon the eastern ramparts. He thus jumped when a voice spoke to him from the darkness of the night.

"Welcome home, youngster."

"Krafus!" Akavish greeted his old mentor. "What are you doing here?"

Akavish could make out spry Krafus sitting on the floor of the rampart, his back resting against the balustrade as he picked his teeth with the tip of his throwing knife.

"I was expecting you."

"How did you know I would return? How did you know it would be here and now?"

"Young cubs often return home to rest from the hunt. How I knew to wait here for you tonight of all nights? I cannot reveal all my methods to you just yet."

"How is father?"

"He also expects you."

"And what will be the manner of my welcome?"

"As you might expect."

"Lovely. How goes his rule over the Canaanites?"

"Surprisingly well. These Canaanites are mercenary in their allegiances, to god or ruler. After you left, Larus killed the King of Ashkelon and most of his family. He spared the oldest daughter and made her his new wife. So congratulations are in order for you as well, on your new mother. The Canaanites do not object to Larus' rule. It seems they are even happier with Larus than with their previous king. Nonetheless, he is easily angered. Do you still wish to see him?"

"I must. We must attack the Israelites. They are a menace and I think only the combined strength of all the Philistines will stop them."

"Beware, young prince. We have all heard stories of the young Philistine boy who fought at Gibeon with stars of death. Larus was not pleased nor did he take pride in those stories."

Akavish walked past old Krafus, towards where he knew the king's residence must be.

"I did what I had to, and so I will do now. I do not fear him." Akavish turned his head towards Krafus, without looking at him.

"You should," Krafus responded to Akavish's receding back. "There is no greater danger to a son than an angry father."

Akavish found the guarded entrance to his father's new home. The guards, recognizing Akavish, let him pass uncontested, with no word, except for an evil smirk on their faces. They looked at him, Akavish thought, as an unruly child about to be spanked. *Well, this child has sharp teeth,* Akavish thought, patting the metal stars inside his garment.

"Enter, my son," was the answer to Akavish's knock on the heavy wooden door.

Big Larus was as large and imposing as ever. He sat behind a table too low for his massive body and was on a wooden chair that creaked under his muscular bulk. His long broadsword lay sheathed at his side. He was studying a papyrus scroll. A lone candle on the table illuminated the room.

"The wayward son returns," Larus stated, not looking up from the scroll.

"I did not feel welcome or wanted," Akavish responded to the implied accusation.

"What makes you think that has changed?"

"Nothing. I was foolish to return."

"You are foolish, period."

"I'm sorry to have disturbed you." Akavish turned and walked back to the door.

"What do you want!?" Larus banged his large fist on the table.

"From you? Nothing." Akavish turned to face his father. "Just perhaps that I would have been sired by another."

"This is how you speak to me!?" Larus stood up and unsheathed his sword.

"I'm not afraid of you."

"Than you are more foolish than I imagined. You have forgotten who is master." Larus approached Akavish with drawn sword.

Risto jumped off Akavish's shoulder to hide in the safety of the shadows. Akavish threw four stars, one at each of Larus' limbs. Larus swatted three of them away with his sword. One penetrated his defense and embedded itself in Larus' left leg. It did not slow Larus down. Akavish readied four more stars but was shocked to see the tip of Larus' sword flying at his head. Akavish ducked. The sword clattered against the stone wall behind Akavish. By the time Akavish looked up again, Larus held his thin neck in a choke-hold with a single hand. Larus raised Akavish and smashed him against the wall, never loosening his grip on his son.

"The Canaanites must be pathetic indeed if they tell tales of your little flying trinkets. Tell me! Why did you come back? It wasn't for love or loyalty."

Akavish's face turned blue from lack of breath. He tried to ply his father's steel grip open with both of his own hands, with no success. Larus finally brought Akavish down to the ground, released his neck, but held him against the wall, holding his hand firmly on Akavish's chest.

"Speak!" Larus commanded.

Akavish panted as he tried to catch his breath.

"I fought the Israelites and lost. My Canaanite allies were annihilated. I want you to unite the other Philistine tribes and challenge the Israelites. Otherwise, they will reach your doorstep as well, and then your brand new city will be lost. I saw them take on five Canaanite armies and destroy them without suffering a scratch. Joshua is the most powerful sorcerer I have ever heard of. I saw him stop the sun itself. I have never heard of anyone having such power."

Larus released Akavish and walked back to his table.

"How did I raise such a fool? Why do you go seeking battles that are not your own? Are you so hungry for death? I am not concerned about the Israelites. This is neither the time nor the place for battle between us. They will have their hands full with the Canaanites on the mountains. It will be some time before they dare attack the coast, and if they do, they will find us challenging targets. I have analyzed reports of their battles, and especially of their losses. I have been in touch with the Amalekites, the first to confront and wound them forty years ago. I have just read of the Moabites and Midianites who brought down a great plague upon Israel, even while the great Moses was alive." Larus pointed at the papyrus on his table. "I have even heard reports about the first battle of Ai, which was a rout for the Israelites. I know their weakness and we shall exploit it when the time comes."

"What is their weakness? How will you fight them?" Akavish asked as he massaged his neck.

"I will not fight them. Whoever has tried a frontal attack upon the Israelites has failed. Their god is strong and protects them. But that is also their greatest weakness. Their god. Their god is demanding. No worship of other gods. No sleeping with other women. They are so strict, they even executed one poor sap and his entire family for his stealing some of the loot of Jericho, which Joshua had declared 'holy'. All we need to do is entice them to sin against their god and his commands, as the Midianites did. The Hebrew god struck the Israelites down himself with a devastating plague."

"How will you get them to sin?" Akavish wondered.

"I will befriend them. I will sell them our wares. I will send our most beautiful priestesses. I will show them the pleasure of our ways and teach them of our gods. Nothing will anger their god more than that. We may not even have to fight. Their god may do the work for us. Do not worry about the Israelites."

"I am the fool?" Akavish asked incredulously. "If you had seen what I had seen, you would not be so confident. They are like a flood in a wadi during the winter rains. They wash over everything and destroy all in their path. They are unstoppable. Strong, powerful Canaanites attacked the Israelites with all their might, but they were as gnats attacking a giant. The Israelites sliced through the Canaanite defense as a sharp ax through wormy wood. They have warriors with superhuman speed and magical powers. Even their children are fearsome warriors." Akavish shivered thinking of his last encounter with Boaz. "You are delusional if you think sitting quietly here and sending them pretty things will conquer them."

Larus pivoted on his feet and slapped Akavish a great blow across the face. From the force of the impact Akavish fell to the floor, a large red welt spreading across his face.

"When will you learn respect?" Larus asked.

"When it is deserved." Akavish answered.

Larus' face turned red and he shook in anger.

"Leave now, before I kill you."

"This is the love of a father?" Akavish picked himself off the floor.

"Are you deserving of love?" Larus retorted.

"Do I have to be deserving of love?"

"Yes. I cannot love someone disloyal or disrespectful."

"Then I guess we deserve each other." Akavish left the room without bothering to close the door. Risto jumped on to Akavish's shoulder as he entered the shadows outside the room.

"So now you come back to me?" Akavish accused Risto. "Where were you when I needed you?"

Risto chattered back something unintelligible. It didn't matter. Akavish was not listening in any case.

18. Boys' Bar Brawl

Akavish, with an unhappy Risto on his shoulder, opened a heavy oak door and adjusted his eyes to the darkness. The tavern was musty and fragrant with pipe smoke that curled around everyone and everything. Red wine gushed generously from large vases and Philistines and Canaanites sat amicably side by side in various states of merriment and intoxication. At the far end of the tavern, a lamb on a spit cooked over an open fire. A young man strummed soothingly on a harp.

Some of the Philistines were recognizable to Akavish; however, the majority of the men were Canaanites. There were also a few Phoenician traders, and two men at a table that could only have been Egyptian, with their white garments and shaved heads. Ashkelon had quickly reverted to a mercantile port under Larus' rule.

Akavish found an empty stool to the right of an ancient looking man. On the other side of the old man, Akavish noted the back of a boy who could not have been much younger than his own twelve years. The boy was absorbed in talking to a tall youth next to him.

Akavish placed his thin frame on the stool. The tavern-keeper ignored him.

"Mead!" Akavish slapped the wooden counter.

"Can you pay for it, child?" the tavern-keeper asked.

Akavish slammed a copper piece on the counter. The copper piece disappeared as a mug of sloshing mead appeared in its place.

"That is a curious creature on your shoulder," the old man said to Akavish.

"What's it to you?" Akavish didn't bother looking up from his drink.

"So young, to drink and be rude," the old man commented. He then addressed a series of chittering sounds at the monkey. Risto jabbered back excitedly.

"At least the monkey is polite to us." The old man flashed a golden smile at Akavish. "The monkey says you've had a rough time and a falling out with your father. Though you are typically rude, he says that you don't usually seek solace in taverns."

Akavish looked at Risto and then at the old man with wide eyes.

"He told you that?" Akavish asked.

"Of course. We are not liars and the monkey is very bright."

Risto nodded in agreement.

"Leave me alone," Akavish said.

"The intemperate are always alone. Taverns are gathering of the lonely. One pretends companionship for brief moments, or drinks, until one can live with the loneliness again." The old man gestured at Risto with his fist; while sticking his thumb and pinky out he placed the thumb on his own nose and then stuck out his tongue. Risto mimicked the old man's movements exactly and chittered some more.

"From the order of Lucian of Sheba?" the old man gave a nod of approval. "We thought so from the accent. This child is destined for mighty deeds? Curious. We have another one here."

The old man pushed his stool back and motioned to the boy next to him.

"Boaz, meet a rude young man."

Boaz and Akavish stared at each other across the space in front of the old man. They each froze for a moment and then pushed off of their stools to stand facing each other, with swords drawn.

"What are you doing here?" Akavish asked as he aimed a cut at Boaz's arm. Boaz parried and returned a stab at

Akavish's stomach. Akavish blocked. The patrons of the tavern turned noisily towards the fight. A short Philistine in the back of the tavern took wagers as to which of the combatants would win. The harpist picked up the pace of his strumming.

"Yered brought us here." Boaz counterattacked. "He said Ashkelon has the best drinks. What are you doing here? Last I saw you was in Gibeon."

"What am I doing here!? This is my home. My father is king here."

"You're the son of a king? Why did you seek me out? Why do you want to kill me?"

"You don't deserve to live." Akavish hammered at Boaz's defense. Boaz blocked every attack. "You are too young to be so famous. Why should tales be told of a ten-year old that makes hardened warriors quake? You're just human, just a little brat. I would show the world that. I am just as good as the famous Boaz. I am better! I will prove it now by killing you."

Akavish grabbed Risto, who was still clinging to his shoulder, and threw him at Boaz's face – a tactic that had served him effectively in the past. A moment after he threw Risto, Akavish followed with a rapid slash at Boaz's sword arm. Risto flew towards Boaz's head, his small claws reaching for Boaz's eyes. Boaz instinctively backhanded the flying Risto towards Akavish. Risto bounced like a stringless puppet into the path of Akavish's sword. Akavish could not stop his violent slash which cut Risto's thin arm, severing it above its hairy elbow.

Risto shrieked in anguish as rivulets of blood streamed onto the tavern floor.

"You animal!" Akavish yelled at Boaz and continued slashing at Boaz in a berserker rage. The patrons of the bar gasped and stepped back at Akavish's fury. The harpist stopped strumming, his attention fully engaged by the duel.

Boaz retreated under the onslaught, as the entire tavern watched, fascinated by the ferocious dance of the diminutive warriors.

"That's a reason to kill me? Just to prove that you're better? What's wrong with you?" Boaz yelled.

"I'll tell you what's wrong, you Israelite slug. I never knew my mother. My father is a vicious bully, whose idea of love is a punch in the stomach, and whom I can never please. If I could kill the young hero of Israel, perhaps that would get his attention, his respect. I gave up long ago on his love."

Akavish assaulted Boaz with a barrage of stabbing attacks aimed at arms, torso and face. With blurring speed, Boaz weaved in and out of Akavish's reach.

"Killing me won't solve anything."

"I don't care. I can think of nothing else worthwhile to do with my life. And now the gods have brought you right to me. Die!"

Akavish disengaged from Boaz, threw a handful of his metallic stars at Boaz's face and then lunged at Boaz with outstretched sword. Boaz dropped to the floor, slicing upwards to intercept the stars. Instead, he sliced into Akavish's sword arm, just below the shoulder. The arm continued its trajectory across the floor of the tavern. Akavish fell onto Boaz, armless and shocked.

"My sword? My arm? Where is it?" Akavish saw his right arm, tightly gripping his sword, a few feet away, next to the lamb on the spit. The tavern patrons gasped collectively at the sudden end of the battle. Akavish fainted as he gushed blood over Boaz.

Yered approached the unconscious Akavish and wrapped up his bleeding stump expertly and quickly.

"Two right arms lost in one night. Jerusalem, they have forgotten. The monkey and the boy are bound tightly. Stand, young Boaz. His own people will care for him now.

Where to?" Yered asked Boaz as he picked him up from under Akavish's body.

"Home. I'm ready to go home," Boaz answered, looking at his sword in anguish.

"You are not going anywhere," a deep voice rumbled. Big Larus stood at the entrance to the tavern, accompanied by half a dozen Philistine soldiers. "No one does this to me, to my family, and leaves unscathed. You will be punished."

Larus lumbered closer to Yered and Boaz.

"We will attempt to stop him. You and the Gibeonite, run!"

Skeletal Yered threw himself at the Philistine giant, jabbing his fingers into Larus' neck, arms and torso. Larus merely swatted the old man aside with a beefy fist to the face. Yered flew into the tavern wall and crumpled into an unconscious heap on the floor.

Tall Shakra waited until Larus passed him and then attempted to stab him from behind. One of the Philistine soldiers intercepted Shakra's blade. Larus whirled around and grabbed Shakra by the neck, lifting him a few feet off the floor.

"A comrade?" Larus asked at the choking Shakra. "But young and strong. Perhaps of some use. Bind him!" Larus commanded as he threw Shakra into the hands of two Philistine soldiers.

"And you, little warrior." Larus turned back to Boaz, standing over the unconscious Akavish. "You deserve a very special torture. But there is no gain in death. What shall we do?" Larus looked up and held his clean-shaven chin. "I know. We shall sell you and your gangly friend to the copper mines at Timna. I hear the Egyptians are always seeking fresh replacements." Larus looked at the transfixed white-robed Egyptians at their table. "For some reason their slaves die very quickly in the mines."

"I'm not going to any mine," Boaz responded. "I did not ask for this fight. He brought it upon himself."

"My son is foolish and headstrong, but he is still my son and I shall avenge the injury you have caused. Guards! Bind him!"

Two Philistine soldiers approached Boaz, one with heavy iron shackles in his hands. Boaz ran to the side and evaded the soldiers. He burst into a sprint, rapidly making his way towards the exit, but not a moment later smashed into Larus' outstretched muscular arm and fell to the floor.

"I will sell you to the slavers," Larus told the dazed Boaz on the floor. "And I shall make a little silver in exchange for the rest of what will be a short, drug-filled and miserable existence in Timna."

Boaz tried to get off the floor only to see a large and heavy sandaled foot approach his face. And then he remembered nothing.

19. Monkey in the Middle

Pain assaulted Akavish's awareness from multiple points. His mouth was dry and sticky. In semi-consciousness he tried to open it, but his thirsting lips would not part. He groaned but no sound reached his ears. He was light-headed. He had trouble organizing his thoughts. He remembered Boaz and a duel. He had been about to kill Boaz, once and for all. But something had gone horribly wrong.

The sharp pain just below his right shoulder reminded him. Boaz had cut off his arm. Tears welled up in his closed eyes. *My arm?* Akavish thought. *Is it possible?*

Akavish felt the bed underneath him and the clean sheets over him. He had been cared for. He still felt pain down his arm. *How is that possible? Was it reattached somehow? Did I dream of losing it?*

Akavish slowly moved his left arm towards the stump that was his right. His fingers drew back suddenly from the place where his arm should have been. Tears fell freely down his face. *It is gone! Yet I still feel the pain!*

Akavish sat up in his bed and opened his eyes. He saw Krafus sitting in a corner of the small room, staring at him with pained eyes.

"Water," Akavish managed to croak.

Krafus brought a copper cup to Akavish's lips and held the cup for him as Akavish fumbled it with his left hand. Akavish drained the cup.

"My arm," Akavish stated.

"Yes," Krafus answered, understanding the question. "It is gone."

"But I can still feel it."

"Yes, warriors who've lost limbs talk of the sensation. They swear they can feel their fingers or move their toes, but it is clearly gone."

"It doesn't grow back, does it?"

"Not unless you're a lizard."

"What happened with Boaz?"

"Your father stopped him and his friend and sold them to the Timna mine. They won't last long there."

"What about Risto? He was also hurt."

"I've not seen your monkey since the fight."

"I must find him."

"You must recuperate first. You nearly died. And it will take you time to get used to your new condition."

"You mean as a cripple?"

"No. Not a cripple. It is true you will be at a great disadvantage, and you can give up on the path of a warrior, but I have known many one-armed men who went on to lead productive lives."

"I am a fighter and that is what I shall do." Akavish got out of bed, only to fall back into it.

"What happened?" Akavish groaned.

"You lost much blood. If you try to get up slowly it might be easier."

"Perhaps I'll rest a little bit longer." Akavish covered himself again.

"Not so dumb after all," Krafus declared as he got up. "I'll go fetch you some food."

*

The boy hunted for green. His singular task in life was to find the green rivulets within the rock. The oil lantern was his only friend in his underground prison. He used a small chisel to cut the innards of the earth. He was careful to examine each crumbly grain of dirt. If he found the green, he was to place it lovingly in the bucket at his side. His masters had warned him not to lose any of the green, any of the precious copper. He had the whip marks to remind him. His back still stung from his recent lashing. His whole body was racked with pain and fatigue. He didn't remember how long he had been digging. Days, months, years? His whole existence seemed a continuous stream of digging. He would collapse to the ground from exhaustion only to be kicked awake a few hours later. Upon awakening he was given a ladle-full of smelly water and a dried crust of bread and a whipping if he didn't start chiseling again quickly.

He tried to remember. Anything. But his mind was a jumble of thoughts and visions that made no sense. His name? He wasn't sure. *Boaz? Boaz. Yes. That sounds right.*

What am I doing here? How did I get here? But he couldn't think clearly. Not knowing what to do and fearing the whip, Boaz kept chiseling with less and less strength.

*

Risto slapped his furry little hand against his side. He rode on Yered's shoulder. The old man had nursed the little monkey's wound and allowed Risto to travel with him. Yered had even tied a thin branch to the stump on Risto's right side. It was small comfort for the loss of his arm, but he somehow felt better with the branch on rather than off.

Risto was furious with himself. He had grown fond of Akavish. Too fond. He had been aware of Akavish's many character faults, but had enjoyed the boy's company and attention. The partnership had turned deadly in their last encounter with the other prodigy, and now both Risto and Akavish had lost an arm. Risto wanted to have nothing further to do with Akavish and decided to follow the eccentric, yet kind old man under him.

"Joshua and Caleb will laugh at us," Yered grumbled to Risto.

Risto chittered at Yered.

"I know, I know. It is the only hope for Boaz and the Gibeonite."

Yered approached the Israelite camp at Gilgal, unarmed, except for a one-armed monkey on his shoulder.

*

"You saw Risto leave with the old man with the golden teeth?" Akavish asked the tavern-keeper.

"Yes. The old man woke up after your father smashed him against the wall. He tended to your monkey and said something about going to Timna."

"To Timna? To the copper mines? What's he looking for there?"

"I presume he wants to find his young friends. Perhaps you should seek some human friends, as opposed to chasing after some jungle animal."

"That animal is my friend. The only one I have." Akavish stormed out of the tavern.

"I'm not surprised," the tavern-keeper said to Akavish's back.

*

Boaz had brief moments of clarity. *I'm being drugged, he realized. That is why my mind is so numb. I can barely think how to get out of this hole. I must retain clarity, but how? I already feel it slipping away.* Boaz continued with his mindless digging.

*

"The son of Job?" Joshua asked incredulously.

"Hard of hearing, young Joshua?" Yered responded.

"Why should I believe your tale? Boaz is a very capable child. I can't believe he would get entangled in a bar fight, and even less so, to be sold as a slave to the Egyptian copper mines."

"You have not met Larus, nor been smashed into unconsciousness, nor taken in iron chains, nor mind-numbed from continuous drugs. The child will die if you do nothing."

"How is it this creature is with you?" Caleb asked. "Last we saw him was atop the shoulder of that deadly little Philistine, who was so intent on killing Boaz."

"The decades in the desert have addled your brains. The monkey tired of the little monster. He is also one-handed now. We make for much more interesting company," Yered pointed at himself. "Send troops to Timna to free them, if you care for the boy's life and that of his friend, the Gibeonite. Otherwise, to certain, though slow and painful death, you doom them. We are ready and willing to accompany you. It would be suicidal for us to go on our own. We are not yet ready to give up our inordinately long life."

"Why should we believe you?"

"Are you willing to take the chance that we are right?"

*

Krafus insisted on accompanying Akavish. They hired camels in Beer Sheva for the long trek south to Timna.

Akavish rode unhappily atop the camel.

"How is one supposed to ride these infernal beasts?" Akavish asked.

"Much like a horse, I suppose. Point them in the right direction and make sure not to fall off."

"They smell and this heat is suffocating." Akavish tried to wipe his sweaty brow, with his lone remaining hand, lost balance, and promptly toppled off the camel, to the dusty, hard ground of the Negev desert.

*

Where is the drug, Boaz thought in his moment of clarity. *The bread? What can they place in that dry piece of bark? The water? No, I've noticed the masters drinking from it as well. What is it? It must be something in the air. Yes. That must be why they cover their faces when they come in the mine. That is it. If I can raise my shirt up to my nose and take it off when they approach…*

*

Caleb led a dozen of his best soldiers south along the shore of the shining Salt Sea. Caleb feared strange Yered was telling the truth and time was of the essence. "Let's hurry!" Caleb shouted as he pushed his mounted troops faster. They galloped, the horses raising a cloud of dust that mingled with the strong salty fumes from the sea.

*

Krafus and Akavish could see the opening to the great copper mine of Timna. The red mountains were a stark contrast to cloudless blue sky. From the south, they could smell the breeze from the Sea of Reeds.

"Let me handle this," Krafus told Akavish as a burly Egyptian overseer approached.

"You come for copper?" The Egyptian asked.

"Perhaps," Krafus answered.

"This one not good for slave," the Egyptian pointed at Akavish's missing arm, "so better be to buy copper."

"We seek information."

"Copper prices have not changed."

"We are seeking a man. A very old man. He may have had an unusual animal with him."

"Don't know what you're talking about. Wasting my time. Leave." The Egyptian turned his back and walked back to the mine entrance.

"Is there a young boy here?" Akavish blurted. "An Israelite, red-head, about ten or eleven years old?"

The Egyptian turned around.

"All are young boys here. I don't care for age, color or nation. Thinking that one-hand can probably also dig." The Egyptian approached menacingly. Akavish noticed the whip in his hand and the large sword by his side. Half a dozen Egyptian guards, showing interest in the discussion, left the mine entrance and approached Krafus and Akavish.

"Never mind," Krafus called out and turned his camel away, motioning to Akavish to follow.

"Not buying copper, not selling slaves, asking strange questions. By Ra! Spies or troublemakers. Deal with each same way." The Egyptians closed in on Krafus and Akavish.

Arrows suddenly protruded from the chests of each of the Egyptians. The Egyptians had just enough time to register surprise as they dropped to the floor, dead.

"Yered spoke the truth," an Israelite voice called out. "There is the one-armed Philistine boy."

Akavish looked up the mountain to see a dozen Israelite soldiers with Caleb, and fresh arrows in bows aimed at him. He was pleased to see his monkey on the old man's shoulder.

"Risto!" Akavish called out. "Come to me." Akavish opened his arms.

Risto did not budge off of Yered's shoulder, but merely glared at Akavish.

"You four," Caleb pointed at soldiers to his left. "Guard the Philistines. The rest, with me to the mine."

Before Caleb could reach the mine entrance, they heard a commotion from deep within the mine. Suddenly, an exhausted, blood-drenched Boaz emerged, with a bloody chisel in his hand. Shakra, the Gibeonite, was behind him, together with dozens of children, teenagers and men, bedraggled, bloody and blinking in the strong desert sun.

"Caleb!" Boaz shouted joyously. "What took you so long? I thought I would live out the rest of a mindless existence down there."

"It looks like you didn't need us after all." Caleb grinned.

"We spoke the truth," Yered added "The child is fortunate."

Akavish stuck his left hand in his tunic, but Krafus grabbed his arm with a vice-like grip.

"Have you learned nothing, child!" Krafus berated Akavish. "Do you wish to die so badly? You would attempt to kill this child, at which you have failed so miserably, while surrounded by four of his compatriots with arrows pointed at your heart?" Krafus released Akavish's arm. "Perhaps you deserve to die. You can put your idiotic and misguided existence out of its short and tragic misery."

Akavish looked back to Risto.

"Risto, please, come back to me."

Risto jumped off of Yered's shoulder, grabbed ahold of Yered's water skin and filled his mouth from it. He then hopped to Akavish. Within arm's reach, Risto spat a gush of water at Akavish's face. Surprised, Akavish spluttered as the water dripped to the dry desert floor. Risto turned his back on Akavish and farted loudly. He hopped back to Yered and jumped onto his shoulder.

"That's incredible!" Shakra exclaimed. "That animal really doesn't like you."

"There is nothing more for you here." Krafus held Akavish's arm tenderly. "Let's go home."

Akavish looked one last time at Risto, his sole childhood companion and friend. He then turned to look at Boaz, and saw him as if for the first time.

Boaz, sensing a change in Akavish, called out:

"Do you still hate me?"

"Probably. But I hate myself more," Akavish answered with the heaviness of truth. "Let's go home," he turned to Krafus.

Caleb motioned for the Israelite soldiers to let them go. Krafus and Akavish cantered their camels northward without looking back.

Caleb and Boaz hugged.

"When I could think, I thought this was my end." Boaz cried. "That I would be doomed to this eternal hellish trance. I'm so glad you came."

"You seem to have escaped on your own."

"If those guards had been at their posts and you hadn't shot them, I'm not sure we would have had the strength to make it."

"Well, we are safe now. Are you ready?"

"Yes, please. Let's go home."

To War with the Eastern Tribes

From the diary of Boaz the Bethlehemite, Elder of the Tribe of Judah. The sixty-eighth year since the Tribes of Israel crossed the River Jordan into Canaan.

"Though consistently triumphant, the natural order prevailed during the remainder of Joshua's battles. The miraculous days of Moses, the manna from heaven, and the lighting-fast conquests of the vast tracts of land east of the Jordan, all became a vague recollection to me. Even the fantastic battles at Jericho and at Gibeon seemed like a distant memory. It took seven years for the Children of Israel to conquer the land of Canaan, and even then, there were significant areas that the Canaanites still held. Thankfully, Joshua excused me from further fighting. Eventually, I was able to play and study as a normal child, reclaiming some of that lost innocence. It lessened the trauma of the death and destruction I had been a part of.

The armies of Israel conquered many cities and killed many soldiers. The idols and their worshippers were destroyed throughout the land. But there was still a vast population of Canaanites that went unconquered and unchallenged. It took a further seven years to divide the conquered land amongst the less aggressive tribes. My tribe of Judah, under Caleb's leadership, was the first to claim our vast territory, stretching southward from Jerusalem over the mountains and down to the desert of Beer Sheva. The descendants of Joseph, namely the tribe of Ephraim and the western half of the tribe of Menashe, secured their territory from the ancient city of Shechem and northwards.

The Reubenites, Gadites and half of the Menashites, the two-and-a-half tribes, as they were called, had their territories on the eastern side of the Jordan, bequeathed to them by Moses himself, on condition that they fight with the western tribes. They had done so admirably.

One story I heard but did not witness, tells how the Reubenites, upon attacking a city and overcoming the initial defense would immediately attack the city's temple, smashing its idols, dismantling the altars and then burning the structure. It seemed this took the heart out of the defenders and made conquest all the easier.

The two-and-a-half tribes had left their families and possessions behind and were always at the forefront of every battle. After the battles of conquest ended, the two-and-a-half tribes pressed Joshua to let them return home, or to proceed with division of the rest of the land to the tribes that had not yet claimed any.

The tribe of Levi, dedicated to the service of God, would receive no tribal allotment. Rather they would be split up throughout cities in Israel and give guidance and instruction to the rest of Israel. The other tribes, Simeon, Yissachar, Zevulun, Dan, Naftali, Asher and Benjamin were comfortable in the camp of Shilo. There was a unity and camaraderie they were hesitant to give up. Joshua berated them:

'How long will you hesitate to go in to possess the land, which the Lord has given you? Appoint for you three men for each tribe and walk through the land, and describe it according to their inheritance. And they shall divide it into seven portions.'

Surveyors were sent to the conquered territories. They measured tribal boundaries. They noted the cities that belonged to each territory. Upon their return, Joshua conducted a public lottery. The names of the seven remaining tribes were written on a small piece of parchment and placed in a burlap bag. The names of the demarcated territories were likewise written on parchment and placed in a separate bag. The princes of the homeless tribes grabbed one parchment from each bag. So the territories were assigned.

The two-and-a-half tribes went back home. I was twenty-four that year. And then we received the news: after a fourteen-year campaign of eradicating idol worship, after having worshipped together with us at the sole Tabernacle in Shilo, we received word that the two-and-a-half tribes had built their own altar on the banks of the River Jordan, on the border of their tribal allotment. This meant war. War with our own brothers.

Joshua dispatched Pinhas the priest and the ten western tribal princes. They went together with the top soldiers and commanders. Joshua said it would be a diplomatic delegation. It was a delegation with hundreds of Israel's most fearsome warriors. And Joshua asked me to go along...

20. Boaz the Coward

"You said *what* to her?" Amitai, his childhood companion, asked, as he and Boaz rode northwards on their donkeys along with the large procession. At twenty-three years old, Amitai was still a bit chubby, with ruddy cheeks, unruly brown curls and an easy smile.

"I told Vered I wasn't ready," Boaz murmured. At twenty-four years old, Boaz was a tall and powerful figure. His red hair had lost none of its luster and his well-formed muscles could be discerned under his tunic. A short fuzzy beard adorned his square jaw.

They were at the front of the contingent from Judah. They rode with the morning sun along the Jordan River. The hot summer days had reduced the power of the River, which flowed strongest in the spring. Pinhas the Priest and ten princes led the tribes from the west side of the Jordan to find the recalcitrant tribes from the east.

"Your cousin? On the day she was expecting you to ask for her hand?" Amitai pushed.

"Yes," Boaz nodded.

"That's bad."

"Really bad," Boaz agreed. "I was told one of Vered's brothers was furious at the insult, and would chase me and force me to marry her."

"Good thing you were asked to join this expedition. That side of your family can be rather foul-tempered."

"Yes. Hopefully, he won't find me amongst the hundreds of soldiers here."

*

"So the coward deigns to accompany us," Ploni, one of Boaz's uncles, caught up with Boaz and Amitai. His voice was loud enough for the rest of the mounted Judeans to hear.

Ploni was ten years Boaz's senior. His arms and neck were heavily scarred from old battle wounds. Ploni had risen to the rank of Captain of a Hundred during the conquest of Canaan.

"You say nothing, little nephew?" Ploni continued. "You crawl out of your hole now that trouble has passed, for a mere diplomatic meeting?"

"A meeting?" Boaz answered in a deep bass. "You call an assembly of hundreds of our best warriors a meeting? We go to fight the other tribes who have betrayed our God."

"Ah, little scholar," Ploni sneered. "How little of the world you know. If you had fought beside those men, if you had seen the leadership, the bravery of Gedel and the others, you would know the eastern tribes would never rebel against God." There were murmurs of agreements from the soldiers within earshot of Ploni.

"But you," Ploni continued, "you are just a studious little coward who believes the first accusation he hears against good and honorable men."

"I follow orders." Boaz lifted his chin up. "We go to investigate the building of a pagan altar by our brothers. They had better have a good explanation, lest we bring down God's very wrath upon them."

"You besmirch the honor of all warriors by riding with us. We do not presume that our brothers are guilty. That is why the priest rides at our head and not a general. We will not raise our hand against our brothers, the accusations will prove baseless. But I guess you can think and do whatever you please. You were always Caleb's pet."

"Have you nothing better to do Ploni, than to fan the flames of old imagined grievances?" Boaz raised his voice.

"Caleb requested that I join the mission. Why are you bitter that I stopped fighting? I still don't understand."

"Bitter? I'm not bitter, young pacifist. I'm betrayed, I'm embarrassed. I'm hurt that the most promising warrior of our people, our tribe, our family, became a coward. We used to retell your adventures with great pride. We looked forward to fighting by your side, to be associated with your glory. But ever since you returned from that mine in Timna, you have proved yourself a weakling. To have such talent as yours and not use it in our struggle is nothing less than cowardice. I think Caleb himself was deeply disappointed."

"You know nothing of Caleb's feelings," Boaz responded hotly.

"Ah, our young firebrand has some flame left in him after all. If only you had used it against our enemies, perhaps there would not be so much land unconquered. I have heard that Joshua himself was saddened by our lack of progress and most likely looked to you as the cause."

"Leave me alone, Ploni, You don't know what you're talking about."

"You *are* alone, Boaz. Cowards always are."

Boaz stopped his donkey and let the Judean soldiers trot ahead. Their swords and saddles clinked around him as they covered him in the dust of the road. None of his tribesmen deigned to look at him. He felt as if they all silently agreed with Ploni. They thought him a coward and wished to avoid this embarrassing member of their tribe.

*

Pinhas positioned the archers in the front of the procession as they approached the river crossing. He and the princes rode behind them, followed by the tribe of Judah, including Boaz and Ploni. In the distance they saw thousands of soldiers massed on the eastern bank of the river. A long row of archers with their arrows notched, stood behind a line of spearmen with raised shields.

"A meeting?" Boaz murmured to Ploni.

"Gedel is no fool," Ploni answered. "He is ready for a fight if we bring it to him, but he is blameless."

"Blameless men don't need an army to explain their innocence."

Some Judeans around Boaz murmured their agreement.

"This formation is proof of his guilt," Boaz continued. "We should attack right away." Boaz removed his sword from its sheath. Other Judeans followed suit. Archers on the other side of the river noticed the movement and aimed their arrows at Boaz and the other Judeans, but did not shoot.

Ploni grabbed Boaz's arm and forced him to re-sheath his sword.

"Stop it, you hothead! If men were to rely on others to uphold their innocence, innocent men would quickly cease to be. People may listen to the truth, but they listen better when there is some steel behind it. Put your sword away before you hurt yourself and wait for instruction from your betters."

A tall grey-haired man appeared in the middle of the formation.

"Hail Gedel, Prince of Reuben!" Pinhas called across the narrow river. Pinhas was flanked by archers and with several hundred soldiers at his back, swords still in their sheaths.

Gedel was a large muscular man with bristly grey hair and a long grey beard. He held a sharp battle ax against his shoulder.

"Hail Pinhas, son of Elazar, son of Aaron!" Gedel responded to Pinhas in his priestly robe. Gedel's voice echoed across the flowing river. A vulture circled above, excited by the meeting of two armies. Several thousand soldiers stood by Gedel's side on the eastern bank of the

Jordan. They were Reubenites, Gadites and half of the tribe Menashe – the tribes of the East.

"What treachery is this that you have committed against the God of Israel, to build an altar, and to rebel this day against God?" Pinhas pointed accusingly at the stone altar across the river, on the eastern side of the Jordan. "Was the plague we received for worshipping Peor so insignificant? Our fathers rebelled against God in the desert and punished thousands of us because of Peor. Will you bring the same destruction upon us again? If you rebel against God today, tomorrow the whole congregation of Israel shall feel His fury. If your land is unclean, then come back over to the land of the possession of God, where God's Tabernacle rests, and inherit amongst us," Pinhas spread out his arms to encompass the men behind him, "but do not rebel against God or us by building an altar besides the altar of God. Did not Achan son of Zerah, the one who stole from the forbidden spoils of Jericho also trespass against holy matters and punishment fall upon all Israel? We lost the first battle of Ai on his account. Will you doom us to lose more?"

"God, Almighty, Lord!" Gedel shouted heavenward. "God, Almighty, Lord! If we have rebelled or been treacherous against God, do not save us today. If we have built an altar to turn away from following the Lord, or to make offerings or sacrifices upon it, let the Lord Himself exact retribution."

"Rather out of fear we have done this thing." Gedel looked across the river into Pinhas' eyes. "Fear, that in days to come, your children will say to our children: 'What have you to do with the Lord, the God of Israel? He has made the Jordan a border between us and you, and you, the children of Reuben and Gad, you have no portion in the Lord.' So your children will cause our children to cease fearing the Lord."

"Therefore we said, let us build an altar, not for burnt-offering, nor for sacrifice," Gedel pointed at the stone altar by his side, "but it shall be a witness between us and you, and between our generations after us, that we may do the service of the Lord. That your children may not say to our children: 'You have no portion in the Lord.' Rather our children shall say: 'Behold the pattern of the altar of the Lord, which our fathers made, not for burnt-offering, nor for sacrifice; but it is a witness between us and you.' Far be it from us," Gedel motioned to the thousands beside him on the eastern riverbank, "that we should rebel against the Lord, and turn away this day from following the Lord, to build an altar for burnt-offering, for meal-offering, or for sacrifice, besides the altar of the Lord our God that is before His Tabernacle."

The western bank of the Jordan River erupted in cheers. The soldiers of the ten tribes waved their fists and saluted Gedel.

"This day we know that God is in our midst," Pinhas pronounced, "because you have not committed this treachery against the Lord. You have delivered the children of Israel out of the hand of the Lord."

Pinhas walked into the shallow waters of the lightly flowing Jordan. His long, flowing white robe billowed in the water, yet somehow did not get wet. Both the eastern and western soldiers looked at Pinhas in wonder as he embraced Gedel firmly.

"Brother," Pinhas said, as he let go his embrace. "We were quite concerned. Concerned enough to fight you, for what on the surface was a grave affront and treachery."

"I know," Gedel whispered. "It was a great gamble. But we were already feeling the distance from our brothers. Do you not refer to us as 'western' versus 'eastern' tribes? Is not the land to the west of the river consecrated? We needed to do something bold, something noteworthy, to keep our kinship, our connection, in Israel's memory."

"How long do you think it will last?" Pinhas asked quietly.

"At the very least, for our lifetimes; perhaps another generation. It is not like in the desert or at camp where we were all together and united against a common enemy. Now every man is concerned for his personal land and his crops and his cattle. The people will not come regularly to the Tabernacle. We shall do what we can to stay true, to feel united, but I fear this new era will present greater challenges."

"It is painful to hear," Pinhas said. "But we shall persevere. Do not forget that the Priests and the Levites shall be amongst each tribe. They can be a uniting force. They will visit the Tabernacle regularly and keep the connection alive."

"I hope so. A war of brothers would be terrible."

"You think it could happen? After our successful conquest?"

"The war is not over, even if we have stopped fighting," Gedel looked at both sides of the Jordan. "Were you not the one who killed the prince of Simeon in the desert? How much fighting and contention did we have when we were united under Moses? We shall have more fighting here, more against our real enemies, and I hope less against ourselves, but fighting we shall have. We shall not stop training our children how to wield a sword, though we would all rather wield the plowshare."

"I shall not leave you on a somber note. Push your people to come to the Tabernacle. When we are united, we are strong and God is pleased."

"Agreed. I shall make the effort. But you and the other princes should visit us as well. And next time, don't come with an army."

*

"You see, coward," Ploni smirked at Boaz. "Your magical powers did not help you read the situation. You were very quick to lift your sword against your brother. If we had followed you, it would have led to horrible bloodshed. *You* are Caleb's protégé?"

"I was wrong, gravely wrong." Boaz's head hung down. "And I apparently needed you of all people to teach me. How could I have been so wrong?"

"You've been stuck in your tent too long, afraid of your own shadow. You've lost whatever judgment you might have once had. You are a coward and until you face whatever childhood fears you carry, you are dangerous and a liability for all of us. I shall report to Caleb of your near-fiasco and let him figure it out." Ploni trotted away, following the procession back south.

Amitai edged his donkey next to Boaz's.

"Are you alright?" Amitai asked.

"No. I am a coward and a fool and it took Ploni to make me see it."

"What are you going to do?"

"I don't know. I'm ashamed to go back, but what else can I do? Perhaps that is part of facing my fears, perhaps I should marry Vered?"

Pinhas approached the two from behind.

"I couldn't help overhearing," Pinhas cleared his throat. "And I saw your impetuous move before, which was truly dangerous. If Gedel had not had good control of his archers, you could have started a war of brothers right here and now."

"What should I do?"

"I think you should avoid the camp for a bit. It is a cocoon that has sheltered you too much."

"Where should I go? I need guidance. Caleb has always been my guide."

"I think you have reached the limits of what you can learn now from mentors. You need to engage with people as an adult."

Boaz hugged his sides and swayed back and forth on his donkey, holding back tears.

"Pinhas, please. I'm confused. I don't know who I am anymore. Help me."

Pinhas looked for long moments at Boaz. He looked to the eastern bank of the Jordan. He looked at the mountain range across that had once belonged to the people of Moab, before Moses and the Israelites had conquered it fourteen years earlier.

"I know," Pinhas concluded, looking back at Boaz and at Amitai next to him. "Seek the tomb of Moses."

"What? The tomb of Moses? Why? Will *he* give me guidance?"

"He gives us guidance every day, through the law that he handed us. However, I think you might benefit more by seeking his resting place. I think if Amitai here would be willing to accompany you, it would be even better."

"I don't have any love-struck women chasing me, or their angry brothers," Amitai smiled. "I'm ready."

"Excellent." Pinhas clapped his hands. "Get to know the tribes on the eastern side better – the ones you were ready to kill. That may be a worthwhile exercise as well."

"And then what?" Boaz asked.

"I suspect the answers will present themselves along the road."

Pinhas turned around and trotted off southward following the back of the retreating western soldiers.

Boaz looked at Amitai. "Are you sure you want to do this?"

"Sounds like a great idea. You're not up to it?" Amitai asked.

"What about Vered?"

"She'll have to work much harder to find you."

"At least it will keep her brother off my back."

"Come, let's go find Moses' tomb. Do you know where

it is?"

"No. I've never heard of anyone having ever found it. Let's cross the river and ask someone on the other side."

21. The Kenite Agent

"You promised my client 200 dinar for that saddle," Raskul, the Kenite agent, demanded, waving his walking stick as he leaned on the tavern table, "and you will pay him for it. It is not his fault your horse grew so fat that she refuses to wear it."

"I ordered a saddle that would fit my horse," Baltar the blacksmith bellowed. "Is it my fault Torash is so incompetent that he doesn't know horses change in size? I will not pay for such poor workmanship." Baltar banged his palm on the table. The patrons of the Bet Shean tavern, all Canaanite, looked at the arguing duo and turned back to their drinks.

From the windows of the tavern, over the heavy fortress walls, one could see the Jordan River to the east. It flowed lazily southward under the humid summer sun. The sweaty patrons tried to forget about the new neighbors that surrounded them, almost on every side. The Israelites had conquered most of the nearby cities and it was just a matter of time before Bet Shean would become a war zone, as heavily fortified as it was. Only a small corridor to the west and a slightly larger one to the northeast, were free of Israelite dominion, allowing the Canaanites of Bet Shean the limited freedom of travel and commerce.

"I would hate for your good name to be soiled by word of your not honoring your contracts and not paying for work done and delivered." Raskul stated.

"Do you threaten me? My word is good when good work is given. I will take this to the magistrate and he will see my point."

"I have an idea," Raskul said pensively, "in order for you to avoid any embarrassment. I understand that you are not happy with the saddle, which is a beautiful piece of workmanship, you must admit, even if it is the wrong size. Return the saddle to me and pay me a small token amount, say 50 dinar, for my client's trouble and efforts, and we shall put the matter to rest. However, I realize that doesn't solve your lack of saddle. As fate should have it, I may just be able to find a saddle of the right size – a highly prized piece, I assure you – and I will of course be happy to get it for you, though it will most likely involve much effort, for a symbolic amount of 250 dinar."

"300 dinar!" Baltar shouted. "What are you? Phoenician? You would take 300 dinar for a 200 dinar saddle?"

"My dear Baltar," Raskul said soothingly. "Your powers of arithmetic are impeccable; however there are several parties involved, so please don't confuse what may be complex for you. 50 dinar is for poor Torash, my client, who worked so hard on that saddle, which is now worthless. It would be a horrible sight for the two of you to go before the magistrate, for accusations to fly and for your good name to be smeared across the streets of Bet Shean. Imagine how much business you would lose. Much more than the meager 50 dinar, which I assure you, will keep Torash happy and quiet. The other 250 dinar is for a superior saddle, one that will fit your sweet horse as a sheath fits its sword. I will take only a sliver of profit for my extensive efforts in locating such a magnificent saddle."

"Humph," Baltar crossed his arms and weighed his money bag. "If it will quiet Torash and get me a badly needed saddle, I will agree."

"Agreed!" Raskul's hand shot out to grab Baltar's and shake it firmly.

"By Ashtar," Baltar grumbled. "This saddle had better be worth it."

"I assure you it is. However, I must insist on payment in advance, both for Torash and for the new saddle. I would hate for there to be a repetition of this misunderstanding."

"This saddle had better be perfect, Raskul, or I shall wring your neck."

"I personally guarantee your satisfaction, and you shall have your saddle by the end of this day. Now for the payment, please."

Baltar counted out 300 dinar into Raskul's palm from the money bag at his side. Raskul discreetly placed the coins in a pouch at his side and tied the pouch tightly.

"With your permission," Raskul bowed to Baltar, "I shall return this defective saddle to Torash with your kind donation, which I shall ensure will keep him quiet, and bring your new saddle forthwith. Thank you."

Raskul scooped up the heavy saddle in one arm and leaned on his walking stick with the other.

*

Two weeks later, Baltar chanced upon Torash in front of the temple of Ashtarte.

"How's the saddle?" Torash asked, smiling.

"Are you addled?" Baltar responded angrily. "That saddle of yours was worthless, yet your agent made me pay you off anyway so you wouldn't take me to the magistrate. Luckily he found me one that fit perfectly, but ended costing me much more. You've cost me 100 dinar, Torash, for your inept work."

"What are you talking about? What agent? I gave that poor Raskul my saddles to deliver. He seemed like a reasonable and intelligent fellow. All he asked for was 10 dinar each to deliver. He explained how much time it would save me and allow me to work on more saddles in that time. It was true. I completed another saddle in the time it would have taken me to deliver the other two and he brought me all the money. I was happy to give him the 20 dinar."

"Raskul did what?" Baltar's face turned crimson as he clenched both fists. "By Baal and Ashtarte! I will kill that man."

"What happened?" Torash asked, perplexed.

"Torash," Baltar breathed heavily out of his mouth. "The day you sent me the saddle, who was the other saddle for?"

"Why, it was for Delmon's donkey." Torash answered, uncomprehending.

"That son of a jackal! Baltar yelled. "I will kill him! I will wrap my hands around his neck and choke the life out of him!" Baltar trotted towards the tavern with Torash at his heels.

*

"Where is he? Where is Raskul?" Baltar shrieked, drunk with rage. His voice reverberated off the tavern walls. "Where is that thrice-cursed agent? I shall squeeze the life out of him. I will pound him and stomp him and crush him until he begs for death. Where is he!!??"

Raskul could hear Baltar from the outhouse and thanked Baal silently that his call to nature coincided with Baltar's wrath. Raskul quietly found his own donkey and slowly cantered out of the city of Bet Shean. He briefly mourned the possessions he had left behind, but he was quickly comforted by the heavy pouch at his side, the earnings from all of his unfortunate victims.

*

Raskul paced his old donkey carefully on the northward road towards Ashtarot. He had crossed the Jordan River and he could glimpse the Sea of Galilee. The swelling in his left leg was acting up. It always acted up when he needed to leave town quickly. He didn't want to go to Ashtarot, but he had few other options. The good people of Bet Shean would surely have burned him alive had they discovered how many of them had been victims of his agency services. He had gotten sloppy. Usually he managed to milk the residents of a city for months, even years. This time, after just a few weeks he had been found out.

His reputation was no better to the west. Which is what now brought him northeast and through the recent war zone between the Israelites and Canaanites. The aggressive Israelites were a people he hadn't truly interacted with and he had no intention of doing so now. Bet Shean was the last free enclave in the area. Raskul just hoped he wouldn't meet any bloodthirsty Israelite warriors before he reached the questionable sanctuary of Ashtarot.

Raskul looked apprehensively up and down the road as he entered deeper into Israelite territory. He looked to his sides to find quick cover, but was disappointed by the sparsely vegetated land of the river bank. He muttered a quick prayer to Baal, to Ashtarte, to Ilu, to Ra, and to the Hebrew God for good measure.

After trotting uneventfully for a few hours, Raskul spotted them just after a rise in the road. But they had seen him as well. Two Israelite warriors; young and armed and heading his way quickly. It was too late to turn back and that would only mark him as prey. Raskul continued to trot nonchalantly and started to whistle a tune, though he sweated profusely in the cooling evening.

"Identify yourself!" a tall muscly redhead commanded Raskul, with extended sword.

"I am Raskul of the Kenite, your humble servant. There is no war between our peoples, so you do not need to threaten me so. I would know your name and mission and whether you are brigands or honorable men. If you are brigands, then let us be done with it, for I am a poor man, a refugee, with no means and less possessions and I would beg for your mercy. If you are honorable men, then I would press you for safe passage in this war torn region."

"We are no brigands, Raskul of the Kenite," the redhead answered, sheathing his sword. "I am Boaz and my companion is Amitai, we are both of the Tribe of Judah."

"Ah, the famous tribe of Judah. I have heard much of your tribe. Of your bravery in battle, and your wisdom and mercy in peace. Let an old man pass unharmed and I will bless your names to all the gods."

"We shall let you go unharmed, but do not invoke the names of your gods."

"Does that offend you, master Boaz? What harm can a good wish and a blessing do? I shall thank your God too. Yahweh you call him?"

"Do not use his name in vain!" Boaz said hotly, reaching again for his sword. "Do not discuss any gods. It is sacrilege to us. Where are you traveling to? Go on and be off with you, before you start naming other gods."

"By Baal and Ashtarte!" Raskul exclaimed. "I have never met such a strange people. You would skewer me just for stating harmless words?"

"I will kill you Kenite, if you don't stay your tongue." Boaz drew his sword.

"Calm, young master, calm. I shall not name any further gods. Not your Yahweh, not Baal, nor Ashtarte. Not the Egyptian Ra or nor even the unpopular Ilu. I swear by all the gods, on heaven and earth, of the trees and rocks and the streams and even the worms, that I shall not name any further gods. I am quite familiar though with the names of a host of demons and lesser angels, which I shall be more than happy to name –"

Raskul found Boaz's sword edge against his neck.

"One more word. One more word, dear talkative man, and I shall have no choice but to slice your neck right here and now. Nod if you understand."

Raskul nodded.

"Good. It is possible to shut you up it seems. While we have your attention, we will ask for directions. If you answer anything other than the question, if you name a god, a demon, a dog, a flower or a gnat, I shall slice your neck with no constraint and consider it a service to my nation and perhaps mankind. Do you understand?"

Raskul nodded.

"Excellent. Intelligent after all."

"Here is the question. Remember to answer simply. I would hate to bloody my sword, but I shall do so if you err by a hairsbreadth. Kenite, which way to the tomb of Moses?"

Raskul's eyes widened. He did not speak. He looked down at the sword by his neck. He put his fingers on the side of the sword and gently pushed it away.

"The vocal chords do not function with steel against them," Raskul said softly.

"Speak. Plainly." Boaz commanded.

"The tomb of Moses you seek. That is a holy site. Hard to find. Only the most determined, the savviest explorers, may be privy to its secrets, its mystery, and its power."

"Do you know where it is?" Boaz spat out through clenched teeth as he brought the blade closer to Raskul's neck.

"No one knows where it is. But I know how to find it."

"Will you take us?"

"For a price."

"What's your price?"

"Land in the tribe of Judah."

"That's impossible."

"Then so will be finding the tomb."

"Is there not something more reasonable you're interested in?"

"How about re-sheathing your sword to start with?"

Boaz sheathed his sword.

"Name a reasonable price," Boaz said.

"What do you have to pay? You don't exactly look like a pair of princes."

"We have a few coins, the weapons we carry, our clothing and our provisions."

"Vagabonds. Not interested. With your permission, please allow me to pass."

"But we must find the tomb of Moses," Boaz pleaded.

"You wish to be guided to the most important, most secret location this side of the Jordan, for a pittance?"

"If you name something we can do, we will perform it."

"Hmm," Raskul looked Boaz and Amitai up and down.

"Here is my offer. It is my final offer. If you don't accept it you shall have to either kill me or let me go. Is that agreed?"

"Agreed."

"I shall agree to guide you in your search for the tomb of Moses, if and only if you agree to be my personal guards, to protect me from all harm, whether deserved or not, until we successfully find the tomb."

"Agreed," Boaz stated. Raskul put out his hand and they shook.

"You too, quiet Amitai," Raskul said with outstretched arm. Amitai looked at Boaz, shrugged his shoulders and shook hands. "Agreed."

"Now swear to it by your god," Raskul ordered. "I will not be offended and I shall hold you to it."

"We swear, by our God, Almighty," Boaz proclaimed, "that we shall protect and guard you from all harm during our search for the tomb of Moses, as long as you guide us faithfully."

"Amen," Amitai agreed.

"That will do," Raskul said. "Now I wish to make camp."

"When we will search for the tomb?" Boaz asked.

"Tomorrow. Negotiating at sword point is hard work. I am weary and it is getting dark."

"How long do you think it will take us to get there?"

"Patience, my young guard. I will disclose more tomorrow."

22. The Claw's Sting

A massive arm fiddled with the delicate metal mechanism. The only light in the dank room was from the blazing fireplace. Shadows danced on the white-skinned form at the workbench. Long greasy hair crowned a balding head that had not seen the sun in many moons. The muscular figure moved his left hand expertly around the metallic apparatus. He pulled and pushed and hammered and twisted the contraption, finally grunting in satisfaction. The mechanism was a long wrought-iron device attached to the owner's right shoulder. The man stood up and swung the dark, sleek, mechanical device with what looked like a claw at the end. The device was situated where an elbow, arm and hand should have been. The claw was composed of two curved blades facing an opposing single one.

"P-p-prince A-a-akavish," a servant stammered as he opened a heavy wooden door, allowing sunlight into the room.

"Curse you, Trigor. Shut that door." Akavish muttered angrily. "How many times have I told you that I hate the Ashkelon sun?"

"Y-y-yes, Master." Trigor bowed his head.

"Bring it to me," Akavish commanded, pointing his claw at the tray Trigor held in trembling hands.

Trigor walked obediently to Akavish.

Akavish grabbed Trigor's arm with his claw and with his healthy left hand grabbed the vial from Trigor's tray.

"What did the apothecary say? Tell me his exact words!" Akavish ordered.

"H-h-he said: T-t-tell that P-p-prince Claw of yours to use this sparingly. It is highly c-c-concentrated. One drop is enough to k-k-kill a man."

Akavish smiled at the last phrase. He poured the entire vial into a thin metal tube that rested within his ferrous arm and closed the tube tightly. The bottom end of the tube narrowed to a needle thin point.

"Now, for our first trial," Akavish said looking at Trigor.

Trigor's mouth opened wide in horror. He tried to back away from Akavish, but the claw held him firmly. Trigor's arm bled as he struggled against the sharp pincers of Akavish's claw.

"N-n-no, Master," Trigor whimpered. "I have served you l-l-loyally."

"I tire of you and your stammering." Akavish twisted his right shoulder suddenly. The thin tube within his claw slid down quickly with a hissing sound. It stopped a hairsbreadth from Trigor's arm. Trigor almost fainted from fright.

"Curse you!" Akavish spat. "The extension is too short. Wait a second."

Akavish hammered and tweaked and pulled on his claw some more, as Trigor writhed in panic.

Akavish slid the tube up his claw until he heard a 'click' sound. He twisted his right shoulder again. The tube slid down and this time penetrated Trigor's arm. Trigor stiffened suddenly and fell to the cold stone floor, lifeless.

"Excellent." Akavish released his claw's grip on the dead servant. "Now, for some field trials."

*

"People are dying in frightening numbers, like mullet in the fisherman's net." King Larus paced the floor of his palace chambers. "You're sure it's not a plague, Krafus?"

"I am certain, my lord," old Krafus advised. "It is poison. But how it's being administered, I cannot imagine, nor for what purpose. I cannot determine the pattern of deaths, except that they were unfortunate enough to wander the streets of our dear Ashkelon alone at night."

"We must stop it!" Larus pounded the stone wall of the chamber. Big Larus was still large. Over the years he had lost some of his height, but more than made up for it around his belly. "It is bad for commerce. The tavern owner has lost more than a third of his business, let alone the brothel and the temple. The priests will have my head if I don't make the streets safe for their evening rituals."

"I'm at a loss. The killer has eluded our patrols and even my own night prowling. We will need additional help, if we are to find this murderer."

"You can't mean Akavish?" Larus looked distastefully at Krafus.

"Even one-armed, my former pupil, your son, Prince Akavish, is a formidable huntsman. It may be good for him to be given a mission and to get some air."

"You ask him then. I still find the sight of him repulsive, and that claw is even more disturbing."

"I will talk to him."

*

"That is horrific," Akavish said to Krafus with great empathy. "Someone is indiscriminately poisoning people at night? How do you know they are random? Perhaps it is a new smuggling cartel? Or secret Egyptian agents, killing off Phoenician sympathizers? You know how the Egyptians have been resorting to all sorts of nasty tricks to regain some of their old glory."

"I'm familiar with all the underground and criminal efforts in Ashkelon," Krafus said, "and I tell you, it is not related to any of them. For Baal's sake, someone poisoned the old cook, Berisol. She was the most innocent, most beloved person I can think of."

"Maybe someone didn't appreciate her cooking," Akavish chuckled darkly.

"Never mind the reason, Akavish. I've given up on determining that. We need to rely on brute force and surveillance and catch this killer, or Ashkelon will turn into a poor, empty husk, with no business, and no people for your father to rule."

"And what rule is that? He sits on his throne and gets fat, living off old glories. He just looks inwards, never thinking of new glories, new conquests."

"And he is wise, young Akavish. He is wise to focus his energies on the prosperity of the city. He is wise to increase trade, to balance the needs of the priests and the merchants and the residents. He is wise to develop loyalty of the citizens to the throne and not rely on fear. Ashkelon is stronger now than it ever was with the Canaanites. Even your mighty Israelites have not dared attack us all these years. It must trouble Joshua greatly that we are part of a strong, robust federation that will not fall so easily. No, Akavish, King Larus is wise to strengthen us from the inside and not seek ill-advised exploits against the Israelites you so hate. Baal be praised! The god of Canaan has been better to us than Zeus ever was. But your father's rule is not the issue. This killer is."

"Leave it to me." Akavish stood up. "You came to the right person. I will track the killer and stop him and deliver the miscreant personally to my father, no matter what I think of Larus' lily-livered reign."

"Just be better-spoken in front of your father. It is to your advantage." Krafus stood and departed the dank, dark room. He did not see Akavish grin broadly.

*

"I have him," Akavish called out from outside the King's chamber. "I have the killer."

"What? Why do you disturb me at this demonic hour?" Larus responded from his bed. "Could this not have waited until morning? Why do you need to bring him to my chamber?"

Larus opened the door to his room.

Akavish walked in with a white-robed body on his shoulder. He dumped the corpse unceremoniously onto the floor of Larus' chamber.

"Here he is, father. As ordered."

"I asked Krafus to handle this. Why do I need to see a corpse?"

"Queasy in your old age? I thought you would want to know about the serial murderer in your precious city. Krafus seemed to think the future of Ashkelon rested in this murderer's hands."

"Yes, yes. Of course. We didn't understand why or even how he was killing such a variety of people. How do you know he is the one?"

"I saw him in the act of murder. I was too late to save his last victim, but he confessed to all the other deaths and even how he did them."

"How did you get him to reveal?"

"I can be persuasive."

"Why did he kill all those people? How?"

"It was quite simple. He was mad. He is Egyptian, as you can tell from the robes. He had a falling out with his slaver partner, also Egyptian, who became his first victim. After that, he seemed to like the power of taking life – those Egyptians seem so obsessed with death – so every night he prowled, seeking lone victims. Their deaths made him feel alive. He justified each death as necessary, even good, to feed his hunger."

"H-how do you know so much?" Larus took a step back.

"Scared, father? This is the knife he used. If you look carefully, you'll see it's coated with a strong poison. All he needed to do was slice his victim's arms lightly and they would die instantly from the poison." Akavish sliced the air between him and his father.

"Careful with that." Larus took another step back.

"Why? Are you afraid something might happen?" Akavish approached with his shiny menacing claw on the right and the poisoned blade on the left.

"I am not afraid of you, Akavish." Larus stood to his full height, meeting Akavish's dark eyes.

"Good. There should never be fear between fathers and sons."

"Of course, but please put the knife away and get rid of the corpse. Thank you for tracking him. You have done me and Ashkelon a great service and I shall not forget it."

"You found him?" Krafus burst into the room.

"Yes," Akavish turned to Krafus.

"Who was he? Why did he do it? How?"

"He was an insane Egyptian slaver," Larus answered. "Akavish has done us a great service."

"I've examined the bodies again," Krafus said, "and I noticed a pattern on each of them. Did you find out how he killed his victims?"

"Yes." Akavish offered the blade, handle first, to Krafus. "He sliced them lightly with this poisoned blade."

"Curious." Krafus held the blade with one hand and his chin with the other. "That does explain things, though each mark was identical."

"How so?" Larus inquired.

"Each body had two slashes on the front of their forearm and one on the back of the arm, and a small circular wound between them – almost imperceptible. I only noticed it because old Berisol bruised so easily. Once I saw it on her corpse, I checked the others."

"What does it mean?" Larus asked.

"It means this madman developed a very unusual and precise killing ritual. I'm just amazed at his consistent accuracy. How did you kill him, Akavish?"

"With his own knife," Akavish responded.

Krafus looked at the arm of the dead Egyptian murderer. The hackles on Krafus' neck shot up. The Egyptian's arm was adorned with a barely visible, but perfectly symmetrical pair of slashes on the front of his arm, followed by a single slash on the back of the arm, and a tiny wound in-between the slash marks.

Krafus looked at Akavish's claw and noticed the two front blades, the one opposing blade and the thin metallic tube inside his artificial arm. He shuddered involuntarily and for the first time in his long and dangerous life, felt fear.

23. Widower's Regret

"I know it is rude of me, but I can't host you," the tall Menashite said at the entrance to his stone house. "I've just returned from Canaan. I haven't been with my wife and children for fourteen years. Try Tzruyim next door. By the time he returned, his wife died of heartache and his daughters had married and moved out. He may appreciate the company."

"Thank you." Boaz stepped back from the house, together with Amitai and Raskul. They noticed the well-tended fields and the large flock of sheep. Down the mountain range, to the west, they could see the blue ribbon of the Jordan River, the border to the newly conquered Canaan. They had trekked southwards and knew they had further to go to reach the reported area of the tomb of Moses.

They walked to a dilapidated shack half a mile away from the Menashite's stone home. The cool autumn breeze escorted them as the sun inched closer to the mountains of Canaan across from them. The field around the nearby shack had grown wild and there were no animals in sight.

Boaz rapped lightly on the door.

There was no answer.

Boaz knocked louder. The door was cracked and broken at the top and bottom edges. The old wood resonated from the knock.

Still no answer.

"Let's leave him alone," Amitai stated. "He might not be in."

"He's in," Boaz answered, closing his eyes, drawing on his powers of Vision. "He's in and in a dark mood."

Boaz knocked again. The door rattled on its hinges.

"Go away!" a broken voice shouted.

"We are travelers. We seek shelter." Boaz stared at the cracked wooden door stubbornly.

"Go elsewhere! I'm in no condition to host," the voice said through the door.

"It seems no one in Yavesh Gilaad is up to hosting," Boaz retorted with some heat. "Are you still children of Israel? Or have you all so quickly forgotten the hospitality of our forefathers? Where are your weary brothers to find rest? Abraham had four doors, west, east, south and north and they were always open. You have only one door and you don't have the decency to open even that? What sort of man are you?"

The door opened violently.

"I'll tell you what type of man I am, you snot-nosed beggar." A giant of a man yelled at the visitors without looking. "I am alone. I fought for a nation. I gave my life for a people and in the end I have nothing. Now leave me alone."

The door closed violently.

"Let us leave him." Amitai grabbed Boaz's arm. "We would be better off outside."

"Though I would much prefer a warm bed," Raskul added. "Your friend may be right. This man is not to be trifled with and your countrymen in this area don't seem particularly welcoming."

"I know him," Boaz said, unmoving. "He was a great warrior. Fearless. It pains me to see him like this."

"Such are the vagaries of war, boy. Some come out unscathed. Some are maimed for life. And many are wounded inside, where it never heals. Leave him be. There is nothing you can do for him. We have our own problems to deal with, namely some shelter before the night winds on this mountain cut into my old bones."

"No. I will not leave him." Boaz stayed his ground. "Tzruyim son of Avigdor, Commander of One Thousand!" Boaz called out. "Come out and face me!"

The door opened slowly.

"I recognized you, Boaz," Tzruyim said softly. "You've grown since the Battle of Gibeon."

"Yes. But what happened to you? What happened to the fearless warrior that braved the arrows of five armies? The one who led his men to capture the wall of Gibeon? When did the mighty son of Avigdor turn into a nasty, inhospitable recluse?"

"Who are you to judge me, boy?" Tzruyim asked.

"Someone who fought by your side," Boaz answered.

Tzruyim sat heavily on the ground in front of his door and covered his face with his large hands.

"Vera," Tzruyim sobbed. "Vera died waiting for me. Fourteen years. All those years of fighting. We won. We conquered, and I returned to ashes just three days ago. No wife. Daughters married without me and gone. My land a shambles, my flocks gone. The neighbors told me how my wife struggled. How she was sad. Always looking to the west for a sign of my return. This is why I fought? This is my reward? Vera..."

Boaz sat down on the ground next to Tzruyim.

"We are cold and we have no place to stay. Can we come in?"

"I just want to be left alone. To mourn in peace. I don't think I'm ready to host. Not without my Vera."

"We just need shelter, Tzruyim. And one should not mourn alone. We will be gone in the morning."

Tzruyim looked distractedly at the ground, as if he had not heard Boaz. The cool wind from the west caressed his large frame. He looked to the west, to Canaan, with sorrow and pain.

"Vera," Tzruyim moaned.

"Just for one night, Tzruyim. Please," begged.

"Fine. For one night," Tzruyim finally responded, still looking to the west. "Though it pains me. I will host for her sake. Yes, she would have wanted that." Tzruyim stood up slowly and walked into his shack, leaving the door open behind him.

*

"You mean all this land is yours," Raskul waved his hand over the simple wooden table they sat at, eating Tzruyim's warm porridge.

"Yes. This was the portion allotted to me, in the day of Moses himself," Tzruyim answered. "I would give it up in an instant to have Vera back."

"What will you do with it?" Raskul asked.

"This land is good pasture land. I need to buy sheep or goats. I prefer sheep."

"I have an offer to make you," Raskul suggested. "A partnership. I will supply you with the funds to restock your flock and you will make me a partner in your land."

"No," Tzruyim kept eating his porridge.

"What do you mean 'no'? We haven't even discussed the terms yet. I assure you, I will give you most favorable conditions."

"No, Kenite. This is ancestral land. This is land that was given to me and that I shall pass on to my children one day. It is not for sale or partnership."

"Enough, Raskul," Boaz muttered. "Leave him alone."

"You are a fool, Tzruyim," Raskul continued. "How will you afford to keep this wasteland? It is worthless. I would give you a handsome investment. Not only would you have the most beautiful of flocks, you can build yourself a mansion, a palace, instead of this miserable excuse for a hovel. Think, man. This is your chance to be wealthy. To receive the reward you so richly deserve. Did your wife die in vain, so that you should bring this property to ruin? Is this how you cherish the memory of your dead Vera?"

Tzruyim dropped the spoon of porridge and stood up. He reached across the small house for the broadsword hanging on the wall. Raskul backed away from the table and looked around in fear.

"Your vow! Your vow!" he called to Boaz and Amitai. "You swore to protect me! What did I say? For a few words this man will kill me? Protect me!"

"You gave a vow to this uncircumcised lout?" Tzruyim hefted his heavy sword and looked at Boaz.

Boaz and Amitai stood in front of Raskul.

"Yes, we did. He promised to take us to the grave of Moses and in return we vowed to protect him."

"This man is a charlatan, and you have given your word to a trickster. Why, he offers me riches that he clearly doesn't have to give, when I can just as easily borrow funds or animals from my willing neighbors. You have done ill by allying yourselves with this Kenite. Your judgment is suspect. You can all stay for the night, but you must be gone by first light. If this Kenite so much as says another word, I will slice his tongue out, no matter who stands in the way. Is that understood?"

"Yes," Boaz and Amitai stated in unison. Raskul nodded his head, still eyeing the massive sword in the widower's powerful hands.

*

"I apologize, Tzruyim, for our companion's rudeness," Boaz said at the door of the shack in the early dawn light. Amitai and Raskul were on their mounts, out of earshot. "He was ill-behaved and I'm sorry I brought him into your home."

"It was for the best, Boaz. He rekindled my energy and helped me think clearly. I will borrow from my neighbors and rebuild myself. I will remarry. I will send for my daughters and offer them the chance to live here, if their husbands are interested. That little thief was exactly what I needed to break my sorrow. Though I miss Vera so deeply."

"Your sacrifice was not in vain." Boaz clutched Tzruyim's large shoulder. "You were instrumental in conquering the land of Canaan and fulfilling God's promise. I'm sorry for your loss."

"Thank you, Boaz. Now go, before my urge to kill that Kenite gets too strong. And beware of him. He is a walking box of mischief. You should be rid of him as soon as possible."

"It is not so easy. We have given him our word and I don't intend to break it. We need him to find the tomb of Moses."

"No one knows where the tomb of Moses is," Tzruyim said. "Why do you seek it?"

"Pinhas the priest directed me to find it. He felt it may help give me some direction in my life."

"You will have an interesting journey, then. If you don't keep the Kenite's mouth shut, he is likely to get all of you killed. Go in peace."

"Thank you."

Boaz walked to his companions and mounted his donkey.

"Splendid." Raskul clapped his hands. "This stop has been invigorating and has given me ideas about business in this area."

"Next time you have a business idea, please discuss it with us first," Boaz requested.

"Why? Are you going to invest?"

Boaz and Amitai merely looked at each other, sighed and trotted on.

24. Mistaken Murderer

The trio rode southward down the ancient King's Road. Their mounts kicking up dust and pebbles in the cool autumn morning. They were low on provisions and would need more for their climb up the uninhabited mountain range further south, where they were told the Tomb of Moses must be.

"*That's* a city," Raskul commented as they saw Bezer in the distance. "And here I was thinking you Israelites only knew farming and shepherding. It's a relief to the senses to come across a center of commerce and opportunity." Bezer was a large walled city, sitting on the desert plain. Wide roads intersected in front of the city. Caravans of merchants entered and exited the large stone gates at a leisurely pace under the hazy autumn sky. Raskul, Boaz and Amitai plodded on their donkeys along the road that hugged the eastern shore of the meandering Jordan River.

"That is one of the six," Amitai mentioned.

"Six what?" Raskul asked

"Six cities of refuge," Boaz answered. "There are three on the eastern side of the Jordan River which Moses named before he died. I was barely ten when he set them up. There are three others on the western side which Joshua established, but all six of them became operational only recently when we completed this stage of conquest."

"What do you need refuge from? You people are the aggressors and conquerors here. Unless you are providing refuge to your victims."

"The peoples we have fought are not 'victims', Raskul. They are enemies," Boaz responded. "As long as they hold fast to their idol-worship, we shall always be enemies and we shall show no mercy. These cities are for our own people, for inadvertent murderers amongst the children of Israel."

"Inadvertent what? How does someone murder by accident? Raskul asked. "I know," he exclaimed, raising his staff, and stabbing at the air. "Pardon me, sir. I'm so sorry for having killed you. I mistook you for a large watermelon. Is that it? And then the bumbling fool is allowed to stay safe in this magnificent city? Why, every cretin will make such a claim. Yes, your honor." Raskul placed the outstretched fingers of his hand on his chest as he addressed an imaginary judge. "That man, with all the jewels and gold that I killed, you see, it was an accident. I thought he was my brother-in-law, whom I truly despise and who owes me a great amount of money. That poor unfortunate soul just had an uncanny resemblance to my ugly brother-in-law. You can't blame me for killing him. I didn't mean it. With your permission I'll keep the dead man's money. He won't be needing it anymore, and I'll settle right here in your cozy city of refuge."

"You don't understand at all," Amitai stated.

"What's there to understand? You Israelites don't make any sense!"

"Accidents happen," Boaz said. "We are a people of laws and justice. We do not kill people just because we presume they're guilty." Boaz swallowed hard and thought of his nearly fatal accusation of the Eastern Tribes. "We give the accidental murderer a place of refuge. The family of the one killed cannot take revenge against the murderer in the city of refuge. But outside the city he can be killed, with no consequences to the avengers. It becomes a prison of sorts for the murderer. He's safe within the city, but can be killed outside of it. But I don't expect you to understand justice, mercy or laws."

As they approached the city gates, a young white-robed man ran towards them.

"Thank God, you made it safely," the young man grabbed hold of the reins of Raskul's donkey and looked apprehensively behind Boaz and Amitai.

"Why of course we made it safely," Raskul retorted. "Why would you think otherwise?"

"You weren't pursued?" the young man asked.

"No. Who are you?" Boaz asked.

"My apologies. I am Hirham, the Priest. We've been expecting you. Come, we have accommodations ready for you and your escorts," the young man addressed Raskul.

"That is as it should be." Raskul puffed up his chest. "Finally, a place that gives me the proper respect. I think I shall enjoy staying here for a long time."

"You are taking your predicament very well," the priest commented as he rushed them into the city, continually looking backwards. "I'm inspired by your attitude."

"Hirham, you are a joy! Please do lead us to our quarters."

The priest led the travelers through the busy city gate. He breathed a sigh of relief as they entered the gates. He spoke in hushed tones to the two armored guards, pointing excitedly at Raskul. "You are safe now," Hirham told Raskul.

"I have never felt safer," Raskul said smiling, "with two strong escorts and an enthusiastic host."

Boaz and Amitai traded quizzical glances.

The travelers passed the city center where merchants loudly offered wheat, barley and a rainbow of other grains and spices. Distinctive jugs of wines and oils were on display in the storefronts. The loud noises and strong smells seemed to overwhelm Boaz and Amitai. Raskul grinned, gleefully taking in the entire stimulus to his senses, his eyes darting from one merchant to another, seeking who might be his next mark.

Hirham led them to a residential street.

"The escorts shall be sharing a room here," Hirham pointed to a rundown hostel for Boaz and Amitai. "And you, sir, this is your residence." The priest indicated Raskul, and led the trio into a new house. The house was simple, but clearly new and well furnished. They entered a small but neat courtyard. On one side there was a pen for animals, on the other side, a stocked storeroom. At the end of the structure, the young priest showed them the living area with a large straw bed to the left, a brand new wooden table on the right and an unused fire-pit in the middle.

"Why, these are the nicest and largest accommodations anyone has ever provided me with. Thank you, Hirham."

"You may be needing it for a long time, and we wanted you to be comfortable."

"How did you know I liked city life?"

"Sir, you are an inspiration. I shall let you get comfortable in your new home and we shall meet again. Make sure not to leave the city gates. I informed the guards and they shall likewise tell the next watch." Hirham departed hurriedly.

Raskul, Boaz and Amitai tied their donkeys in Raskul's new pen and walked in to the living area, each one grabbing a chair and sitting at the table. A bowl of fresh fruit awaited them in the center of the table. Raskul grabbed a fresh fig and bit into it hungrily, the juice flowing down his grey stubble beard. Boaz and Amitai each grabbed a fig, said a short benediction and bit into the figs neatly.

"I have never been received so royally!" Raskul exclaimed as he placed his feet on the table.

"Raskul, do you forget our mission, or your promise?" Boaz accused.

"No, no, no, my dear Boaz. We are very close to Moses' tomb. I can smell it. He died very close to here. Everyone has said so. I expect it is no more than a few hours journey further and we shall be free of this mission and I shall be able to return and settle in this most welcoming of places. Oh, this is so good." Raskul bit into another juicy fig.

"Fine. We shall spend the night here in Bezer and leave first thing in the morning. But why they should honor you so, is still a great mystery to me."

"Don't look a gift horse in the mouth," Raskul laughed. "At least that's what they used to say in that poor city the Greeks destroyed."

*

Raskul, Boaz and Amitai cantered towards the city gate at first light. They replenished their supplies with dried fruit and freshly baked bread. As they approached the gate, the guards looked at them in surprise. They lowered their spears blocking the exit.

"What goes on here?" Raskul asked. "How dare you block my way? Do you know who I am?"

"You are not allowed to leave the city," the tall guard on the left said, not moving his spear.

"I am an honored resident of this great city and I shall not be denied passage. Now move aside or I shall call that pleasant Hirham." Raskul dismounted and pushed at the spear, but it did not budge.

"We *should* call Hirham, as he is the one that prohibited your departure," the guard responded and nodded at his fellow. The squat guard on the right ran into the city.

"Are we allowed to leave?" Amitai asked pointing at himself and Boaz, who also dismounted.

"Yes. We were expecting the two of you to leave once you saw him comfortably settled."

Boaz and Amitai looked at each other with questions on their faces.

"They can travel, but I cannot?" Raskul asked furiously.

"What is the problem?" Hirham asked from behind as he approached with the squat guard.

"This buffoon has misunderstood your orders and is not allowing me to leave with my companions," Raskul placed his fists on his hips.

"The guards have understood perfectly. You are not allowed to leave."

"This is ridiculous!"

"Calm yourself, sir. You know, you are the first. And I'm sure the process may seem strange to you. The truth is, I was so excited when I heard, though of course it was a tragic circumstance, and then when I spotted you outside the walls, I could barely contain myself to finally fulfill the mission of this city."

"What are you talking about? What am I the first of? What mission?"

"I hate to discuss this publicly as I do not wish to shame you in front of others."

"Speak it, man. What am I the first of? Why do you imprison me in this city?"

"You are the first inadvertent murderer to be given sanctuary in our city of refuge," Hirham whispered.

"Me? What proof do you have? How do you make such an accusation? What is the sentence?"

"It was reported yesterday, that an older man, with an unkempt, shaggy appearance, and a criminal look, had accidentally killed a man in Yaazer. They said you had been attempting to break into a house with an ax. The ax-head flew off the handle and killed your accomplice. His family vowed to kill you."

"I never killed anyone! I've never even been to Yaazer. These two will vouch for me."

"You are not the murderer?" Hirham asked, clearly disappointed.

"No! I may be guilty of many crimes, but murder, even inadvertent, is not one of them."

"Is this true?" Hirham looked at Boaz and Amitai.

"Yes, he is probably guilty of many crimes," Amitai smirked.

"We have been his companions for weeks now and he has not been in Yaazer all this time," Boaz added.

"Oh! What a horrible, horrible mistake!" Hirham cried. "To have assumed you were the murderer. I am so sorry." Hirham fell on his knees and grasped Raskul's hand. "Please forgive me, sir. In my enthusiasm I have shamed you terribly."

"It's no matter," Raskul said magnanimously. "Usually, I am the one who brings shame upon myself. Now, if we could discuss a permanent arrangement in that quaint house."

"That's not possible." Hirham stood up and cleared his throat. "The house is reserved exclusively for the inadvertent murderer, where he would live out his life or stay until the death of the High Priest, depending on the findings of the court, of course. I'm sorry. It's best you go on your way, before others make the same mistake I did."

"Let us go, Raskul," Boaz said. "We have wasted enough time here with all the confusion."

"Fine. Goodbye, young Hirham. I forgive you. I actually enjoyed all the attention. This inadvertent murderer will be a lucky guy to be in your care."

"Goodbye, sir. I'm still inspired by you." Hirham bowed to Raskul.

Raskul, Boaz and Amitai mounted their donkeys and trotted out of the gates of Bezer.

A cloud of sand approached them quickly on the road. They could make out three riders. The middle rider was a bedraggled, mean-looking, grey-haired man, escorted on either side by two younger men. Behind them, half a dozen angry men rode hard in pursuit.

"That must be the inadvertent murderer," Boaz commented.

"Don't assume," Amitai said.

"Seriously," Raskul agreed. "Do you think I really look like him?"

"You're not that good-looking," Amitai quipped as the harried riders passed them in a hurry.

"I hope he enjoys the house. I'm going to miss it," Raskul lamented.

"He will miss his freedom," Boaz noted as the angry posse passed them in pursuit.

"Freedom is overrated. Give me security. Give me comfort, and I will gladly give up these so-called freedoms."

"That is why you cannot understand Israelites. We cherish our freedom. The lashes of the slave masters still resonate in our bones. But you are not Israelite."

"Thank God," Raskul answered, as they left the city of refuge behind them.

25. Filial Regicide

The flower must be somewhere here, Akavish thought, as he scanned the tall grass with his torch ablaze. His eyes had developed the ability to see well in the dark. Nonetheless, he appreciated the warmth if not the light of the torch. The two perpetual guards waited for Akavish outside the grassy area. Ever since Akavish had "discovered" the poisoner of Ashkelon, guards followed him wherever he went.

The papyrus he received had described the Azalea flower as highly toxic. *A white flower with pink spots that blooms in the spring. It could grow beneath trees.* Akavish cut at the tall grass with his sword as he meandered through the swampy valley half a day's ride from Ashkelon. His thoughts were as dark as the night he so loved. He thought of power, of the power of death. He had become accustomed to his nightly murders in Ashkelon and missed the thrashing of his victims in their last moments of life. He fed on their dying breath and now dreamed of more violence.

Akavish reached a sandy clearing and proceeded. As he walked over the soft sand, his left foot was suddenly difficult to lift, and he found himself quickly sinking. *Quicksand!* Akavish thought. He grabbed quickly at an overhanging branch and pulled himself up.

Perfect, Akavish thought. *Why bring death to him? Bring him to death.*

Akavish hacked away at the overhanging branches around the clearing, making sure there were none within reach of the sandy bog. He then placed several branches across the bog, testing what amount would carry his weight, but not more. Satisfied, Akavish rode his horse back to Ashkelon, happier than he had been in a long time.

*

"It is a shame. Krafus would have loved to accompany us," King Larus said hesitantly, his enormous belly shaking lightly as he sat on his throne.

"It cannot be helped. We should not wait." Akavish answered. "Are you afraid?"

"I do not fear a nighttime excursion. But Krafus is wise in these matters and he is a resourceful man to have around."

"By the time he returns from his mission, the tunnel may be lost."

"Are you sure about this?"

"Certainly. It is a passage that only opens with the full moon, as we will have tonight. Beyond the entrance I glimpsed great treasure. Bring some trusted guards with you, if you want."

*

Akavish removed the shiny arm from his shoulder. In its place he attached an older, duller version. It was slightly rusted, though the claw was still sharp. He left his dark home and walked merrily through the streets of Ashkelon as the sun touched the horizon.

Akavish arrived at the palace early in the evening and saddled his horse. He took his father with him and two escorts and rode to the place he had spoken of.

After the third hour of riding, Akavish lowered his eyes, and spotted the place nearby.

"Stay here with the horses," Akavish said to the escorts. "We shall conduct our business and I shall return."

Larus took the burning torch and Akavish led the way with the sword to cut through the tall grass.

And the two of them went together.

Then Larus spoke to Akavish, his son, and said, "Son."

"Here I am, my father."

"I have fire on this torch, but where is this entrance you are looking for?"

"The gods will provide the answer, my father." And the two of them continued together.

They arrived at the place which Akavish had prepared. Akavish made a big show of cutting at the tall grass. He walked gingerly over the camouflaged branches of wood hidden in the sand, and muttered a silent prayer to the dark gods.

Larus followed Akavish, but the wood underneath did not bear his weight. A muffled snap was the first sign that the trap had been sprung. By the time Akavish had turned around, Larus was already up to his knees in the sand, moving his legs ferociously.

Larus called out from the sand, "Akavish! Akavish!"

"Here I am."

"Stretch out your hand to me, my son."

"You are too far away, and there is nothing here I can use to reach you. Let me run to the horses and bring them here."

Akavish ran around the bog, through the tall grass growing on the solid ground.

He reached the two guards, standing by the horses.

"Help! Help!"Akavish yelled, waving his sword frantically at the horses.

The horses, frightened by the terrifying movement, bolted away.

The reins of one horse were caught in a nearby thicket.

"What is the matter?" one of the guards asked.

"The King is caught in a bog! Only the horses can help! Steady the horse, while I free it."

Akavish sliced his sword down on the reins of the horse, just an inch away from its nostrils. The horse reared on its back legs, front hooves clawing at the humid night air. The horse galloped off before the soldiers could catch it.

"Never mind the horses, let's return to the King!"

The guards followed Akavish back to the bog. Larus was neck-deep with a frantic look in his eyes. His face and arms were covered by the sticky sand. His left arm still held the burning torch aloft.

"Son. Help me!"

"I shall enter the sand. Guards! We shall form a chain. You, hold on to the tree." Akavish pointed at the shorter of the two. "Then you," Akavish commanded the taller one, "clasp his arm tightly and you will clasp mine."

They formed a human chain. The three men and the one metal arm reaching into the quicksand. Larus grasped the claw. The sharp pincers cut into the flesh of Larus' hand, but the big man held on firmly.

"Thank you, son. I thought I would die. For a moment I thought it might have all been a devious plot you hatched. Forgive me for doubting you."

"I forgive you, father," Akavish whispered as he grinned broadly. "I forgive you for your stupidity in trusting me. I forgive you for the years of harassment. I forgive you for your lack of attention. I forgive you for all your sins."

"What are you talking about, Akavish. Just pull me out of here. Your claws are slicing through my hands!"

"I forgive you, father, because I am finally, once and for all, getting rid of the source of all my problems. Goodbye. May your afterlife be as unpleasant as your death."

Akavish twisted his artificial arm quickly and the device came off his shoulder. The sudden release of tension pulled Akavish back to ground with the two guards.

"My arm!" Akavish cried for the guards' benefit. "It came loose!"

Larus' head dipped beneath the surface of the sand, as well as the torch and Akavish's iron arm.

With one final effort, Larus raised his head above the sand and splurted out, "Son!"

Larus descended into the quicksand, never to be seen alive again.

"Father!" Akavish cried. "Father." Akavish fell to his knees beside the quicksand and cried in the moonlight.

After a few moments, one of the guards put his arm on Akavish's healthy shoulder.

"You did everything you could, Akavish. It was a terrible accident. But he is gone. We must return to Ashkelon and inform the people. Their king is dead, but thankfully we have a new king."

The guards could not see Akavish's smile.

"Long live the King," Akavish whispered to the sand.

26. The Tomb of Moses

"I could have sworn I saw the cave on this ridge," Raskul snarled through his gnashed teeth. He, Boaz and Amitai climbed Mount Nevo on the eastern bank of the Jordan. They had left their mounts at the foot of the mountain. They could see the rubble of Jericho across the river, far below. Moss and weeds grew over the broken, abandoned city.

"There!" Amitai's sharp eyes pointed at a ledge several hundred paces higher. "Do you see an opening there? Perhaps that is it?"

"Let's keep climbing," Boaz ordered. "It's recorded that Moses could see the land all around, so he must have been close to the top of the mountain."

"Moses must have had long legs to climb this pathless mountain. I'm a merchant, not a goat," Raskul complained. He sat on a large rock and crossed his legs as he massaged his left knee. He kicked at the soft dirt with his sandal. "I'll wait for you here."

"Then I take it our arrangement is over?" Boaz said. "We are free of your 'guidance' and you of our protection."

"You're here, aren't you?" Raskul fumed. "You wouldn't have made it here without me."

"We probably would have been here sooner and with less hassle," Amitai interjected.

"Watch your smart mouth, boy," Raskul raised his walking stick. "I'm not so old that I can't give you a whack on your head."

"We are of course indebted to you for your accompaniment," Boaz raised his hands placating Raskul. "But I suspect we are better off parting ways and absolving each other of our promises."

"You will not get off that easily, sonny boy. You promised to protect me until we found the Tomb of Moses. I will sit here comfortably until you find the tomb. You can then take me to it, so I will see it with my own eyes, and then we can discuss a new arrangement. I'm not some mountain ram to go prancing around seeking this elusive cave. Have some respect for an old man."

"The condition for our protection was your leading us to the tomb faithfully," Boaz replied. "We have yet to find it and you have been less than faithful. In fact, you've been nothing but a major nuisance, delay and distraction. We are clear of our promise to you. Goodbye, Raskul."

"Okay, okay," Raskul walked after Boaz and Amitai. "If you wanted me to accompany you so badly, you just had to say so. No need to get insulting. I will not be so easily parted from my sworn protectors."

"Are you deaf as well as dumb?" Amitai asked. "We're finished with you, Raskul. Go back to your snake pit and leave us alone."

"How rude! I thought you Israelites claimed to be the paragons of morality and goodness. This is how you treat your humble servant? What injury have I caused you? You ungrateful wretches. I cared for you as a lioness for her cubs. Those delays were not my fault. Those items that went missing were not my fault. I don't know how they ended up in the hands of those merchants; they must have fallen out of your backpacks. It's not a coincidence that I knew them. I know many people from many nations."

"Hello, Raskul," a commanding voice bellowed from in front of them. A big, dark burly man climbed down the mountain accompanied by a dozen swarthy Midianites, all with curved swords. A dozen other Midianites closed quickly on Boaz, Amitai and Raskul from behind.

"Trasha," Raskul greeted the Midianite leader nervously. "What a coincidence to meet you here. What brings you to this scenic mountain range?"

"The two healthy specimens you brought us, of course. How did you describe them? 'Strong, young, but not too bright.' That's exactly what we look for in prospective slaves."

"Trasha, I'm hurt that you would accuse me of such a thing."

"I'm sure the silver in your pocket is easing your conscience."

"You sold us!?" Boaz turned to Raskul.

"I'm sure this is a misunderstanding that can be easily remedied. I suggest we go along with Trasha and his men and work this out."

"Does your treachery know any bounds?" Boaz accused Raskul.

"Yes, Raskul." Trasha smiled. "It's very naughty of you to betray your friends like that. In fact, one bad turn deserves another. We shall take our silver back from you Raskul, now that we have the slaves."

"What!?" Raskul exclaimed. "You would cheat me of fairly delivered merchandise?"

"It's an ancient Midianite custom. We never pay for what we can take by force. Isn't that right, boys?"

The Midianite men grunted in agreement, grinning and raising their swords higher.

"See," Trasha nodded approvingly. "We are devout in the practice of our traditions. You can consider us holy men. Now will you descend with us peacefully, or shall we have to hurt you a bit first?"

Boaz closed his eyes in response. He remembered Caleb's training. He remembered how he had used Isaac's Sight to perceive the aura of his enemy. He saw the aura of the Midianites in front and behind him. They were a sickly green of greed and a dark red of blood lust. On his left was Raskul with a maelstrom of colors; green greed, yellow fear, orange anger, purple pride and pale shame. Boaz did not give himself the time to analyze. On his right, Amitai was a steely blue of courage with a soft mauve of apprehension.

"At my signal," Boaz whispered, "hit the ground and cover your eyes. Then follow me to the high ground."

"What is your answer, Israelite?" Trasha asked impatiently.

Boaz opened his eyes. "My forefathers were slaves for too long to want to repeat the experience. We decline your kind invitation."

"You have verve, Israelite," Trasha laughed. "Perhaps I'll keep you as a personal slave. Ever since your people left Egypt there has been a regional shortage of slaves. Do you know how much I can get for a healthy slave? And an Israelite one? That would be a prize."

"This discussion is no longer amusing," Boaz raised his sword. Amitai mirrored the move. "Either move aside or die."

"The dumber ones always choose the hard way," Trasha said to his men. "Take them, with no limb loss!" Two dozen Midianites closed in on Boaz and Amitai. Raskul made himself very small and curled up next to a large stone.

"Now," Boaz barked.

Amitai fell onto the ground and covered his eyes with his arm.

Boaz closed his eyes and stabbed his sword into the soft ground of the ridge. He rapidly spun in place as his sword made a deep circle in the ground. The movement shot a whirlwind of dirt towards his attackers, blinding them. The Midianites clutched at their faces, rubbing the dirt out of their eyes, some of them dropping their swords.

Boaz somersaulted in midair, launching over the attackers ahead of him, up the mountain, and slicing at the Midianites with his blade. By the time he landed uphill of his attackers, three had fallen dead. Others looked around in a daze, searching for their prey.

"Get uphill and use your arrows," Boaz ordered Amitai. Amitai ran past the opening Boaz created, as the surrounding Midianites spat dirt and rubbed at their eyes.

Boaz attacked the Midianites closest to the edge of the ridge, kicking several over the ledge and slashing at the rest, and then kicking them over as well. They screamed and yelled noisily as they fell off the mountain. Within the space of a few moments half of the Midianite marauders had been slaughtered.

Amitai calmly picked off any Midianite approaching Boaz. Boaz pounced on the ones inward from the ridge that had cleared their eyes and regrouped. One of them had taken out his bow and arrow, shooting at Amitai and forcing him to take cover.

"You are a most formidable fighter!" Trasha exclaimed. "You could lead an army! Let me arrange it and I promise you riches beyond your dreams."

"Stand down or die," was Boaz's only response.

"How do I know you won't just kill us?" Trasha asked.

"You don't. Vile creatures can never understand honor," Boaz accused Trasha as if it were a death sentence.

Chilled, Trasha dropped his sword. The half-a-dozen other Midianites followed suit.

"Now leave this mountain and make sure never to come within sight of me. If I see you again, I will kill you. If I hear that you or any Midianite attacked an Israelite, I will hunt you down and kill you."

"You will hold me responsible for all Midianites? That is an impossible task."

"Yes. Do you seek fairness? I can save us both the effort and kill you now."

"You are persuasive. What is your name?"

"My name is 'The one who killed Trasha the Midianite, because he was too dull to save himself.' Now leave before I decide to take that name."

Trasha ran down the mountain, followed by his men. Boaz walked towards Raskul still hiding by the rock near the edge of the ridge.

"Boaz, that was masterful!" Raskul stood up and opened his arms wide. "You've saved us all."

"Leave, Raskul." Boaz leveled his sword at Raskul.

"What? Me? Your trusted guide and companion? You don't believe that liar Trasha. Midianites are known for their deception."

Boaz slashed at the pocket of Raskul's garment and caught the silver pieces that dropped out with the edge of his sword. He placed the silver in his palm.

"This is all you received for us?" Boaz asked. "I would have thought we'd be worth more than six silver pieces."

"That's my money!" Raskul reached for the silver.

Boaz raised his sword again. Amitai approached, arrow notched and pointed at Raskul's heart.

"What are you waiting for?" Amitai asked. "This snake sold us to slave-traders."

Raskul backed away from the threatening duo. He tripped on a stone and fell backwards over the edge of the mountain. Boaz dropped his sword, dived for Raskul and grabbed him by the ankle before the traitor disappeared from sight.

"Boaz, Boaz! Please don't let me go!" Raskul cried. "I'm sorry. I know I'm a miserable lout, but please, spare me. Have mercy!"

"Drop him," Amitai said. "If you let him live, he will just backstab us again or get us into other trouble. Is it worth saving his life just to jeopardize ours again?"

"I swear! I swear by all the gods! By everything I hold dear, I will never harm you, betray you, or even think of betraying you again."

"Your word is meaningless." Boaz let go of Raskul's ankle and grabbed it with his other hand. He hoisted

Raskul up and dumped him unceremoniously on the soft ground.

"Go. I never want to see you or hear you again. Say a word, and I will skewer you right here. Go!"

Raskul scampered down the mountain.

"You are too kind," Amitai said.

"Perhaps. The Midianites may not be so gentle with him if they meet up."

"But that's not why you let him go."

"No. I let him go because I don't want to kill unless I really have to."

"I understand."

"Truly?" Boaz looked at his friend.

"Yes, I do. Come, let's find that tomb and get off this inhospitable mountain."

Boaz and Amitai turned and climbed towards the mountain peak.

*

"I give in," Amitai raised his hands as they reached the peak for the third time. "We've been up and down and over this mountain like a priest checking for lesions. Every time we think we see a cave entrance it turns out to be a mirage. Those rumors must be true. No one can find the tomb of Moses."

Boaz sat on a rock near the summit of Mount Nevo. He looked west towards Canaan, saying nothing.

Amitai, noting his friend's silence, sat next to him on the rock and looked out across the clear sky. He could see the shore of the Great Sea in the distance.

"Do you remember when we tried to stop Moses from climbing this mountain?" Boaz asked, gazing westward.

"I'll never forget that day," Amitai said. "The way he was so gentle with us and then threw those gooseberries at us to occupy our hands and then jumped over us after we let go of him. He seemed relieved, even eager to move on."

"Do you realize that this was Moses' last sight before he died?" Boaz added. "He saw all the land that God gave us. South, west, north, east," Boaz pointed. "And the promise has been fulfilled, mostly. A nation of escaped slaves now controls the land that we can see from here. Joshua has led us well."

"What are you thinking?" Amitai asked.

"I'm thinking that Pinhas is wise, and knew what he was doing when he sent us on this wild quail chase."

"Why did he send us then? I thought by seeking the tomb of Moses you would get guidance?"

"That is exactly what he said. He didn't say that at the tomb we would receive guidance. I think he meant that just the process of seeking would provide guidance. He must have known that it can't be found and he also must have known we would come across bandits of one kind or another and that I would be forced to fight."

"Is that bad?"

"I've been petrified of fighting ever since I escaped the copper mines of Timna. When I fought as a child, it was instinctive. I was killing simply because I was put in a place to kill. It was without thought and it was part of this grand, national, God-ordained process. I couldn't do it anymore. Then, when we went to confront the two-and-a-half tribes, my instincts were all wrong and I was ready to fight with no cause. But now with these Midianites I had no choice. And I was good at it. Very good at it. I could have killed all of them had I wanted to. But I held back. It felt good to kill those evil creatures, but it felt equally good to be able to stop, and especially to not kill that leech, Raskul. I have never found someone so distasteful, except for Akavish, of course. I would take the company of acerbic Ploni any day over Raskul. But I still couldn't justify killing him when he was not an immediate or direct threat."

"We may yet regret your mercy."

"Perhaps, but now my mind is settled and my path is clear."

"Really? Now what?"

"I have special training and skills that I should put to good use."

"But the war is over."

"Yes, but there are still bandits like Trasha and his friends roaming our lands. I aim to deal with them and secure our roads and villages."

"What about Vered, or some other cousin that will want to marry you? Don't you want to settle down? Work the land? How long will you hunt these ruffians for?"

"I don't know. Until something more pressing comes my way."

"I'm with you then."

"Truly?"

"Where you go, I shall go. Where you sleep, I shall sleep."

Boaz lifted Amitai in a bear-hug.

"I'm glad I saved your life all those years ago. I never knew what a true friend I had."

Tears rolled down Amitai's face.

"Ribs," Amitai gasped. "You're crushing my ribs."

Boaz gently placed Amitai back on the ground and let go.

"On second thought, maybe it's safer to go home," Amitai smiled.

"Come on," Boaz slapped Amitai on the back. "Let's hunt some Midianites."

And the two friends ran down Mount Nevo, not noticing the cave entrance right next to them and the white-bearded spectre looking fondly down at them.

27. Ambush of the Ammonites

Amitai stuffed dried leaves and twigs into the little pouch. He sat on the leaf-strewn ground of the forest, with the tall oaks above him and his supplies around him. He poured oil liberally into the pouch making sure it moistened the flint stone protruding slightly from the bottom of the fist-sized burlap bag. He added various other pieces of leaves, roots and bark. Satisfied, he tied the pouch tightly and proceeded to prepare another one.

"How many are you going to make?" Boaz asked his friend.

"As many as I can," Amitai answered, not looking up from his work. "These little smoke balls have helped us much in the past. You never know when you'd like to disappear from enemy sight."

"You worry too much. We've had one successful interception after another, with not even an injury, except for Gidal, who stubbed his toe on a root, if you want to count that. Our militia has become so popular I've had to turn recruits away. I can see enemies in the dark and from a distance."

"Nonetheless, it doesn't hurt to be prepared. I'm going to give at least two of these to each of the men."

"That's over forty balls. Whatever makes you happy, Amitai. We'll start marching at nightfall. I'm looking forward to tomorrow's attack. We've been building up to this for some time and it should put a stop to Ammonite attacks."

*

Boaz closed his eyes and scanned his periphery with Isaac's Sight. His men had the dull grey of tiredness, mixed with a strong blue of confidence and a bright orange of excitement for the coming battle. He noticed a lone figure in the trees above their position in the forest. It was the alert, anxious yellow of an enemy, an Ammonite. The Ammonite had followed them from a respectful distance throughout the night. Boaz extended his vision to Nurad, the town they were about to attack. Only one soul was awake in the darkness before the dawn. He was colored an aggressive red of anticipation.

They were just over the border from the tribal region of Gad. Boaz and his growing militia had destroyed multiple bands of raiders. Boaz's success attracted new volunteers every month. After two years of trekking up and down the borders of the Israelite territory, he had made the land safer from bandits. The last battle had even seemed too easy. The Ammonites had retreated quickly, some of them appeared to have been sleeping before the encounter.

The Ammonites had been foraying into the Gadite territory and stealing flocks and anything else they could get their hands on. Boaz had decided to take the battle to Nurad, the base from which the Ammonites had been attacking.

From his hiding place in the forest, Boaz and his twenty men waited for dawn to break. His men were good, but fighting on a moonless night on their enemy's home ground would be too risky. They waited as the pale red dawn colored the land.

Nurad beckoned to Boaz. Its undefended homes called out and dared Boaz to raid them. The lack of walls indicated either there was nothing to defend or that the Ammonites here feared nothing.

Boaz raised his hand and gave the signal to attack. His militia moved stealthily out of the forest and approached Nurad.

An unusual bird call was the first thing to alert Boaz that something was wrong. A second bird call responded from the town ahead. Boaz signaled to halt and closed his eyes again. Suddenly, he sensed hundreds of souls waking quickly to consciousness. Not only in Nurad, but also in the forest behind them. *Ambush!* Boaz thought. *Somehow they anticipated our coming and hid their troops from my senses.*

"We're surrounded," Boaz said urgently.

"Where?" Amitai, ever at Boaz's side, asked.

"It's a trap."

In moments, a fully awake and totally armed force surrounded Boaz and his men. Boaz counted a ring of over five hundred soldiers, all with notched arrows pointed at the small Israelite group in the middle.

"Your harassment of our men is over," an old man called out. He was thin and hunched over, with a wispy white beard. "Surrender peacefully and I promise all of you a quick and clean death. It's not pleasant being hacked to death."

"Now what?" Amitai whispered to Boaz. Boaz noticed that his men had all turned pale. They had never faced such a hopeless disadvantage before. *I walked them right into this trap,* Boaz moaned to himself, *and I have no idea how to get us out. I can't just surrender. Think! Fast!*

"Before you calculate whether to resist or not," the old man continued. "I'd like you and your men to consider the following. Boaz, we know of your extraordinary senses and supernatural speed and we have prepared ourselves accordingly. As far as the rest of you, according to my reports you are all human and can be killed as well as any man. The way back to the forest is blocked. Except for the trail you took to reach us, we have dug deep trenches throughout the length of the forest. At the bottom of the trenches are rows of sharpened spikes. The trail you came through is now defended by over two hundred men. Go ahead, Boaz. Close your eyes and confirm."

Boaz closed his eyes and noted the two hundred souls, eager for blood. There were even more enemies spread out through the forest and throughout Nurad. *There will be no easy escape,* Boaz concluded. *These Ammonites have laid an impenetrable trap.*

"You see, Boaz. Your activities have been bad for our livelihood. It is nothing personal, but we realized, while you Israelites might find our way of doing business distasteful, your consistent destruction of our raiding parties needed to be stopped. We have banded together to lay this trap and to stop you once and for all."

"How will you stop me?" Boaz asked, stalling for time.

"I thought you would never ask!" the old man said cheerfully. He chirped an authentic sounding bird call. Two soldiers exited a nearby house and walked towards the old man. In between them walked a woman. Boaz was shocked that he recognized her. Her bright red hair matched his own. Vered! His dear cousin. The woman he had thought to marry but was too cowardly to face. Vered. How in heaven did she get here? He thought incredulously. We are far from the tribe of Judah, where she should be safe on her father's land.

"You can't imagine the trouble and expense it took to find and capture a relative of yours. One that we heard you are particularly fond of," the old man explained. "She's a feisty one, but we've taught her some manners."

Boaz noticed bruises on Vered's pretty face. She looked at Boaz with both joy and misery.

"Now, Boaz," the old man drew a dagger, held Vered in front of him and rested the dagger against Vered's neck. "Surrender or I kill your lovely cousin."

Boaz knew what he had to do.

"On my signal, form a ring with your shields, set your smoke balls," Boaz whispered to his men, "and head back to the forest. I'll try to get Vered and draw their fire."

"Old man," Boaz responded. "You bring out some redheaded wench and call her my cousin? You think that will hold me captive. She doesn't even look Israelite."

The old man seemed taken aback for a moment.

"Really? If she is nothing to you, then you will not object to killing her? Here," the old man pushed Vered towards Boaz. "Shoot her where she stands. Then I will be convinced there is no relationship. Be mindful, that there are five hundred arrows trained on you, and if you miss by a fingerbreadth, it shall be the last arrow you shoot."

Boaz notched his arrow with a prayer and aimed at Vered. *How are we going to pull this off?*

"Now!" Boaz barked as he took aim at the old man and let loose his arrow. The old man moved quickly for his age, but the arrow still struck him in the shoulder. At the same moment the rest of the Israelites scraped the bottom of their smoke balls with flint, and threw them between themselves and the Ammonites. Amitai threw one at Vered. They were all quickly enveloped in a thick cloud of white smoke.

Hundreds of Ammonite arrows flew at the surrounded Israelites who had raised their shields. There were too many arrows, though. Boaz, with his superhuman speed managed to avoid the arrows as he raced to Vered. He lifted Vered up and kept running past the wounded old man and into the town of Nurad. He leapt, with Vered still in his arms, on to the flat roof of a one-storey house.

"Stay hidden until I come to get you," Boaz said tenderly.

"Nice to see you too," Vered responded, but Boaz had already gone.

Gidal was the first of Boaz's men to fall. One arrow penetrated his thigh, bringing him to the ground. From alternate sides, a second arrow hit him in the lower back, while a third penetrated his lung. Tarel, to Gidal's right, tried to lift his friend's prone body, only to be shot as well.

Boaz could sense the lives of each of his men disappear. He cried as he ran and slashed at the ring of Ammonite archers. He had felled two dozen before the Ammonites realized what he was doing. One of the Ammonites whistled a shrill signal. Those closest to Boaz dropped to the ground in unison. Those directly opposite Boaz shot at him as the only target. Boaz dropped quickly to the ground, as he could not outrace all the arrows. The Ammonites next to Boaz then jumped on him. Before he knew it, his arms and legs were pinned down by three soldiers on each appendage and five on his torso.

The rest of the Ammonite army concentrated their fire on the retreating Israelites. Body after body fell. The retreating circle of shields got smaller and smaller as they left dead kinsmen in their wake. Boaz felt each death as a stab in the heart. Six, seven, eight of his men, butchered. Boaz struggled against his captors, but the more he fought, the harder they held. Tears fell freely down his eyes. In his mind he could taste each death, the disbelief that they were gone forever. *It is my fault. My pride and arrogance. Gidal, Tarel, Chanin, Leskiah, Elmol, Darnes, Bitam, Altor. Gone. And more if I can't help.*

Boaz relaxed his struggle, realizing the futility. *What can I do? God! Help us!*

The Ammonites on Boaz also relaxed their pressure on him, though still holding his limbs firmly. From the corner of his eye, Boaz noticed Vered approaching rapidly. She carried a heavy iron cauldron. With fire in her eyes, Vered smashed the cauldron onto the Ammonites on top of Boaz. Six men fell over and crashed into the other Ammonites holding Boaz. Freed, Boaz grabbed his sword and moved like a whirlwind, killing all the Ammonites around him. He lifted the panting Vered in his other arm and sped along the line of Ammonites who were shooting at the retreating Israelites. His sword slashed faster than the eye could follow. Cursing and crying Boaz mowed down a hundred men in the fastest burst of speed he had ever reached in his life. The Ammonites, with all eyes on the retreating Israelites, had assumed Boaz had been successfully subdued. Boaz got closer and closer to the forest entrance, leaving a path of cloven and dismembered Ammonites along the way.

The Israelite ring reached the entrance to the forest under heavy fire. Amitai led the retreat and had the men release the last remaining smoke balls at the Ammonites, blinding them. Amitai ordered a charge. The Israelites, now within sword reach of the Ammonites, hacked at them through the smoke. Boaz reached his men just as they had broken through the Ammonite ring and into the forest.

"Amitai!" Boaz breathed heavily. "How are you?" Amitai had a broken arrow shaft protruding from his left shoulder and another one in his thigh. Most of the men had at least one or two arrows in them.

"Clear the troops ahead and we might yet have a chance."

"No!" Vered said suddenly. "There's a better way."

"Speak quickly," Boaz commanded.

"There is a cave nearby. I escaped one day and hid there overnight. They never found it. They caught me the next day as I tried to go further."

"Good," Boaz nodded. "Amitai, follow Vered. I'll try to recover the fallen."

"Save the living." Amitai looked at Boaz sternly. "The dead can wait."

"You're right," Boaz agreed, fresh tears moistening his eyes. "I'll engage the troops in the forest, while you make for the cave. I'll then double back to the town and see what I can do."

"That's more reasonable." Amitai clasped Boaz's arm. "Don't blame yourself. Let's salvage what we can and then figure out what went wrong." Boaz nodded silently and sped deeper into the forest.

Boaz took cover behind a large oak and closed his eyes to assess the situation. He could see his remaining men, a dark grey of deathly exhaustion following Vered. Boaz was amazed by Vered's aura. It was a shiny white, indicating a bravery and purity of purpose that reminded him of Joshua or Caleb's aura. It was tinted by a deep purple of energy and determination. *What a woman!* Boaz thought in awe.

He could sense the Ammonites from Nurad regrouping and entering the forest. Boaz had destroyed half of their troops. The remaining soldiers were shocked by the carnage Boaz had left in his wake. Boaz could sense the red hot anger of the old man. *That brilliant, conniving, old tactician almost killed us all. And we're not out of it yet.* Boaz turned his attention deeper into the forest. Two hundred fresh troops closed in towards the escaping Israelites. Boaz would have to deal with them first.

28. Battlefield Romance

With a fresh surge of energy, Boaz ran in the opposite direction of his men, parallel to the approaching troops. He ran until he could circle around them unnoticed. Boaz still carried the sling from his childhood battles. He grabbed a handful of sharp stones and slung them with violent force and deadly accuracy at the back of the Ammonites' heads. Two, five, eight, fourteen. The Ammonites fell to Boaz's unrelenting attack. He moved and shot, moved and shot, so the Ammonites thought they were under attack by an entirely new hidden force. After the fiftieth Ammonite fell, the troops disbanded, fleeing chaotically in all directions.

Boaz returned to the edge of the forest in time to hear the fleeing Ammonites yell.

"There is another army of Israelites! They are bigger and more numerous! Flee!"

To encourage their fear, Boaz pelted the Ammonites at the forest entrance with a volley of his deadly rocks. They ran to Nurad, to the safety of its buildings, leaving their dead behind.

Boaz waited until the battlefield between the forest and the town was clear of the living. Hundreds of bodies littered the field. But only eight of them interested him: Eight that he recognized in death. Eight that he loved and missed. Eight that he would never forgive himself for having led them to their deaths.

He took a deep breath and ran to Altor, bringing his body under the protection of the trees. He repeated his sprint seven more times, ending with Gidel. Happy, clumsy, loyal Gidel. Boaz thought his heart would break to think how much he would miss Gidel.

Still carrying Gidel, Boaz searched for the live auras of the rest of his men, hiding in the nearby cave.

"I got them," Boaz announced as he laid Gidel's corpse tenderly by the cave entrance.

Boaz took six of the men that were still able to walk to bring back the other bodies. Amitai lay collapsed on the cave floor as Vered tended to his wounds. Boaz closed his eyes for a moment. *I don't see his aura! That's how they must have tricked us. They must have realized that I don't see the auras of the sleeping.*

Minutes later the men returned, carrying their dead and laid them in a row by the deep cavern entrance.

The musty cave interior washed over Boaz, carried by a slight breeze.

"There may be another way out," Boaz commented.

"We figured that already," Vered answered while treating Barlo's wounded abdomen. "But first we need to care for the wounded. We'll place a guard by the cave entrance until we're ready to move again."

"Good thinking," Boaz agreed, further impressed with this cousin of his. *I don't know why I never really noticed her before.*

Boaz then collapsed on the floor face first. During the battle, he hadn't realized an arrow had hit him and now protruded from his back.

*

"How long can he sleep for?" a sweet female voice said in Boaz's dream.

"After his superhuman feats, he's usually either ravenous or exhausted." Boaz recognized Amitai's voice.

"Two days seems excessive." It was Vered. *How could I not recognize her voice?*

"I've never seen him do as much as he did in Nurad. He may have lost much blood from that wound as well. Let's give him another day."

"Silly boy. He was always foolhardy."

"You disapprove?" Amitai asked, offended.

"Do I disapprove of Boaz trekking up and down the land looking for a fight?" Vered raised her voice. "Do I disapprove of being kidnapped from home and being threatened and beaten? Do I disapprove of him trying to make up for the wars he didn't fight? Of course I disapprove. Are a few lousy sheep worth eight men's lives? You tell me!" Vered pointed harshly at the eight fresh graves in the cavern.

"Each of the men joined our militia willingly, knowing it was dangerous."

"Did they? Boaz was invincible. Boaz was unstoppable. The men probably thought that just to walk in Boaz's shadow would keep them from harm."

"Perhaps. But now we know better. I suspect, Boaz now most of all. He will take this very hard."

"Good. Maybe he'll come back home where he belongs."

"You care for him."

"Of course I care for him. He's my cousin."

"No. You care for him more than that."

Vered blushed in the dark cave. Boaz couldn't see her in his dream, but he could feel her warmth.

*

"Wake up," Vered commanded Boaz, shaking him roughly. "Enough sleep. If we don't get proper care for Barlo, he may die from his wound."

Boaz groggily opened his eyes. In the dim light of the cave he could make out Vered's fiery hair. "This is the most pleasant sight I've woken to in many a year," Boaz said.

"Flattery will get you nowhere," Vered lied. "We've been waiting on you. Everyone else has been ready to move. You've been sleeping for three days. We found an exit far down this cavern that is within the territory of Gad. If we leave now, we should be able to get help for Barlo in time."

"What happened to me?"

"You had an arrow in your back and you collapsed from exhaustion."

"You saved me." Boaz gazed into Vered's eyes with admiration.

"No. The arrow was not fatal. Just hit some muscle."

"You did save me. When the Ammonites had me pinned down."

"I couldn't just let them kill you."

"I can't just let the Ammonites or the Midianites or the Moabites or anyone else kill and pillage our people."

"Haven't you had enough?"

"Perhaps. I'll have to think about it. I'll have to analyze where we went wrong and adjust accordingly."

"Will you ever give it up?"

Boaz closed his eyes. He looked closely at Vered's swirling aura: That same deep majestic purple of energy and determination. Now it was mixed with a light pink of hope and anticipation, and a warm red he had never seen before. *Is that the color of love?* He could almost hear her heart beating, she was hanging on his every word. Underneath it all was that bright white of purity and bravery. *I wonder how other men find their soul mates without Sight,* Boaz wondered. *I can live with Vered's aura for the rest of my life.*

"I will give it up for the right person."

"And who might that person be?"

"The person who saved my life. The person who stood by my side. The person who confronted my enemies unflinchingly. I would spend the rest of my life with that person."

"You want to spend the rest of your life with Amitai?" Vered teased.

Boaz smiled.

"No, Vered. As soon as I have resolved this failure, as soon as I'm sure our militia is well organized, manned and led, I would spend the rest of my life with you. Would that be agreeable to you?"

"As long as it won't take too long. I won't wait around for you forever."

"You don't make a man's life easy."

"Is that what you were looking for in a wife?"

"I had hopes."

"You talk too much, Boaz. Let's get Barlo some care and then you can tell me how much you adore me. Get off your lazy back and let's move." Vered turned abruptly and helped lead Barlo deeper into the cavern, to the exit beyond.

Boaz was startled by Vered's curt answer. He closed his eyes and noticed the growing glow of happiness within her. *Even with the Sight, I may never understand women.*

Boaz followed her towards the light at the end of the tunnel.

29. King Akavish

Akavish sat on his new throne in his father's throne room. He had burned his father's heavy wooden throne and constructed a dark copper one instead. Akavish loved the feel of the cold metal on the skin of his one healthy arm. Even more, he loved clanging his iron arm on the chair and watching the cringing reaction of the attendants in the throne room. The large stone chamber was regularly filled with people though he was never quite sure why they were there. He frequently cast suspicious glances upon them.

His latest arm was a marvel of technological genius. Akavish could now choose from a selection of poisons, a built in cross-bow, or a dart-launcher. He was still working on installing a mechanized sling for his famous stars of death. All his weapons were, of course, deliciously poison-tipped.

"But my king," Bardes, the chief servant, pleaded on his knees in front of Akavish, "you are asking me to burn down my son's house. He meant no disrespect or attack when he bumped into you. He merely tripped on a loose cobblestone. Please reconsider."

"My decision is final." Akavish placed his ferrous arm on the servant's shoulder. Silence pervaded the room. "I do not appreciate being argued with. If you cannot carry out my orders, I shall find someone else more loyal."

Good help is so hard to find, Akavish thought, as he flicked his mechanical arm, stinging to death his third chief servant, in as many months.

Bardes collapsed to the ground and writhed in pain for a few seconds before freezing in a most unnatural position. *Why don't people listen to me, understand me?* Akavish griped to himself.

"Remove him," Akavish commanded the other court sycophants hanging around in the throne chamber. "And send his family the usual payment with instructions to leave Ashkelon before nightfall. I don't want any moping or vengeful relatives about. Burn all their homes down." Two servants hauled the dead Bardes out of the throne room.

"Aldas," Akavish pointed at a young man in the corner of the throne room. "You look reasonably intelligent. I name you my new chief servant. Fail me, and your end will be as swift as his." Akavish gestured at the departing late chief servant.

Aldas trembled as he walked to Akavish's throne and knelt at his feet.

"King Akavish," Aldas intoned. "Your merest whim shall be as an ironclad command."

"Well spoken. Now fetch Krafus. He should have been back from his mission by now."

*

"Congratulations on your promotion, Aldas," said Krafus, as he sipped slowly from his mead in the tavern hall. "I hope you last longer than your predecessors. I'm in no rush to see Akavish. I need to consider the information I've learned and how to use it. It's a shame Bardes' son was a bumbling fool and couldn't kill Akavish when he had the chance."

"Akavish seems to sense every plot and move against him and is somehow able to protect himself. He suspects you most of all."

"I know, but he still hesitates to kill me. He still likes to hear what I have to say. We must be careful with this latest piece of information. I'm sure it can serve our purposes."

"What is it?"

"After many years of silence, Akavish's old nemesis, the Israelite Boaz, the one who cut off his arm, is being spoken of again."

"What do they say?"

"He has organized a militia that is exterminating band after band of ruffians. He has vanquished Midianites, Ammonites, Moabites, all with growing success and popularity."

"How will this help us?"

"Akavish's blood will boil when he hears of his old enemy's success."

"Then I would rather be elsewhere when you give him the news."

"Are you fearful, Aldas? Perhaps you should leave Ashkelon if you cannot confront our tyrant."

"We are doomed if we do not bring the madman down. He is crazed enough that he would hunt me down if I abandoned this city. He has wrecked it and our livelihood. Commerce has slowed to a crawl. Sailors are docking at Ashdod instead of here and all the merchants are taking their business there. He has burned down half the city. Soon there will be nothing left to save."

"Have faith, Aldas. There is an additional bit of news that is sure to drive Akavish mad and send him to chase his old adversary. Boaz will have to destroy Akavish for us. Boaz has ever been fortunate. His god smiles upon him."

"What news? How will you break it to him?"

"Come and see. I'm looking forward to the pain it will inflict upon Akavish."

*

"Welcome back, Krafus," said Akavish, as he clanged his metal claw on his copper throne.

"Hail, King Akavish, Ruler of Ashkelon, Scion of Larus and Battler of the Israelites," Krafus announced with great pomp as he approached the throne, staying out of reach of the menacing claw.

"Stop it, old man. Just tell me what you've learned."

"As you wished, I've studied the movements of the Israelites and they are no threat to Ashkelon or to any of the other Philistine cities."

"Let me be the judge of what is a threat. Details. Give me details."

"Joshua, their great sorcerer and leader, has retired. Their regular army has disbanded, with each man awarded land. The Israelite soldiers are all busy planting their fields and grazing their animals. They were actually quite orderly about parceling the land, dividing by tribe and then by family. They have not succeeded in conquering all of the Canaanite cities though. Several do pay homage and taxes to the Israelites and there are even a few that are still independent."

"So war has ended for the Israelites?" Akavish asked, confused.

"There is one who still fights."

"Who?"

"You know him."

"Boaz?" Akavish's pulse quickened.

"Yes. He has created a militia that has been attacking the various bands that have been stealing Israelite flocks. Boaz has demolished Moabite, Ammonite and Midianite raiders. Apparently he single-handedly destroyed an Ammonite stronghold. He is feared by his enemies and loved by his people."

Akavish's face turned red as he forgot to breathe. Shaking with rage, he raked his throne with his claw, rending the air with the piercing shriek of metal on metal. All in the throne room scrambled to cover their ears. Krafus tried to hide a grin.

"I should have killed him when I had the chance," Akavish finally said.

"You can't mean to pursue him now?" Krafus asked.

"And why shouldn't I?"

"We need you here. You have duties to your city, to your people."

"My people hate me and plot to kill me, with you at the head of the conspiracy. Boaz has love and fame and glory. It should have been mine. Instead he leaves me a cripple and is adored by his people. Why should I not kill him?"

"Remember he always bested you when you met. If anything, now that he's an adult I have heard that he has become an even greater warrior and leader of men. If he was incredible as a child, he must be formidable as an adult and a commander of battle-proven soldiers."

"Perhaps you are right. I am king, am I not? I have the fear and obediance of my people. Why should I seek trouble with the Israelite? Let him play soldier with the nations of the east. I am comfortable here, and as you say, the Israelites are no threat to us. You are wise as always, Krafus."

"I'm pleased that you follow my guidance, King Akavish. However, I did not finish my report."

"Proceed."

"Boaz is to be married this summer."

"What!?" Akavish jumped out of his throne. "To whom? How? How does a professional soldier have time for marriage as well? Have the gods poured all their blessings upon my enemy?"

"Yes. He is marrying the love of his life. A beautiful woman from his tribe. I believe she is even a relative. It is reported that they make quite a handsome couple." Krafus paused and looked at Akavish's claw and balding, greasy head with open distaste, as if to say: *You were handsome once too. Now, what woman would want you, unless you forced her or threatened her family*?

"More. Tell me more," Akavish grunted through gritted teeth.

"His success has not only been military and romantic. He has started a bakery. The most famous in his tribe. He has become quite wealthy for a young man."

"How? When? Is there nothing the gods have not granted him? Why do they tease me like this? There is more. I sense you are withholding more. Tell me!"

"Joshua will be at his wedding. And so will Caleb, and all the princes of Israel. Joshua has no sons. It is rumored that Joshua may appoint Boaz his successor as leader of all the Israelites, though I still don't know how succession works amongst these people."

"Enough! I've heard enough! We shall destroy Boaz. It is against all nature for a being to be so blessed. I shall be the weapon of the gods," Akavish raised his claw heavenward, "and exact justice and retribution from this insolent Israelite. By Baal and Ashtarte! We shall be there for his wedding celebration. We shall annihilate Boaz and the entire Israelite leadership. They will not expect an attack at so joyous an event in what they consider peace-time. Then all of the Israelite lands will be ripe for the picking. I shall become Akavish the Great. Akavish the Conqueror. All will fear my name, not just the worthless citizens of Ashkelon. I will trample upon the dead carcass of Boaz and then kill his bride. Or perhaps his bride first. Yes. He should see her die first. This is what I was meant to do. Krafus, tell the other cities. There will be enough land for everyone. Promise them vineyards and olive groves and flocks and herds and wide pastures. We cannot live long enclosed in these cities, relying just on the sea. We must expand eastward and this is our opportunity."

"Excellent, your majesty. I shall send word immediately." Krafus could barely contain his glee as he left Akavish.

"Aldas!" Akavish called for the new chief servant.

"Yes, your majesty." Aldas approached.

"Call for the blacksmith and the apothecary. I need more darts, arrows and especially stars of death. Lots of stars of death. And much poison. This is going to be a massacre!" Akavish spoke with such joy, even those in the room that wished him dead couldn't help but smile.

30. House of Bread

"Stop it!" Vered giggled, as Boaz threw a sprinkling of flour at his bride-to-be.

"You've been in the sun too much," Boaz smiled. "We need to get you back to your beautiful pale self."

"Am I less beautiful because I like the outdoors?" Vered asked in mock anger. The two of them were kneading dough in Boaz's bakery, in the town of Bethlehem, amidst the rolling hills south of Jerusalem. The bakery was a simple stone structure. A large brick oven with a roaring fire dominated the back wall. An open ledge at the front faced the bustling main road of Bethlehem. A wide wooden table in the middle of the bakery was filled with kneaded dough. On the side of the table were large sacks of freshly ground flour and basins of clear spring water. The hot oven warmed up the entire bakery, taking away the chill of the early morning in the Judean Mountains. Their wedding day was just three weeks away.

Boaz, realizing he had yet again stuck his foot in his mouth, couldn't figure out how to extricate himself. *Flattery,* he finally thought. *Shameless flattery always does the trick.*

"You misunderstand, my love. You are beautiful when you are pale, as well as when you are bronzed by the sun."

"First you call me ugly, and now you call me a fool, saying I misunderstand you?" Boaz couldn't help hearing a sharper edge in her voice. He was never sure when she was teasing and when she was serious. He needed to pacify her, for his own sake, before he was bewildered even further.

"No. I mean, yes. I mean, you are beautiful under all circumstances. And of course you are no fool. You are one of the smartest women I've ever met."

"Are you implying that women are generally not smart? You're saying I'm smart for a woman? Is that like saying you walk well for a cripple?" Vered threw the dough she was kneading hard on the table.

"No! That's not what I mean at all!"

"Then say what you mean! Why are you so cruel and insulting?" Vered took her apron off. She dropped it onto a nearby stool, raising a thin cloud of white dust. She walked to the washing basin to clean her hands, arms and face.

Boaz stood with his mouth ajar. Just moments ago they were teasing each other playfully and now she seemed truly angry. He closed his eyes for a moment, trying to sense her aura.

Her white essence was bright, but there was a swirling mixture of colors as well. Red anger, yellow fear, but also blue and green and purples he did not understand.

"Vered, my dear," Boaz said calmly. "What's the matter? Why are you angry with me? What have I done?"

"You're going to leave me," she said, not looking at him.

"Nonsense. I have no such plans."

"My mother said men from your militia would be coming to look for you today, asking you to return."

"How does she know that?"

"She's friendly with Amitai's mother, who got word that her son is arriving today. Why else would he come suddenly to Bethlehem from his command?

"They don't need me anymore. I saw to that. Amitai is doing a fantastic job. He's a better tactician than I ever was. He has experienced, dedicated men. He said not to worry, and I will take him at his word."

"But what if he does come? Promise me you will not go off with them," Vered pleaded.

"We agreed, Vered. I would only go if they absolutely need me. How often can that happen? We've destroyed the major thieving groups, any survivors are disbanded and disorganized and Amitai has them all on the run. I don't fear any major problems for a while. Relax, Vered. I'm not going anywhere."

"You promise?"

"I promise. Come, let's get this batch in the oven and clean up. Customers will be arriving any minute."

Though not cheered, Vered scooped up the dough she had kneaded and placed it carefully in the wide brick oven. Boaz, with his renowned speed, gathered his portion of dough and placed it quickly yet gingerly into the remaining empty spaces in the oven.

The smell of the baking bread brought a smile back to Vered's face.

"This is a good batch," Boaz said, changing the topic.

"Yes. You're getting better and faster. We've also received more orders for delivery."

"It's amazing."

"It certainly is," a gruff voice interrupted them from the front of the bakery.

"Father," Boaz said to the tall red-headed man with the long beard. Salmoon son of Nachshon had adjusted well to the conquest of Canaan. He much preferred tilling the earth to wielding a sword. In an agrarian existence he no longer worried about the shadow of his famous warrior father, Nachshon the Daring.

"Good morning, son. It warms the heart to see you up before dawn, working on something not life-threatening, close to home. I haven't heard of anyone dying from baking yet."

"Good to see you as well, father. How can I be of service?"

"Oh, nothing. I just wanted to check on you and Vered before I went to prayers. Don't be late. It's good you're making a living, but don't forget that God is the true Provider."

"I won't forget, Father. As soon as I've helped Vered sell our first batch, I'll be right there."

"Good. And a wonderful day to you, Vered."

"Thank you, Salmoon," Vered curtsied.

Boaz's father strode away as a dozen women of all ages, carrying empty baskets, approached the bakery. On the narrow road, Boaz could see other men in prayer shawls walking towards the local sanctuary for morning prayers.

With long, flat sticks, Boaz and Vered quickly scooped the hot, fresh bread out of the oven and placed them on the ledge at the front of the bakery.

"That will be three coppers, Marta," Boaz said, as a matronly woman filled her basket with the steaming loaves.

"My sons love your bread," Marta replied with a shy smile, as she dropped three small copper pieces on the counter. "My husband said he doesn't mind spending the money to give me a reprieve from baking all these years. God bless you, Boaz."

"Good day to you, Marta. Thank you."

Boaz finished selling the first batch, as Vered started kneading a second one. The initial crowd of women dissipated as the ledge was cleared of the fresh bread.

"I'd better head to the sanctuary," Boaz said, as he wiped the bread crumbs off the ledge with a rag. "My father will be annoyed as it is."

"Boaz!" a panting breath approached the bakery.

"Amitai! What are you doing here? Are you okay?"

"We need you," he said, catching his breath. "We found a Moabite stronghold right on the border with the Reubenites. They have deep caves in the mountain and I need your Sight to tell us how many there are."

"Oh, no you don't," Vered chastised Amitai. "Don't barge in here right before our wedding, demanding Boaz help you. You have enough men. You don't need him."

"I'm sorry, Vered," Amitai said, looking down. "It's just a matter of timing. We followed them to their caves and I left my men to keep an eye on them, but if Boaz could tell us how many there are and where they're located, it could save lives. He doesn't even need to fight. I can have him back before the wedding."

"Don't even think about it, Boaz." Vered looked at Boaz sternly.

"Amitai, can this wait a few days?" Boaz asked.

"You know as well as I do that every day we delay gives these criminals more time to regroup, build themselves up and prepare for their next attack. While you are busy baking bread, they get stronger every day."

Boaz looked at Vered.

"If you leave, Boaz son of Salmoon," Vered said. "Don't bother coming back."

"Vered…"

"No, Boaz. No. This is it. This is when you decide between your friends and me. Do you want to be a professional soldier or do you want to be a family man? Let's see. Let's see where you stand. Better I should find out now, than once we're married. Well? What's it going to be?"

"Vered, they need me. You heard Amitai. This may save lives."

"Boaz, I need you. I cannot live in constant fear of you dying in one of those raids. Wasn't the raid on Ammon close enough?" Tears streamed down Vered's face. "Why does Amitai need to chase and attack every thief in the land? Give them a break. Give yourselves a break. When are you going to build a home? Do you want to be a professional soldier all your life?"

Boaz looked from Vered to Amitai.

He closed his eyes and saw the raging inferno of colors within Vered. A hot, red anger with a sickly orange of despair. Her bright white had been muted by confusion, longing and fear. He could sense Amitai's grey guilt and steely blue need.

Vered is right, Boaz thought. *And I need her too.*

"Amitai," Boaz said, as he opened his eyes. "You'll have to find another way."

Boaz could feel Vered's love and gratitude over the heat of the bakery ovens.

"I'm not leaving Vered," he continued. "We need our calm and quiet until at least after the wedding. And for the first year I will certainly not be leaving her."

"You're nice and safe here in Bethlehem," Amitai responded with some anger, "but on the periphery they bring the fight to us."

"I've retired from fighting. Now I'm just going to focus on my work and my bride and some serenity."

"What happened to our leader? What happened to the Boaz that was afraid of no man? What happened to all those ideals of defending our people?" Amitai asked pointedly.

"I need a break, Amitai," Boaz answered. "I'm entering a new stage in my life, together with Vered. I promised her. Please understand, Amitai. When our existence is really threatened I will be there, but these bandits are more of a nuisance than anything else. It is important to deal with them, but now it needs to be without me."

"This is disappointing," Amitai said. "Now I'm not sure what we'll do, but if your decision is final, I will have to find another way."

"You will, Amitai," Boaz assured his friend. "You'll invent some new contraption that will smoke them out, or make the cavern collapse on them, or somehow give yourselves an advantage."

"Interesting idea. The men will be disappointed though. I'd better head back." Amitai turned grumpily.

"Don't leave angry," Boaz said. "Here, take a loaf for the road." Boaz handed Amitai a warm loaf of bread.

"Thank you, Boaz. I don't agree with you, but I respect your decision. Vered, I wish you much joy and happiness. I hope that one day I'll find someone so passionate about me."

"It's easier if you're not holding a sword," Vered answered. "Women want farmers and shepherds, not warriors."

"I hear you. Once I find and train my successor, I'll give up the sword. In the meantime, I'll excuse myself from you lovebirds, as I have some Moabites to deal with. Goodbye and may God be with you." Amitai and Boaz clasped hands and hugged. Amitai then departed without further word.

"Thank you," Vered said to Boaz meaningfully.

"Thank you," Boaz responded. "I'm sorry I made you angry and even considered going."

"Well, we have a lot of work to do before the wedding and I need to get this second batch of dough in the oven."

"The wedding will be glorious," Boaz said encouragingly. "Nothing will ruin it."

Boaz and Vered looked at each other lovingly, not knowing their wedding day would prove to be the bloodiest day of the year.

31. Monkey Business

"Hurry up over there," grey-haired Raskul called ahead irritably to the front of the line. He leaned heavily on his cane. "We don't have all day. Some of us have important matters to discuss with the Ancient One."

Raskul stood in a line snaking up a mountain. The line was composed mostly of ill or impoverished people. He recognized most of the nationalities: Moabites, Ammonites, Midianites, Edomites and even a rare Egyptian. All had come to this lone mountain on the southeastern edge of the great Sea of Salt. Yered, the Ancient One, with his magical monkey, had gained a reputation for being a miracle worker. He was also known for providing good, if sometimes cryptic, advice.

They moved slowly. Finally, Raskul saw that the line led to a shallow cave where Yered sat on a large stone, cross-legged, with the small magical monkey on his shoulder. The Ancient One wore long white cotton robes, stained here and there with remains of mead. He had no hair on his bronzed head, except for two thin lines of white tuft that were his eyebrows. The monkey had luxurious black and white fur and his eyes shone with intelligence. Instead of a right arm, a long wooden contraption, with a fake wooden hand at the end, was affixed to the monkey's shoulder.

"Next in line," Yered called.

"Ancient One," a young man limped to him on one healthy leg, supported by crude crutches. "My leg was cut off in a fight with the Israelites. I have heard that you can help bring it back."

"I am not a finder of lost limbs. You were foolish to fight against Israelites and are fortunate to be alive. See Achira the Moabite. He can construct a fake limb. He is the best. Expensive, but worth it. Three coppers for advice." Yered extended his hand and the young amputee dutifully dropped three coppers in his dark, wrinkled hand.

"Next in line!" Yered called.

Only two people now stood between Raskul and Yered. A middle-aged man and an old woman. Now Raskul was able to get a better look at the Ancient One. He noticed the sun-darkened wrinkled skin on the wiry figure. He could not take his eyes off of the shiny golden teeth and wondered how he might steal them.

"Ancient One," the thin middle-aged man in rags approached Yered. "I keep losing at the bone games. What advice can you give me?"

"You are a foolish man with a foolish question and a waste of our time. Stop gambling. One copper."

"What? For that? I wait in this endless line for hours, that is all you say and you still want me to pay? You're a fraud." The man turned away.

"Risto," Yered nodded at the monkey. The monkey jumped onto the man's head, curled his tail tightly around the man's neck, deftly took five copper pieces out of the man's pouch and jumped smoothly back onto Yered's shoulder.

"That's for wasting Risto's time," Yered told the coughing man. "Further argument or time-wasting shall cost you more."

The man walked away without another word, keeping his eyes on the monkey until he was out of sight.

"Ancient One," the old toothless woman hobbled towards him. "I have a terrible pain in my joints, and the roots that used to ease the pain no longer work. Can you help me?"

"We can help. It is expensive. Twenty coppers for the medicine."

"Twenty coppers!?" the old woman exclaimed. "How do I know it will work?"

"Next in line!" Yered called.

"Fine. I'll pay you. Here it is." She counted out twenty coppers into the Yered's hand.

Risto the monkey, jumped onto Yered's lap, opened a panel in his own wooden arm and chittered excitedly at Yered.

"You suggest Alkanel?" Yered addressed Risto while pointing at the long hollow container in the monkey's wooden arm. The container was divided into multiple tiny partitions, each with a small amount of crushed herbs.

"The anise, perhaps," Yered continued.

Risto waved his good arm passionately.

"No," Yered said forcefully. "Buckthorn is not the solution to everything. We know you like celandine, but for joint pain silverweed is the best."

Risto screeched pointing his healthy finger angrily at the herb compartments.

"Fine. Thyme and silverweed," Yered concluded.

Risto nodded, satisfied, and took a pinch of herbs out of two of the compartments.

"Wait," the old woman put up her hand. "What magic is this, from a monkey's false arm?"

"Not magic," Yered answered. "Medicine. Herbs of healing. Storing it in the monkey's arm, with his vitality, keeps it fresh and potent. Effective for hard-to-find herbs. Very valuable. Therefore expensive."

Yered removed a large fresh fig leaf from a pile next to his stone, placed the herbs in it and folded it tightly closed.

"When you reach home, mix the herbs in a large jug of water. Drink one mouthful of that water, morning and night. Good luck."

"Thank you, Ancient One. Thank you." The old woman departed holding the folded fig leaf as if it was gold.

"Next in line!" Yered called.

Raskul approached, shaken by the treatment he saw the Ancient One give his clients, yet determined to ask his question.

"Ancient One," Raskul said. "I have an enemy. A powerful enemy. But I don't know how to defeat him."

"Curious. A man may be measured by his enemies, unless he is so foolish as to make an unnecessary one."

"This enemy betrayed me. After I led him faithfully and cared for him, he double-crossed me and left me to fend for myself against a band of ruffians. I was fortunate to escape with my life. I have had no peace or success since that day. I always fear that he will hunt me, or kill me. But now I may have an opportunity to exact my revenge. He is to marry and I would spoil his happiness."

"Ah, revenge is sweetest when least expected. What do you seek from us?"

"I don't know how to beat him. He is unnaturally fast, can sense where his enemies are, and can predict their moves. I have seen him best a band of cut-throat brigands single-handedly. How can I hurt such a man?"

"Hmm, the description is like that of a boy we once knew."

"Will you help me or not?"

"Fifty coppers."

"What if your advice is unsatisfactory?"

"Next in line!" Yered called.

"Fine, fine. Here's your money." Raskul grudgingly counted out the pieces from his pouch. "How does one best such an enemy?"

"Come as a friend."

"That's it? That's what my fifty coppers gets me?"

"We have a no complaint policy, or Risto will take more," Yered said. "Curious. Who is this enemy?"

"Boaz of Judah. He is to be married next week in Bethlehem. And perhaps you are right. He always put on airs of being merciful. I shall come as a friend to share in his joy." Raskul's words dripped with malice as he bowed to Yered and departed.

Yered looked at Risto and saw old wounds and memories in his eyes. Risto chittered urgently.

"Yes, Risto. We must attend the wedding."

32. Prenuptial Warfare

"Oh, Vered!" her cousin Naomi gushed, "you look stunning. The gown looks so good on you!"

"Thank you, Naomi. I'm so happy," Vered answered as she kissed her cousin in greeting. "I can't believe this day is here. I was afraid Boaz would play at being soldier forever."

Naomi examined Vered's dress in her home as outside, the wedding preparations occupied the entire city of Bethlehem.

"Well, you've certainly gotten him to settle down," Naomi said. "With the bakery and all, I understand he's already a wealthy man."

"It doesn't hurt, but I'm happiest that his fighting days are over. Amitai tried to get him for one last mission, but Boaz refused. I was so relieved. I promise you, I was ready to leave him if he had gone with Amitai."

"Well, I'm hoping Elimelech will finally muster the courage to propose to me," Naomi sighed. "That will make me your aunt, you know."

"Can we still be friends?" Vered teased.

"Maybe even neighbors." Naomi hoped.

"I'm just looking forward to some peace and quiet with my new husband."

"Well, now that he's resigned from the militia and is busy with the bakery, what's the worst that can happen? An overbaked loaf?"

The two girls laughed as the summer sun climbed the sky of Bethlehem.

*

Raskul rode his donkey cautiously on the road to Bethlehem. He passed the city of Hebron uneventfully and tried to enjoy the view of the rolling vineyards and olive groves of the Judean Mountains. The cool summer breeze dissipated the heat of the afternoon sun. Nonetheless, he was anxious about the coming encounter. In the distance he could make out the walled city of Bethlehem surrounded by acres and acres of wheat fields.

A rider on a chestnut horse approached Raskul from behind. Thundering hooves and a cloud of dust escorted a tall man with a flaming red and white beard and a broad grin.

"Greetings, traveler," the man called out as he matched Raskul's pace.

"Greetings, my lord," Raskul nodded to the princely man.

"My name is Caleb. Who are you?" The man inquired.

"I am Raskul of the Kenites," he said, adding quickly, "no enemy of the Israelites."

"Welcome, Raskul. What brings you to the tribe of Judah?"

"A wedding."

"You're an acquaintance of Boaz, then?" Caleb asked jovially.

"A f-friend," Raskul stuttered.

"I'm his uncle and am also traveling to Bethlehem. Let us ride together to the city."

Neither of them noticed a hunchback figure in a long cloak riding behind them. From the folds of the cloak, a hairy tail peeked out.

*

"Why do we need to be on duty today?" Eran complained to Yashen.

"Someone needs to." Yashen yawned.

The two of them stood on the eastern tower of the city gate. The gate of Bethlehem was a large stone arch with two heavy oak doors. The gate faced north, towards nearby Jerusalem. They could barely make out the walls of Jerusalem through the summer haze.

"It's a waste of time, I say," Eran continued. "We should be down there mingling with all the guests."

Yashen looked at the stonework city plaza inside the gates where a growing number of people gathered. Long tables with freshly baked cakes stood next to the stone homes that surrounded the plaza.

"The whole Nachshon clan makes it look like a meeting of redheads," Yashen commented. "I'd be interested in a Benjaminite brunette myself."

"I think Naomi is the prettiest girl in town," Eran sighed. "But looks like Elimelech has already made his move." He pointed at the two redheads standing close to each other.

"Good day, men," a commanding voice called to them from the gate.

Eran and Yashen turned around to see an old man with a long flowing white beard. Next to him was a middle-aged bearded man, with bright eyes. Both rode gray donkeys.

"Our Master, Joshua. High Priest Pinhas. Welcome," Eran blurted.

"Thank you, young man. What is your name?" Joshua, the old leader of Israel, asked.

"Eran son of Haser."

"Eran," Joshua instructed. "Though I know you would much rather be down at the celebration, I would advise you to take your duty seriously. We have been blessed with years of peace here, in no small part thanks also to the recent efforts of our groom. Nonetheless, we must remain vigilant."

"Yes, Joshua," Eran said. "Though I hear rumors of a new warrior leading the militia together with Amitai."

"Ehud of Benjamin. I have met him. Cunning and sharp. But I've also heard rumors of the Moabites regaining their strength and for some reason I have an ominous feeling today. Keep your eyes open."

"Yes, sir!" Eran and Yashen responded.

"Good. Carry on." Joshua commanded and rode off with a smiling Pinhas.

*

"Hello, Boaz," Raskul said nervously.

Boaz turned around from talking with his uncle Ploni.

"Raskul?" Boaz said, surprised.

"Yes, I thought I'd join you on this day of celebration."

"Why, thank y-. Wait. Someone give me a sword! I vowed to kill you on sight, you backstabbing, traitorous wretch. How dare you come here on this day? Ploni, fetch me a sword."

"Now, now, now, Boaz." Raskul raised his hands. "Let's not be so hasty. I swear, I won't swear by any of the gods, which I know annoys you so much. You are a forgiving people. A gracious people. Is this how you would treat an old journey-mate?"

"What's the matter, Boaz? What did he do? He seems like a pleasant enough fellow," Caleb asked.

"He tried to sell me and Amitai into slavery. He is a snake that should be killed without hesitation. Ploni, what are you waiting for? Run into my father's house and get me my sword."

"On your wedding day you will kill a defenseless man?" Ploni asked.

"Perhaps you're right. Get some rope and let's bind him and I can kill him tomorrow."

"One moment, Boaz," Caleb interceded. "I realize this man has done you great wrong, and had terrible intentions, which in the end did not materialize. He has come to you on your wedding day, knowing your anger towards him, in order to make amends. I think that in the spirit of this day you should forgive him."

"Fine. Ploni, please bring me my sword in any case. I don't trust this uncircumcised lout for a moment. His coming is a bad omen. The sword will be a good reminder to keep him from wagging his idolatrous tongue. I will slice it off, Raskul, if you so much as think the wrong way."

"You are kind as always," Raskul mock bowed. "Where is your mate Amitai? He was always the better spoken one of you two."

"Amitai is at the front leading the militia. If it weren't for criminals like you, he might have been here to celebrate with me."

"You are too harsh, Boaz. I never actively harmed someone. Perhaps I tried to make some silver off the misfortunes of others, but I never lifted a finger against someone in anger."

"No, just out of greed. You are incorrigible, Raskul, and I will be happy once you leave."

"May I stay to see you successfully married?"

"Yes. But one wrong word and you will regret having ventured to Bethlehem."

"Enough, Boaz," Caleb interjected. "I'll keep an eye on your friend. I see Joshua and Pinhas have arrived and the guests look ready. Let's get started."

*

Eran and Yashen looked dutifully to the east, across the Jordan River from where the Moabites would logically approach, while keeping half an eye on the northern road from Jerusalem. The eastern front was quiet as the sun started its slow descent to the west. A group of twenty cloaked horsemen trotted leisurely towards the gate. Eran was the first to notice them approaching.

"More friends of Boaz?" Eran pointed out to Yashen.

"Must be. They are heavily armed. Either some militiamen or some former captains of hundreds or thousands. But why are they so covered up in this heat?"

"Something is not right. They are wearing heavy armor under their cloaks. Where is that trumpet. Pass me the trumpet, Yashen." Eran said urgently. Yashen reached for the trumpet in the corner of the tower and handed it to Eran.

Suddenly, from amongst the riders, a giant of a man completely covered in armor and a metal helmet galloped at breakneck speed towards the gate. He aimed his right arm at the two watchmen. An arrow shot out of the man's arm and hit Eran in the shoulder before he could blow the trumpet. The trumpet clattered to the floor as Eran fell, writhing in agony. Yashen reached for the trumpet, but was pierced by an arrow to the abdomen before he could touch the bright metal instrument rolling on the floor. The last thing he saw was an army of thousands approaching Bethlehem from the west with scaling ladders and a large battering ram.

The other horsemen raced after their leader towards the open gate of Bethlehem.

*

Boaz stood under the wedding canopy that was erected close to the gate of the city. It was constructed of a large white shawl supported by four long wooden poles. Joshua and Caleb held the front poles and Elimelech and Ploni held the back ones. A large assembly filled the town square. A band consisting of a lyre, harp, flute and drum played a happy melody. Fluffy clouds caught the rays of the setting sun, painting the sky in a rainbow of colors. The bride's great-aunt wept joyfully.

Vered walked around Boaz slowly seven times, smiling shyly. They were both in white. Boaz wore a new long white tunic and Vered was in a flowing dress of white cotton, with gentle white lilies adorning her flaming red hair. Boaz and Vered's parents stood under the canopy together with Pinhas, who was officiating. "Do you have the ring?" Pinhas asked.

"Elimelech?" Boaz asked his uncle.

"Of course, of course. Here it is." Elimelech retrieved an unadorned gold ring from his pouch. As he handed the ring to Boaz, they were distracted by the sound of loud galloping. The ring dropped and Boaz bent down to pick it up. An arrow whizzed by where he had been standing and struck an elderly man beyond the canopy. It hit the man in the leg. The man immediately fell to the ground, where he convulsed and then stopped breathing.

"We're under attack! Take cover!" Joshua commanded as he lowered the canopy to cover the wedding party. Several more arrows punctured the large shawl. One hit a woman's arm. In seconds she was on the floor, dead. Pandemonium erupted as guests and neighbors screamed and ran in all directions.

"Poison!" Caleb yelled, as he looked at the victims.

They all saw the twenty horsemen approach the gates with a metal giant in the lead.

"Caleb," Joshua ordered, stepping naturally into the role of command. "The gates. Pinhas. The walls. Fly. Elimelech, Ploni. Organize the men. Boaz, with me. The rest of you, into the houses."

Caleb moved like a blur to the gate. He closed one door before the invaders arrived. As he was closing the second one, he saw the metal giant would make it in. He was surprised to see an older, familiar-looking attacker motion with his hands for the rest of the riders to slow down. The intruder made it past the swinging door. Caleb shut and bolted the gate shut. The metal giant kept galloping towards the wedding party and the fallen canopy. Caleb raced after the rider and launched himself at him, knocking him off the horse. The rider clanged heavily on the plaza stonework, cursing as he stood himself up. Caleb rolled as he fell and was on his feet in a moment facing the invader.

"I'm not interested in you, old man," the intruder with the metal face said. Only two slits for the eyes and one for the mouth revealed darkness within. "But I'll kill you just as well." He pointed his arm at Caleb, turned a dial on it with his left hand and a metal dart shot out. Caleb ducked and the dart struck a young boy who had been running for cover. The boy fell, convulsed, and was still.

Caleb launched himself at the intruder and tackled him to the floor. Caleb struck a series of blows at the metal clad warrior to no effect. The intruder tried hammering at Caleb with his iron arm, but Caleb was faster.

"Out of my way! It is Boaz I want!" the intruder bellowed.

"Akavish, isn't it? Caleb breathed heavily as the mechanical arm missed him by a hairsbreadth. "And that was Krafus with you."

"Yes. I am King Akavish of Ashkelon and soon I will rule your people as well."

Akavish grabbed Caleb with his massive healthy arm and tried to stab him with his deadly claw. Caleb wriggled and punched, avoiding the claw, but unable to escape Akavish's grasp. Frustrated, Akavish threw Caleb above him into the air and then shot three darts in rapid succession at Caleb's falling body. Caleb managed to contort his body and avoid all the darts, but as he fell he struck his head on the side of Akavish's iron arm, and collapsed to the floor, unconscious.

*

Pinhas, the High Priest, tied his golden headband around his forehead, closed his eyes for a moment as he stood behind the wedding canopy and then quickly levitated. He flew towards the gate tower, as he watched Caleb reach the doors. Townspeople were yelling and running throughout the plaza and in the streets and alleyways of Bethlehem. The beautifully arranged feast tables were knocked over. Fresh wedding cakes were trampled and jugs of wine smashed as the residents ran either to confront the enemy or to hide from them. Boaz and Vered remained with Joshua behind the downed canopy.

Pinhas saw two dead watchmen at the eastern tower, where he landed. On the western side thousands of Philistine troops ran towards the walls of Bethlehem. Pinhas spotted the tall scaling ladders and the massive, metal-tipped battering ram. Elimelech and Ploni approached the stairs to the eastern tower.

"Elimelech," Pinhas called down. "Assemble your men at the western wall. The first wave of attackers will be there in moments. Ploni. You will need to get men to reinforce the gate. The Philistines have a gargantuan battering ram and your oak gates will not last long under their onslaught. Go! I'll see what I can do from the air."

Pinhas took to the air as the first ladder abutted the wall. Half a dozen men were on the ladder and one reached the top of the wall before he reached them. Pinhas flew feet first into the Philistine on the rampart and knocked him over the two-storey wall. He then grabbed the top of the ladder, and with all the Philistines on it, pushed it backwards. Ladder and soldiers fell on the troops below. Pinhas flew and knocked over ladder after ladder, weaving in and out of a rain of arrows from below, until Elimelech reached the rampart, followed by a few dozen defenders.

"There are thousands!" Elimelech stood gaping at the hordes massing under the walls.

"You're just in time," Pinhas landed, exhausted. "I need a rest. Keep the ladders off as long as you can. I see they are massing on the eastern wall. I will hold them off until we can get reinforcements on that side. God be with you." Pinhas flew to the eastern wall of the city as half a dozen new ladders landed simultaneously on the western wall, followed by a barrage of arrows.

*

Joshua calmly observed the maelstrom of metal jousting with Caleb. He noted the dead victims of the poisoned arrows and darts. He closed his eyes and sensed the thousands of Philistines crashing against Bethlehem like stormy waves upon the shore.

"Looks like your childhood nemesis has returned with some friends," Joshua said to Boaz and Vered, all hiding behind the pockmarked wedding canopy.

"Akavish with Philistines? That metal monster is Akavish?" Boaz asked, incredulous.

"He has an amusing way of celebrating your wedding. We need to stop them, but we're going to need some help. I'm going to pray. Guard me while I focus my attention. Salvation will come from the sky."

Without further word, Joshua stood up, closed his eyes and turned his head heavenward. Boaz stood up, with sword in hand, watching for any arrows that might threaten Joshua as he concentrated on his communion with God.

"You know this attacker?" Vered pointed at Akavish struggling with Caleb.

"He has wanted me dead since I was a kid. Last I heard he was king of Ashkelon."

"Was he upset you didn't invite him to the wedding? I told you to double-check your list."

"Not funny, Vered. People are dying because of this madman."

"Well, I'm sorry, my hero, but if I don't make light of the situation, I will panic out of sheer terror. What's Joshua going to do?"

"He said salvation will come from the sky. I don't see anything. Stopping the sun won't help us this time."

"I see clouds forming," Vered pointed at a dark cloud moving in from the north. "Perhaps he'll make it dark."

"No! Caleb has fallen. I must help him. I must hold off Akavish. Watch Joshua, my love."

"Boaz, wait! How am I supposed to protect him?" Vered called to Boaz. But he had already jumped over the canopy and was speeding towards Akavish. He knocked the tip of Akavish's claw away from Caleb's unconscious body.

"Your timing was always miserable, Akavish," Boaz stated as he smashed his sword against Akavish's helmet.

"I think I might have gotten it right this time," Akavish responded as he swung his claw at Boaz. "Great audience. All your nobles, princes and leaders ripe for the picking. Tell me, can I congratulate you on the wedding or was I too early? Can I kiss the bride?"

"You sick man. You stopped the wedding." Boaz's sword clanged off Akavish's armor. "Are you causing all this bloodshed on a mere vendetta? You've dragged your people into this as well?"

"My people are mine to do with as I will. Your wedding was merely a good opportunity to attack." Akavish kicked Boaz away from him, aimed his arm, and shot a barrage of darts, arrows and stars of death.

Boaz's sword moved faster than the eye could follow, picking each deadly object out of the air.

"You have become faster," Akavish said. "But you will not find a way to harm me. It is just a matter of time until you fall." Akavish shot a second barrage of weaponry at Boaz. They all clattered to the ground, repelled by Boaz's blade.

The sound of steel against oak resonated throughout the city as the battering of the gates began. Women ran around screaming for their missing children. Men argued with their wives as they tried to get their weapons and go to the gate and walls. Horses neighed and livestock squealed as they sensed the fear of the people. Another table toppled, spilling fresh bread and old wine under the feet of rushing passersby.

"My people shall be here soon and then it will indeed be a celebration," Akavish exulted. "Where is that bride of yours? I would have you watch her die in agony before I end your miserable life." Akavish turned away from Boaz and walked calmly towards the downed wedding canopy.

*

Vered grabbed one of the poles of the canopy and looked around frantically for signs of attack. She kept an eye on the duel between Boaz and Akavish.

"Can I be of assistance?" a leathery voice addressed Vered from behind. "We've never been properly introduced. I'm Raskul, an old friend of Boaz."

"I've heard of you," Vered pointed the pole at the older man, grateful for a manageable threat. "Stay away from me, or I swear I'll knock you on the head."

"So violent! A fitting bride for Boaz. And one who swears. A woman after my own heart. But you misunderstand me. I am just here to help. And it looks like you can use help."

"Boaz said you were a greedy old man, capable of great mischief."

"He would, and I am." Raskul edged closer.

"Stay away, Raskul." Vered backed away, noticing for the first time the long knife at Raskul's side.

*

Ploni didn't mind battle. He had fought in one successful battle after another with Joshua, soundly defeating the kings of Canaan. But this was different. He had never been in a siege before. Never had to wait for an enemy to breach his last physical defense. This is what it must have felt like to be on the receiving end, he thought.

"Hold the doors!" Ploni called out, as together with a dozen men they held the crumbling oak doors against the Philistine battering.

"They're breaking!" someone yelled. "The next hit will break through!"

"HOLD!" Ploni yelled, as he pressed his body against the door.

The metal of the battering ram crushed wood and bone as it smashed through the doors of Bethlehem. Ploni and the men around him were thrown from the gate like rag dolls. Ploni lost consciousness as hundreds of Philistines poured into Bethlehem.

Akavish smiled behind his helmet as he heard his troops at his back and aimed his claw at the redheaded girl in the white dress.

33. Wedding Crashers

Yered, still cloaked, watched the wedding proceedings from a nearby alleyway. Risto clung to his back, completing Yered's disguise as a hunchback. Yered kept smacking Risto's hairy tail as it flicked in and out of the cloak. Both Yered and his simian pet were surprised by the speed of the Philistine attack upon Bethlehem and the large armored man who had made it through the gates.

"That's your former master?" Yered asked Risto as they watched Akavish fight Caleb near the city gate.

Risto nodded affirmatively.

"He has become frightening."

Risto agreed and spat a few choice curses, caressing his own prosthetic wooden arm.

"He is most dangerous. Stopping him will lessen the danger. Raskul is a small threat." He pointed at the Kenite slowly making his way towards the fallen wedding canopy, as guests and residents ran for cover. A dark wave of arrows rained down on Bethlehem from outside the walls, momentarily blotting out the sun. Most of the residents had cleared the plaza, but a number were caught in the deadly deluge, groaning and arching their backs as the shafts penetrated their limbs. Bodies of Bethlehemites fell dead or injured in the city plaza. Joshua stood in the center of the plaza, immobile behind the large white shawl. He stood with eyes closed, head and palms heavenward, guarded by Boaz, with Vered standing next to Boaz.

Risto jumped up and down under Yered's cloak.

"Patience, Risto," Yered told the monkey. "We will only enter the fray and reveal ourselves when absolutely needed."

Risto chittered wildly, pointing at a fallen Caleb on the ground. The clear blue skies suddenly turned overcast, with dark heavy clouds rolling in, as Boaz ran to intercept Akavish's claw before it impaled the unconscious Caleb. Boaz knocked the claw aside with his sword, but could not get through Akavish's metal armor and helmet. However, Akavish was unable to injure the faster Boaz. Akavish finally turned from Boaz and walked towards Vered with his claw pointed at her.

"Ah, what a lovely creature," Akavish pronounced. "It will give me great satisfaction to rob you of her. Pay attention, Boaz. Watch helplessly as your bride dies in writhing agony."

The entire city shook, as the Philistine battering ram smashed through the wooden gate of Bethlehem, scattering the Israelite defenders. A river of Philistines poured into the city, with Boaz the only one in their way to stop their surge.

Yered saw Raskul approach Vered menacingly. Boaz looked wildly between the approaching Philistine army and his bride. Tears welled in his eyes as he tried to decide where to go. Vered was threatened by both Akavish and Raskul. Joshua stood oblivious as a statue next to Vered. Thunder rumbled in the previously clear summer sky.

"We are needed," Yered said as he removed his cloak. "Time to split up."

Akavish aimed his claw at Vered and reached for the lever that would launch his poisonous projectiles.

"Boaz!" Yered yelled. "We shall protect your woman. You focus on fighting the Philistines."

Risto jumped off of Yered's back and with a wild screech launched himself at Akavish's head, blocking his view. Akavish tried impaling the monkey with his claw. Risto climbed to Akavish's back and wrapped his tail around the eye slits of Akavish's helmet.

"Risto?" Akavish hollered incredulously. "You are stopping me? After all these years, this is how you greet me? I will squash you as the insignificant creature you are!"

*

"Greetings, seeker," Yered addressed Raskul's back.

Startled, Raskul turned around. "Ancient One? What are you doing here?"

"Preventing harm that we encouraged."

"What harm is that?"

"Revenge. You are appearing as a friend to an enemy."

Raskul's face turned crimson. "I meant no harm. Just introducing myself to the lovely bride of my old friend."

"Who are you?" Vered aimed her wooden pole at the ancient Yered.

"An acquaintance of Boaz. Yered son of Job." He smiled, showing his golden teeth.

"You, I've heard well of." Vered lowered her pole. "You saved Boaz from the mines of Timna."

"We have come to save again. You are in mortal danger." Yered pointed at Akavish struggling with the monkey on his back.

*

Boaz looked from the rapidly approaching Philistine army, to Akavish and to Vered. *There is no way I can split myself to tackle Akavish and his army. What do I do!?* Boaz agonized. Then he heard Yered's call and saw a wooden-armed Risto flying at Akavish's head. *Thank you, God!* Boaz thought fervently. *Please keep her safe.*

Boaz ran into the approaching Philistine army and slashed recklessly into their front. Half a dozen soldiers fell from his first blow. Suddenly, an eerie silence blanketed the city. Electric crackling filled the air. The clouds above became dark as night and then an explosion filled the sky. Thunder and lightning rocked the walls of Bethlehem. Waves of water poured from above. Judeans and Philistines looked in apprehension at the wrath from the heavens, and then reengaged their foes.

Philistine soldiers slipped on the wet stones as the front line came to a standstill under Boaz's onslaught. Boaz fought with a fury he did not recall. *You come to my home?* Boaz thought angrily at the intruders. *You threaten my family? My bride? On my wedding day!?* Boaz slashed and hacked through the Philistine lines, moving like a whirlwind. Dozens of Philistines fell to Boaz's ferocity.

*

Elimelech ran back and forth on the western ramparts of Bethlehem, killing one Philistine invader after another. His men were holding up against the endless barrage, but he knew they would shortly falter. More scaling ladders were propped against the wall, uncontested. More Philistine soldiers were reaching the ramparts and engaging his men. Most of the dead on the ramparts were Philistine. The number of the Philistine dead outnumbered the Israelites living. *But soon the living Philistines will overwhelm the defenders of Bethlehem,* Elimelech realized. *Zuki has fallen, and his brother Achi with him. Lerel will never walk again and Drami will never see. Avli will not return to his pregnant wife and Brenyah will not rejoin his nine children.* Elimelech mourned each friend, relative and neighbor that fell to the Philistine arrows and swords. Yet he pushed on, encouraging his men with his spirit and his sword. Somewhere inside of him, though, his spirit broke. He could not bear this tragedy, this hardship, this pain. *Why, God?* he asked, as he stabbed a large mace-wielding Philistine with his sword. *How can you let this happen? Why must we suffer so?*

As if in response, a bolt of lighting struck one of the Philistine ladders, incinerating the dozen soldiers on and around it. Then another flash struck from the sky followed rapidly by yet another. Three, four, five fires burned in the pouring rain against the walls of Bethlehem.

Thank you, God, Elimelech thought, as the tide on the western wall turned in the Israelites favor. *But why the suffering?* Elimelech looked at his dead and crippled men. *I cannot bear to see my people suffer.*

*

Ploni awoke to the sound of thunder and the cold rain on his body. He saw the throngs of Philistines march through the broken gate, felt his own broken bones and fainted from the pain.

*

As he flew around repeated volleys of arrows, Pinhas toppled as many scaling ladders as he could. Philistines fell heavily to the ground crushing other attackers below. But more ladders replaced them and more arrows were aimed towards him amidst the thunder and lightning. The torrent diminished the flying priest's visibility and he could barely make out the arrows speeding towards him as the deluge completely soaked him.

Finally, an arrow shot Pinhas out of the sky. He landed hard on the eastern ramparts. He lost consciousness amongst the dead wet bodies of the Philistines and Israelites. Philistines overran the eastern wall, killing the last Israelite defenders on that rampart, and poured into the city. Krafus smiled from outside the gates where he could see his soldiers joining the phalanx in the plaza.

*

"No!!" Akavish howled at the rain, "the water will dilute my poison!" With his healthy hand, Akavish finally grabbed hold of Risto and threw him into the sky. Akavish shot his remaining poisoned darts at the monkey. Risto twisted mid-air and avoided the deadly barrage as he landed safely on one of the courtyard houses.

"Blasted monkey. I will deal with you later. First to kill the bride, while Boaz is occupied with my men." Akavish stepped over the still, prone body of Caleb, pointed his claw at the redheaded girl and let loose his stars of death.

*

Joshua felt the cold rain on his closed eyelids. God had given him the keys to the skies and he was determined to use it well. He sensed the thousands of Philistines attacking the walls. Through his closed eyes he saw the hundreds pouring through the destroyed gate. He felt every Israelite death and injury. Elimelech, leading the defense on the western wall - the hardest hit - was on the edge of despair. Joshua flicked his wrist and lightning struck a ladder filled with Philistines right next to Elimelech. Joshua moved his fingers again and another lighting bolt struck a Philistine ladder. Again and again Joshua expertly moved his fingers like a conductor guiding an invisible orchestra. Lightning fell upon critical attack points, stemming the tide of the Philistine invasion. He noted the curious monkey struggling with the metal beast, and the slowly stirring Caleb on the ground. He was pleased to see Boaz holding the center. He sensed Vered confronting two men. He turned his attention to the eastern wall in time to see Pinhas shot down and the wall overrun. *We shall need assistance from another source,* he told God, *the bolts are not enough,* as he continued to conduct the lighting from the sky.

*

"I must protect Joshua," Vered said to Yered and Raskul as she stood closer to the praying leader amidst the thunderstorm. "He is bringing the lightning and the rain, and that is probably the only thing giving us an advantage." She looked anxiously at Boaz sprinting amongst the Philistine army, mowing down line after line of soldiers. *How long can he last?* she wondered fretfully.

Raskul followed Vered's gaze and saw her fear and longing for Boaz. He had never seen such a look of love. At once he was both amazed and insanely jealous of Boaz. *Look at him risk his life,* Raskul thought in wonder. *Look at his speed. His deadliness. One man against an entire army. Scribes shall write of this. And she loves him, she truly loves him. What a woman. Brave and beautiful! How could I come between such love?*

"Go to safety," Raskul commanded, as he drew his long knife and faced the Philistines by the gate. "I shall watch over your leader."

He turned in time to see Akavish launch a whirling metallic disc at Vered. Time slowed down for the Kenite. He knew the disc meant death. He could picture its poisonous tips ripping into the flesh of Boaz's bride. He thought of his entire miserable life and how he had betrayed every single being he'd come in touch with. The parents he had run from, the wife and children he had abandoned, every single person whose trust he had taken advantage of. For decades he had corrupted the basic human trust of people from all walks of life. In that fraction of a second, as the spinning star of death flew towards Vered, Raskul knew what he had to do. He needed to do one good thing in his life. His life needed to mean something. He would save this woman. He would preserve that beautiful love that he had witnessed and he would sacrifice his life to do so.

Raskul jumped in front of Vered. The star of death cut Raskul's arm but continued traveling and embedded itself in Vered's shoulder.

Both Raskul and Vered fell to the floor writhing in agony.

*

Boaz's heart shattered as he saw Akavish launch his star of death at Vered. He was amazed to see Raskul jump to intercept the star and then heartbroken to see him and Vered collapse. Something in him died. Unconsciously, he slowed down. *What do I have to live for now?* he thought morosely. One Philistine tripped him. A dozen fell on him. He was trapped under an avalanche of soldiers. *This is it,* Boaz thought. *Both of us die on our wedding day.* He shed a tear in the pouring rain.

Then he heard the trumpeting. It was a ram's horn. *Amitai! That's Amitai's horn. The militia. He has brought the militia.*

"Boaz," he heard Vered call out softly. *She still lives! There is hope! I will not die by these uncircumcised heathens!* Boaz hacked frantically at the Philistines covering him, and then spun wildly, slashing at the bodies around him. He launched himself off the ground powerfully and cut all around him like a tornado through a field of wheat. He saw Akavish walking to the downed Vered, apparently to finish the job. He saw Yered and Risto tending to Vered. Boaz ran at Akavish and tackled him, both falling to the ground, the metal of Akavish's armor banging loudly on the wet stones.

*

Yered whistled loudly and shrilly as he kneeled next to the prone bodies of Raskul and Vered. In moments Risto was on his shoulder, jabbering heatedly.

"Yes," Yered agreed. "They're both poisoned. We have seconds. Give me your arm."

Risto opened the panel on his wooden arm.

Yered ran his finger quickly over the small compartments in Risto's arm. "Thyme, Silverweed, Anise, Celandine, Alkanel, Buckthorn. Yes. Buckthorn. It's the only hope for poison. It will take a few moments."

Yered took the crushed leaves, placed them in his mouth and chewed them vigorously with his golden teeth.

"Risto. Fetch a cup and water," Yered commanded. Risto shut his wooden arm closed to keep his store of leaves dry and hopped away. He returned moments later, sloshing water in a clay mug.

"Ancient One," Raskul groaned. "Save her first."

"That was my intent," Yered answered through a mouthful of saliva and leaves. "Though we did not expect such a noble act on your part. You are fortunate that the rain diluted the poison. Otherwise, you would already be dead."

"Boaz," Vered moaned, her eyes fluttering in and out of consciousness.

Yered placed the chewed leaves into the cup and stirred the mixture with his finger. He lifted Vered's head and brought the cup to her lips.

"Drink fully. It may save you."

Vered drank greedily from the cup and lost consciousness, the grimace of pain easing from her face.

"I feel my life ebbing," Raskul croaked. "There is no time."

"Hold on a few more moments," Yered ordered, as he stuffed fresh Buckthorn leaves in his mouth.

"No. I have been a scoundrel my entire life. I would rather leave having done something good. Farewell, Ancient One." Raskul forced a dry raspy cough.

"You're in such a rush to die?"

"It is better this way. Even from all my betrayals I learned it is best to leave while riding high." Raskul coughed painfully. "I shall never do better than this. Just tell Boaz to inform my family, if they still remember me."

Raskul closed his eyes, breathed a last rattling breath, and was still, forever.

"Bah!" Yered spat the leaves on the ground. "We hate the taste of Buckthorn. Waste of good leaves."

He turned to see Boaz struggling with Akavish, the regrouping Philistine army, and the lightning blazing across the sky.

*

"You will not succeed." Boaz smashed his sword ineffectively against Akavish's armored side.

"I already have. Your gate is broken. My army is on and within the walls. Your bride is dying in painful agony and shortly so will you." Akavish answered with a slash of his metal claw to Boaz's head. Boaz ducked, kicking Akavish in the midriff. Caleb, on the floor behind them, opened his eyes and looked at the fighting in a daze.

They heard the ram's horn again.

"You hear that, Akavish?" Boaz said triumphantly. "God sends us our salvation."

Smoke exploded amongst the Philistines at the gate. The rain, thunder, lighting and smoke completely disoriented the Philistine soldiers. When the smoke cleared, Akavish was shocked to see the Philistines split into two, with a wedge of Israelites cutting a swathe through the Philistine ranks. Boaz saw Amitai and young Ehud at the lead, cleaving the Philistine army.

"I will not be denied!" Akavish head-butted Boaz with his metal helmet. Boaz, dazed, took a step back. Akavish pointed his claw at Boaz, ready to fire.

"Hey! Ugly!" Ehud called out. Ehud was a short brown-haired youth with a muscular build. He wore a simple, but blood-smeared, rain-soaked tunic, and held a short sword in each hand. Akavish turned to look at the new voice.

"Yes, you, metal-face," Ehud continued as he approached Akavish. "I'm talking about you. Are you so horrific that you need to hide your face behind a mask? Is this the powerful King Akavish that is too cowardly to show his face?"

"I will kill you miscreant, for your affront." Akavish fired his stars of death at Ehud. Ehud spun out of the way, letting the stars kill Philistines behind him.

"You'll have to do better than that, ugly."

"Die!" Akavish yelled and ran at Ehud.

Ehud ran at Akavish, a sword in each hand and jumped into the air. With one sword Ehud knocked Akavish's claw aside. The other sword he stabbed into a crevice above the metallic arm.

"You blasted Hebrew!" Akavish yelled. "How dare you touch our royal being? You will die!"

A recovered Boaz launched himself at Akavish. The armored Philistine turned away from Ehud and fired the rest of his arsenal at Boaz. Boaz spun in the air, knocking the stars, arrows and darts away with his sword. As Boaz was about to make contact with Akavish, he stabbed his sword into the eye-slit of Akavish's helmet.

"Argh!!" Akavish screamed in agony, as the tip of Boaz's blade blinded his right eye.

"Now, Ehud. His arm," Boaz called.

Ehud, together with Boaz, grabbed the sides of Akavish's claw and pulled forcefully. Caleb, fully awake, crawled behind Akavish, and grabbed both his legs. Boaz braced his own leg onto Akavish's chest for leverage as Akavish struggled against the Israelite warriors, with Boaz's sword still stuck in his eye-slit. Finally the mechanical arm came off, revealing a pink fleshy stump that ended a few inches below the shoulder.

As Caleb kept Akavish's legs pinned to the ground, the large Philistine screamed again and clawed the wet air uselessly with his healthy hand. "My arm! My arm!"

"Do not fear, my poor sick, loveless, one-armed freak of a nemesis." Boaz said, turning the heavy metallic device around. "You thought the power of your arm could conquer all your enemies, but your hatred blinded you to everything. Our God has promised us this land. He is the power in our world, not your sophisticated devices. We shall not be removed from this land nor be defeated so easily. Die, sick man. Die!"

Boaz slammed the edge of the claw into Akavish's pink stump. The force of the impact let loose the five different poisons and acids that Akavish had stored in his arm and launched the rest of his stars of death and arrows at point-blank range. Akavish's shoulder exploded inside his armor, leaving a blackened stump of dripping flesh. There was not enough flesh for all the different and now combined poisons Akavish had carried. A wave of black ooze quickly disintegrated Akavish's chest, appendages and finally his head. A sickly, dark vapor wafted up to the thunderous clouds. Nothing remained of Akavish except for an empty armor and his iron claw. Caleb rolled away from the steaming armor.

"Good." Ehud kicked the empty armor. "I had no interest in burying this monster anyway."

"The fight is not over." Boaz clasped Caleb's arm, raising him from the floor and turned back to the gate. Fresh Philistine troops arrived from the eastern wall, amidst the lightning and rain.

From outside the gate, Krafus raised his hand.

"Retreat! Retreat!" the Philistines called. "Akavish is dead! Retreat!"

Just as quickly as they had attacked, they pulled back.

Amitai and the Israelite militiamen pulled further into the city, letting the Philistines depart unchallenged.

"Make sure it's not a trick," Boaz told Ehud. "I'm going to Vered."

Boaz ran and reached Vered, who was very still on the floor. Caleb followed behind him.

"She shall live," Yered said to Boaz.

"What about Raskul?" Boaz asked.

"Dead. He saved her life. He had good, deep within him."

"I told you he was likable," Caleb added.

"I will treasure this act of his, no matter how poorly I thought of him," said Boaz.

"Raskul asked that you inform his family," Yered added. "It was his dying wish."

"Then I shall find the family of Raskul the Kenite and tell them of his noble deed," Boaz vowed.

The lightning and thunder stopped. The clouds dissipated quickly on a gentle southern breeze. The sun was a bright red on the western horizon. Joshua awoke from his trance, his robe and white beard soaked. "It is over. They have retreated. That was close."

"Thank God," Boaz said.

"Indeed," Joshua agreed. "Now we need to tend to the wounded and bury our dead. Yered, we are in your and your monkey's debt once again. You have come to us unbidden in our time of need. First to rescue Boaz and now to save Bethlehem and all of us. May God grant you all the blessings of your father Job, on you and your descendants."

"Pfah," Yered spat. "I've received plenty of blessings. Though we are happy that you acknowledge our father. We have come to clear our conscience. Bless the monkey instead."

"Very well. Monkey, may God ease your pain." Joshua touched Risto's arm. "And may He reward your noble actions."

Risto jumped up and down excitedly on Yered's shoulder.

"Yes," Yered agreed with Risto. "This youngling is well spoken. Risto thanks you and to you and your people wishes well. It is our time to depart. Farewell brave warrior," Yered bowed to Boaz. "May you have a long and blissful life with your bride. She is an uncommon woman. Treasure her."

Yered walked to the exit of the city, with Risto on his shoulder, waving his tail merrily in the air.

34. Bride of War

The healthy Judean soldiers covered the corpses of their comrades and neigbhors and moved them outside the gates of the city. Residents tended to the wounded. Two weary soldiers took the body of Raskul, while Vered's parents returned to tend to the bride, asleep on the floor.

At the broken gate of Bethlehem, Yered bowed to an old Philistine walking in, escorted by Amitai and Ehud. The two Israelites and the Philistine in the middle reached Joshua, Caleb and Boaz.

"I am Krafus of Ashkelon," the old Philistine announced to them. "And I ask for parley. I wish to explain and to apologize, for we did not pursue this battle on a whim. We have been ruled these last years by a tyrant, the metal warrior Akavish. Our people have been in mortal terror of him. His madness, his paranoia, his hatred of the living, and his random murders almost destroyed our city and our people. We tried to depose him, to kill him, but nothing worked. Then we played on his hatred and fear of you Israelites, and you in particular, Boaz, in the hopes that you would do what we could not. If you did not kill him, we would have gained your territory. But our hope was that you would succeed. That is why we retreated as soon as the tyrant was destroyed. We had no wish to fight your lightning and sorcerer's powers. We thank you. You have done us a great service."

"You have done us great harm," Joshua said, "to bring war to our homes. I do not believe that the Philistines are so peaceful or benevolent that you do not harbor further ambitions against us. But I see that you have achieved your prime mission of eliminating your ruler. Admirably crafty. He thought he had his army with him, when they were ever at a distance. Go in peace for now, Krafus. We accept your apology, but not your explanation. We shall ever be wary of you Philistines. Ehud, see Krafus safely out of our walls."

Krafus bowed to the Israelites and left towards the gate with Ehud.

Boaz hugged Amitai.

"You came just in time," Boaz said. "I thought this was the end. It was worse than when the Ammonites ambushed us at Nurad."

"I didn't want to miss your wedding. How is Vered?"

"She will live. She rests."

"I've had enough resting," Vered said feebly from the floor. "What happened?"

"We won," Boaz answered. "Akavish is dead and the Philistines have retreated. Raskul, Yered and Risto saved your life. Raskul died. He tried to stop Akavish's star of death with his own body."

Pinhas, Elimelech, Boaz's parents and other friends and relatives returned to the wet and fallen wedding canopy. Pinhas winced with every step, a broken arrow shaft still protruding from his shoulder.

"High Priest," Vered addressed Pinhas from the ground as her parents helped her sit up. "Would you still marry us? The marriage contract was penned for today and the sun has not yet set."

Pinhas looked at Joshua and then answered Vered. "Today and this week will be a time of bereavement for many of us. All of us have relatives and friends that have died today. Do you still wish to proceed, knowing that your week of celebration shall be a week of mourning for everyone else?"

"I share in the sadness and the mourning," Vered said, standing up unsteadily, supported on either side by her parents. "But I want to show our city that this attack cannot stop us, will not stop us. They dared attack us unprovoked, and by the grace of God we were victorious. I will not compound our grief by denying our joy, our celebration."

Joshua smiled and nodded at Pinhas.

"I take it neither you, nor Boaz has lost immediate relatives."

Boaz's father, Salmoon, spoke. "I have not seen my brother, Ploni. I do not know if he is amongst the living or the dead."

"I saw him, brother," Elimelech said. "He was badly injured at the gate, but he lives."

"I will not hold up the sun for this," Joshua said, "so I suggest we conduct a brief ceremony. The bride, groom, and their immediate families should have a modest celebration. The rest of us shall help with burying the dead, caring for the sick and comforting the mourners. This was a heavy blow for us, but the spirit of this new couple will soften the blow and put a smile on the face of the mourners. Life does go on!"

"Boaz, the ring?" Pinhas asked.

Boaz searched the ground and, incredibly, found the ring right where he had dropped it. Joshua, Caleb, Elimelech and Amitai raised the tattered canopy above the couple.

"Boaz, place the ring on the second finger of Vered's right hand and repeat after me: Hereby you are betrothed to me with this ring, according to the law of Moses and Israel."

Boaz gave the bloody sword he was still holding to Amitai and then gently slid the ring onto Vered's extended finger. Though wet and dirty, Vered glowed joyfully.

In a powerful voice, Boaz declared: "Hereby you are betrothed to me with this ring, according to the law of Moses and Israel!"

"Betrothed, betrothed, betrothed!" everyone sang.

Boaz took Vered's hand. "Finally," he said.

"Yes. Finally. I'm glad you had your sword handy and just as glad you've given it to Amitai. Let's go."

Vered and Boaz walked hand in hand to their new house.

"May they build a steadfast house in Israel," Joshua blessed the departing couple.

"Amen," everyone answered, as the sun set on the city of Bethlehem.

35. Assembly and Prophecy

"Do you feel it, Pinhas?" Joshua asked the High Priest. They stood together at the top of the rock-strewn mountain, outside the city of Shechem in the valley below. The hills of the Tribe of Ephraim, Joshua's tribe, rose dramatically around them. They were on the border of the desert. Some of the mountains were green and verdant and others sparse and bare. The morning sun rose steadily. The night's dew still glistened on the short grass, between large boulders where Joshua and Pinhas stood.

"I feel the apathy," Pinhas replied.

"It is worse than that. It is the contentment. They are satiated and they no longer rely on God. Each man has his own field, with peace all around. I fear my Master's other prophecies will come true."

Joshua had aged considerably. He was nearly one hundred and ten years old. The once vibrant, powerful warrior, the commanding general, the leader of the tribes of Israel was now little more than a withered white frame of skin and bones.

"So soon?" Pinhas, with a fully white beard, asked with some surprise. "Moses made his prophecies sound like they were for a distant future. Surely we are not there yet."

"There were many layers to my Master's prophecies. Is not the word of God eternal? There are cycles. And cycles within cycles. Mysteries and secrets, that only future generations will understand and uncover. The next cycle will start soon – at most another generation. We must do what we can."

"That is why you've called them again?" Pinhas asked, pointing at the masses of people climbing up the mountain.

"Yes. The last convocation was not satisfactory. The judges and princes gathered, but with no conviction, and they left with no enthusiasm, no commitment. I must press harder. My time is coming near and I will not have another opportunity. And there are two I must instruct further and strengthen."

"Boaz and Ehud?" Pinhas asked.

"Yes, they are critical for the next cycle. If they fail, the future may be harsher and more precarious than needs be."

"I don't understand," Pinhas admitted.

"Neither do I," Joshua laughed. "God directs me and gives me certain images and directions. I get glimpses of the tapestry of our future and our past, and both Boaz and Ehud have pivotal roles. It is their free choice that shall determine the course of the major threads. God's plan remains intact, yet the hue, the pattern, the entire fabric of our history will be shaped by their actions."

"That is why you choose this place, Shechem?" Pinhas asked.

"Yes. Our forefather Jacob needed to strengthen the tribes and the first generation. He needed to purge them of the idolatrous compulsion. He succeeded right here on this mountaintop, beside this tree." Joshua pointed to the ancient terebinth tree near him. "If we dig deep enough, we may even find the old idols and jewelry Jacob buried here. I pray that we can draw from Jacob's success and the energy of this place."

Two men approached Joshua and Pinhas, ahead of the crowd. One was a tall redhead, with hints of grey; the other was a squat young muscular brown-haired man.

"We are here, Joshua, Pinhas," Boaz, the redhead, announced as he and Ehud bowed to the leader of Israel and to the High Priest.

"Welcome, Boaz son of Salmoon of Judah, Ehud son of Gera of Benjamin. You are worthy representatives of your tribes."

"We are but minor judges in our tribes," Boaz responded. "There are more senior judges and princes amongst us. We merely answered your summons to arrive early at the mountaintop."

"Well answered," Joshua said. "I wish for the two of you to see what I see. To see the assembled princes and elders and judges of the tribes of Israel. I feel that this is a sight that shall not occur again for many generations. I want you to remember it and draw strength from it. But do not stand right next to me. That would be improper. Perhaps stand next to the terebinth here and observe. Remain after the assembly leaves, as I wish to speak to each of your further."

"I don't understand." Ehud cleared his throat. "Why will there be no more assemblies? Who will lead after you?"

"Sharp as always, Ehud." Joshua smiled. "How is your blacksmithing work progressing?"

"Well, I am busy with pots and pans, rakes and hoes and a constant stream of domestic and agricultural tools. I still can't compete with the Philistine blacksmiths but I'm getting better. Would you like to order something?"

"No, no, Ehud. Thank you. But I will answer your question. There is no one to appoint to succeed me and the tribes would not accept anyone other than from their own tribes. Boaz, would your proud tribe of Judah accept someone from Ehud's Benjamin? Ehud, would your tribe allow someone from Menashe or even your neighbor Ephraim to rule over you? It is not like the days in the desert or even of the conquest. Each man, each family, each tribe is comfortable on its own land. Too comfortable. They will not follow or heed anyone else. They barely heed me or Pinhas. That is, until trouble returns. Then they will need strong leaders."

"When do you expect trouble?" Ehud asked.

"Not in my day," Joshua chuckled dryly. "But that's enough for now. The assembly is congregating and I would not have them wait. Go stand by the tree."

Joshua moved slowly to the top of the mountain, supported by a large wooden staff. Pinhas stayed behind, but still in sight of the massing crowd. Boaz and Ehud walked quickly to the shade of the large terebinth.

Joshua gazed upon the congregated representatives. Twelve princes faced him and bowed low when he approached. The seventy elders stood behind the princes in their somber woolen robes. Behind them, further down the slope of the mountain, stood the judges and officers from every city and village of the twelve tribes of Israel, hundreds strong. Joshua recognized the older ones: The ones who had entered Canaan with him from the desert, the ones who had fought side by side with him to conquer the land God had promised.

Joshua felt the spirit of God permeate him. He stood tall and spoke powerfully:

"Children of Israel!" Joshua's voice reverberated off the surrounding mountains, filling the valley with his voice. "Thus said the Lord, the God of Israel: Your fathers dwelt in antiquity beyond the River. Terah was the father of Abraham, and the father of Nahor; and they served other gods. I took your father Abraham from beyond the River, and led him throughout all the land of Canaan, and multiplied his seed, and gave him Isaac. I gave unto Isaac, Jacob and Esau; and I gave unto Esau Mount Seir, to possess it; and Jacob and his children went down into Egypt. I sent Moses and Aaron, and I plagued Egypt, and afterward I brought you out. I brought your fathers out of Egypt; and you came unto the sea; and the Egyptians pursued after your fathers with chariots and with horsemen unto the Red Sea. And when they cried out unto God, He put darkness between you and the Egyptians, and brought the sea upon them, and covered them; and your eyes saw what I did in Egypt; and you dwelt in the wilderness many days."

Ehud whispered to Boaz. "What's with the history lesson?"

"Hush," Boaz answered. "We need reminding. We don't think of what God has done for us often enough."

"I brought you into the land of the Amorites," Joshua continued, "that dwelt beyond the Jordan; and they fought with you; and I gave them into your hand, and you possessed their land; and I destroyed them from before you. Then Balak the son of Zippor, king of Moab, arose and fought against Israel; and he sent and called Balaam the son of Beor to curse you. But I would not hearken unto Balaam; therefore he even blessed you; so I delivered you out of his hand. And you went over the Jordan, and came unto Jericho; and the men of Jericho fought against you, the Amorite, and the Perizzite, and the Canaanite, and the Hittite, and the Girgashite, the Hivite, and the Jebusite; and I delivered them into your hand. I sent the hornet before you, which drove them out from before you, even the two kings of the Amorites; not with thy sword, nor with thy bow. And I gave you a land whereon you had not labored, and cities which you built not, and you dwell therein; of vineyards and olive groves which you have not planted do you eat."

"We know all of this," Ehud said impatiently. "What's the point?"

"Listen, Ehud. Listen."

"Now therefore fear the Lord." Joshua raised his arms heavenward. "And serve Him in sincerity and in truth; and put away the gods which your fathers served beyond the River, and in Egypt; and serve you the Lord." Joshua clenched his fist angrily. "And if it seems evil unto you to serve the Lord, choose you this day whom you will serve; whether the gods which your fathers served that were beyond the River, or the gods of the Amorites, in whose land you dwell; but as for me and my house, we will serve the Lord." Joshua stopped suddenly and looked impassively at the twelve princes in front of him. The entire assembly broke into surprised and angry murmurs.

"Did he say what I just thought he did? I can't believe it. He's giving us a choice to serve the other gods?" Ehud whispered.

"It must be a test," Boaz answered. "He wants to strengthen the people's resolve."

"He's going to have a riot on his hands."

"Let's see what the princes do."

The judges and the elders seemed insulted and furious at Joshua's offer.

"What does he mean?" an elder from Naftali asked. "Our people have free choice to worship other gods? This is the disciple of Moses? He would encourage us to leave our worship of God? Blasphemy!"

"Joshua does not mean it," the Prince of Zevulun answered, turning to the masses behind him. "He senses our people's weakness, our lack of resolve. He prods us to see how deep our apathy is. We must answer him."

"We are dedicated to God and to the instruction of Moses," the Prince of Yissachar stated.

"Then we must say so," the Prince of Zevulun said to the crowd. "We all must say so. Unequivocally. It is nice that Joshua gives inspiring speeches, but it is not enough. He must hear from us. All of us!"

And the people shouted back to Joshua, as if in one voice:

"Far be it from us that we should forsake the Lord, to serve other gods; for the Lord our God, it is He that brought us and our fathers up out of the land of Egypt, from the house of bondage, and that did those great signs in our sight, and preserved us in the way we went, and among all the peoples through the midst of whom we passed."

Ehud whispered to Boaz. "This is amazing!"

"Yes. Joshua has accomplished his purpose. They are showing some resolve after all."

The assembly continued shouting: "And the Lord drove out from before us all the peoples, even the Amorites that dwelt in the land; therefore we also will serve the Lord; for He is our God."

The people of Israel stopped speaking. Complete silence enveloped the mountain. All waited for Joshua's reaction. Joshua looked upon the assembly, an imperceptible smirk on his face. He closed his eyes, looked heavenward, nodded and opened his eyes to address the children of Israel.

"You cannot serve the Lord; for He is a holy God; He is a jealous God; He will not forgive your transgressions nor your sins. If you forsake the Lord, even after all the good that He has done for you, and serve strange gods, then He will turn and do you evil, and consume you."

"Is he out of his mind?" Ehud could barely contain himself. "What does he want from them? A pact in blood? Their firstborns? I'm impressed they haven't stoned him yet."

"No. Joshua is not satisfied yet," Boaz explained. "He is driving the point home. He is renewing Israel's allegiance to God. He hopes their commitment will endure. This is his way."

The Princes conducted a heated discussion with the Elders and the Judges. They would make another unified statement. Louder and more passionately than before, they cried out in unison:

"Nay! We will serve the Lord!"

Joshua finally smiled and declared:

"You are witnesses against yourselves that you have chosen the Lord, to serve Him."

Without prompt or discussion, the entire assembly, hundreds strong, raised their fists to the sky and screamed:

"We are witnesses!"

"Now therefore put away the strange gods which are among you," Joshua pointed at the assembly, "and turn your heart unto the Lord, the God of Israel."

"The Lord our God will we serve," they answered, "and unto His voice will we hearken."

Joshua nodded. He stretched his hand towards Pinhas standing near him. Pinhas presented an old scroll to Joshua, and held up a writing tablet for him to place it on.

"I am now writing these words, this new covenant, between you and God," Joshua said as he wrote on the scroll. He handed the scroll back to Pinhas and looked around the mountaintop. He spotted the largest boulder he could find, a large gray stone, the height of a man and as wide as two men standing together. Joshua approached the stone with his staff and slashed at it with the tip of his staff. A red gash appeared through the middle of the stone sending off hot sparks. The crowd stepped back and murmured in amazement. Joshua then placed his staff on the ground, bent his knees and dug his hands under the massive stone. The frail-looking old man lifted the stone and walked it across the mountaintop to the large terebinth. The congregation was silent in awe. Joshua dropped the stone next to the large tree. It landed with a loud thud and sunk a few finger-breadths into the grassy ground.

Under the shade of the tree, the children of Israel could make out a faint glow surrounding their leader.

"Behold!" Joshua called out, standing tall and firm, with no sigh of exertion on his face. "This stone shall be a witness against us; for it has heard all the words of the Lord which He spoke unto us; it shall therefore be a witness against you, lest you deny your God! Now go, every man to his home and his inheritance. But remember this day. Remember the pact we have reforged with God. Remember it and tell it to your children. God bless you and watch over you!"

The assembled stood, smiling at Joshua, clapped each other on the back and in general seemed pleased with themselves, as if successfully passing a test. They slowly disassembled, each group heading to their own tribal lands. Some of the princes and elders stayed behind, waiting to speak with Joshua.

"Wow!" Ehud breathed. "Was that what it was like at Mount Sinai?"

"I'm not that old," Boaz said. "Though this was certainly awe-inspiring."

"Let's see what else Joshua wanted to tell us."

The two walked briskly back to Joshua and Pinhas, ahead of the princes. Joshua motioned for Boaz and Ehud to approach and for the princes to wait and keep their distance.

"Ah, the next leaders," Joshua said to Boaz and Ehud. "What did you think of our assembly?"

"Inspiring," Boaz answered.

"Amazing!" Ehud replied. "We should do it more often."

"I wish," Joshua smiled. "But such monumental occasions would then lose there efficacy. I wonder when the next one may occur." Joshua looked far away, pensively. "Never mind. Back to the business at hand. I will give you some advice for the future."

Joshua closed his eyes, his face concentrating intently, his head bobbing up and down as if following some invisible current. He opened his eyes and looked at Boaz.

"My dear young warrior. You have seen more battle and death than most. Your skills and Caleb's training served you and us well. You will have a more domestic life now, but there is one more task you will need to do, one courageous act that will set the stage for a unified Israel."

"What act? What unity? Are we not unified now?"

"All I can tell you is that your act will be one of kindness. An unexpected kindness that will be placed at your feet and that will take great strength and resolve. It will go against what everyone around you will say. As for unity, we are unified now just in name, and with my passing, even that unity will disintegrate for generations to come. Only a special personality, in future days of tribulation, will have the power, the charisma, the will, to unify all of Israel. He shall come from your seed, Boaz."

Boaz stood, mouth ajar, uncomprehending.

"On to you, Ehud son of Gera. Your fighting career has not ended. One day you shall lead your tribe. The sons of Benjamin shall follow you into battle. You will need all your prodigious cunning and skill to overcome your enemy. Most of all, you will require faith. Faith in God and the instruction of Moses. Faith in His enduring love for the children of Israel, even when we sin. He will bring oppressors onto Israel whenever we stray from His path. It is as my Master Moses has foretold. You will see the cycle. The cycle of oppression, of God's salvation through a chosen one and then tranquility until we stray again. After your battle, yours will be the period of the greatest tranquility. Make sure, in your old age, to tell the next leader of this cycle. You will know who it is just as I know it is you. Give him strength, that he not forget God, when all around have."

Ehud blinked rapidly trying to absorb Joshua's prophecy.

"Who is my enemy? How can I prepare?"

"I cannot reveal more," Joshua smiled suddenly as if understanding some divine joke. "I will hint at his identity, but it will confound both of you for the rest of your lives. Your enemy, Ehud, is Boaz's future father-in-law. Your killing and defeating him will enable the monarchy of Israel to rise."

Ehud and Boaz looked at Joshua in utter confusion.

"Now don't go around killing every prospective father-in-law," Joshua added. "And don't you worry, Boaz. Vered and you shall have a long and happy life together. But I have said enough. Perhaps too much. To answer your second question, Ehud. There is no preparation. The evil shall rise slowly and unchecked. The apathy shall grow. The compulsion to worship other gods will rise again, slowly but surely. The only preparation is to remain strong, dedicated, faithful. Keep the spirit and the belief alive in others, though at times you may feel as if you are the only one. Never give up hope! Deep inside every Israelite is an unshakeable faith in God, as you've seen today. Time and foreign influences will cover it in layers of idol-worship and materialism, but one call to arms, one strike against an oppressor, will cut through all those layers and reveal the true sons of Israel inside. Now go, both of you. I have things to discuss with Pinhas and the princes before I depart this world and you are both needed in your homes."

Joshua hugged Boaz and Ehud tightly, then released them, holding back tears.

"Farewell, Boaz, Ehud. Be strong and of good courage!"

Epilogue: The Death of Joshua

From the diary of Boaz the Bethlehemite:

Joshua's death struck me hard. He had always watched over me, ever since we crossed the Jordan River all those decades ago. I felt as if the heavy weight of a runner's baton had been thrust into my hand. I felt unworthy, unprepared and unsure. Unworthy of any of his attentions, unprepared to exercise any leadership, and unsure how to do so.

Joshua died shortly after the assembly at Shechem. Many turbulent thoughts went through my mind on that cold rainy day on the peak of Mount Ephraim. There were precious few of us that came to escort Joshua's body to the lonely grave. What an embarrassment! The man who had commanded the legions of Israel, buried by a handful of his loved ones. Where were all the princes? The elders? The judges? The captains of hundreds and thousands? The people of Israel? How quickly you forget your leaders. I felt eerily that Joshua's dark prophecies were already coming to fruition.

How much I shared with others on that day, how much I told myself and how much I remembered from snatches of conversations with Joshua, I do not recall. This quill and papyrus that I use to record events are poor substitutes for the images and memories of a racing and selective mind, but they are better than naught.

Joshua reached the age of one hundred and ten, the same as his illustrious ancestor, Joseph son of Jacob. It seemed to me that Joshua and Joseph bonded more in death than in the lives that were centuries apart.

Joseph, a prince and viceroy of Egypt, had known wealth and luxury most of his life. In Egypt, Joseph had been the unofficial leader of his brothers, the future tribes.

Always aloof though, always somewhat apart. He was the first of the brothers to die, prophesying the Exodus from Egypt.

Joshua had been a prince of his tribe and the official leader of all of Israel. His whole life had been lived humbly, first as the servant of Moses, never leaving his side. Upon the death of Moses, Joshua resided in his simple campaign tent, until the conquest and division of Canaan were complete. He was a man of the people, understanding them well, relating to their pain and frustration, perhaps even better than his master Moses had. Moses had been too close to God. How could a man who spoke directly with God, whose own face radiated the Divine glory, understand or appreciate the petty concerns of mere mortals? Joshua understood. Though divinely inspired, he was a step removed, a step closer to us humans.

Joseph had died in Egypt, yet his bones had been lovingly escorted by Moses himself throughout the sojourn of the Children of Israel through the desert.

Joshua had recounted to me once how Moses delivered Joseph's bones, along with the mantle of leadership to Joshua. Moses was dressed in his old robe and carried his staff. Joshua was in battle gear, with light leather armor and a sword at his side. They stood on the dusty plains of Moab, looking into the land of Canaan from across the Jordan River. Moses entrusted the remains of Joseph to Joshua and had one of their last conversations:

"Bury him in Shechem," Moses had instructed Joshua. "Oh, that I would have the privilege," Moses moaned quietly. "Oh, that I would tread the land of our forefathers, as you are about to, Joshua."

"Is there no chance?" Joshua asked.

"No. God will not change His mind. His decision is final. I must accept it."

"Will we ever meet again?"

"In death, certainly; and at the resurrection."

"You see it? You see The End?" Joshua asked, pushing his Master on this subject one last time.

"Yes, Joshua. But I cannot reveal it. Not even to you. It is too heavy a burden, and you shall have many a burden dealing with the present."

"Will the sharing not make it lighter, even in your final hours?"

"Perhaps. But I take many things to the grave. You must be strong and of good courage, Joshua. God will be with you and guide you. You will defeat the kings of Canaan. You will see the tribes victorious and settled – each family in their portion."

"Yet I would know the future," Joshua insisted.

"I will tell you a bit of your future." Moses closed his eyes for a moment and opened them again, looking far away. "You will be buried in the allotment of your tribe, not far from your ancestor, Joseph. You will conquer all whom you attack and all the Kings of Canaan will fear you, though you will not attack all. Israel will not be worthy. I bequeath to you our stiff-necked brethren, and they shall not change. There will be the camaraderie of battle and camp life, but that will dissipate after you have inherited the land, and each family and tribe takes matters into their own hands. You must keep them united while you live. United and dedicated. Idol-worshippers will surround you. Our people will become enamored by their corrupt ways. You must remain ever vigilant. Build up the barriers as strong as you can, for eventually they will fall. But do not be saddened. Your name shall be one of the greatest in the narrative of our people. All will recall you as The Conqueror. Your story shall be a pillar of our history. I am proud of you, Joshua. Of the man you have become and the destiny you will fulfill. You have been loyal, dedicated and courageous, and those traits will serve you well in your mission."

"Is there more?" Joshua asked, sensing Moses' pause.

"There is much more. God will reveal exactly what you need at the right time. He only shows the future when it serves a purpose. And congratulations on your marriage."

"You jest, my Master? There is no one among the daughters of Israel that has agreed to marry me."

"I do not jest. There is one who is not amongst us that will join our people. She is brave and beautiful, inside and out. You will meet her quite soon and the two of you will enjoy the rest of your life together."

"Who is she? How will I know?"

"You will know her when you see her. If I close my eyes and concentrate, I can sense her aura shining like a beacon from across the river. All in its right time."

"I will miss you greatly."

"I shall miss you as well. But never doubt yourself or that this is your task. It has been decreed from heaven. If I have been compared to the sun, then you are the moon and after you, many stars shall follow until the moon rises again."

"I don't understand."

"It is not our task to understand, merely to accept."

"You understand."

"I am in a unique position that will not be repeated in human history."

"Is it better to understand?"

"It is both consoling and painful at the same time."

"You speak in riddles."

"I speak the truth, which is often a riddle that only time and experience will solve."

"I am ready then," Joshua stated.

"Of course you are." Moses and Joshua embraced, tears streaming down both their faces. Moses' tears reached his long snow-white beard, while Joshua's tears touched his own light blond beard.

So ended the account that I recall from Joshua.

*

There was a period of great tranquility after Joshua died. It lasted until the elders of that generation passed away. Slowly, rumors of Moabite strength emerged. Canaanite cities that Joshua had not attacked exhibited greater strength, greater independence. Some Canaanite cities, who had previously demonstrated their subservience by paying a yearly tax to Israelite tribes, now stopped doing so. With the growing strength of the idol-worshippers around us, more of our people conducted business with them. "What's wrong with their money?" many would argue.

Israelites started buying products from the idol-worshippers: beautiful Philistine pottery and expert metalworking, distinctive Moabite rugs and fancy Ammonite garments. Finally, Israelites started doing business with Canaanites. "They are right here," the merchants explained. "Why do I need to go to the coast or cross the Jordan to get my goods? The fabrics from Megiddo are just as good – and cheaper!"

Israelite merchants met with their Canaanite counterparts in their taverns, though still careful not to drink their wines. Mead, however, they consumed together with them freely: "No one uses mead for idol libations. A friendly drink or two won't hurt."

Judges protested the growing friendship with Canaanites to no avail.

I knew that the situation had sunk into troublesome waters when I heard a young Judean farmhand curse as he walked into Bethlehem with a bull in tow: "By Baal, you lazy animal! I'll have you slaughtered for your meat if you don't move!"

Disturbed, I approached the young man.

"What did you say?"

"Nothing, sir," the young man replied, startled. "I was just berating my bull for moving slowly. He is a strong animal. Are you interested? He can plow an entire field in half a day."

"Did you just swear in the name of a false god?" I pressed.

"What? That? It's just an expression. Everyone in my village says it."

"Do you realize that it is prohibited? That the Law of Moses, that God himself commanded us not to use the names of the false gods?"

"Really? I'm sorry. I meant no harm. Have a good day."

The young man moved along as quickly as he could. I wasn't sure if he was embarrassed or just uncomfortable under my glare.

How quickly they forget! Joshua is gone just a handful of years and already the next generation is weak in the Law of Moses. Where are the Levites? Were they not charged with teaching the Law? But I digress. I wanted to write about Joshua. To remember him and what he accomplished, rather than harp on how matters worsened in the years that followed his death.

All of the prophecies regarding Joshua were fulfilled. He was buried not far from Joseph. He married the beautiful Rahav of Jericho and lived happily with her until the end of his days. He vanquished all that came in his path. The Kings of Canaan trembled at the mention of his name. Each of the twelve tribes was settled in their inheritance. The Levite cities and cities of refuge were established. The Children of Israel dwelt in the land promised to our forefathers. The land promised at the Exodus from Egypt. The land promised at Mount Sinai. The land promised throughout the forty years of desert wandering. The Children of Israel dwelt in the land in peace and security, prosperous and comfortable. Israel succeeded in abandoning the miraculous existence of the desert, the manna, the magical well, the protective clouds, the clothing that never wore out. We moved to an existence of working the land. Of waiting for the ground to give birth to its produce. Of gathering the sheaves and grinding the wheat. Of mixing and kneading and baking the dough. Of seeding the ground and rotating the crops. Of waiting upon the right fruit in the right season. Grapes, olives, figs, pomegranates, dates – a land blessed with abundance. Cows and goats and sheep roamed throughout our land.

Once, I chanced upon a particularly productive cow on the western bank of the Jordan River, where palm trees grow wild. It was at the crack of dawn when the sleepy farmer went to milk his cow. He was not paying attention as the milk from the cow overflowed his wooden pail. The milk trickled down the hill and flowed over ripe dates that had fallen from a palm tree. The milk mingled with the honey oozing from the dates. Then I knew we were indeed in a land flowing with milk and honey. As Moses had promised and Joshua fulfilled. We shall ever remember you, Joshua, Conqueror, Leader, Servant of God, Father, Friend.

Acknowledgements

This book is the product of many years of dreaming and of many hands helping, inspiring, pleading and pushing along the way. Some of the people who come to mind, but not nearly all include:

To my parents, who transmitted their love of Tanach (Bible) to me at an early age.

To all of my teachers, from kindergarten through graduate school and beyond.

To my wife, Tamara, who always believed.

To my kids to whom this book is dedicated. An author couldn't ask for better fans.

To my father-in-law, Josef Tocker, for his constant and fanstastic graphical support and beautiful cover design.

To Rachel Nachmani, for the original, versatile, hand-drawn map of Canaan.

To Dr. Avi Shmidman, for his overnight editing of the stories as I sent them out to my weekly email list.

To Rabbi Joshua Amaru, who kept me honest on the biblical details.

To Dr. Yael Ziegler, for her taking the time to share with me her amazing grasp of the biblical narrative.

To my mother, Nira Spitz, for her excellent line-editing.

To Judy Labensohn for her writing coaching and to Elana Greenfield for her writing workshop. Some of the excercises from the workshop made it into the manuscript!

To Julie Grey, scriptmaster extraordinaire, for her fanstastic story editing and support.

And to everyone else who encouraged me, challenged me and believed I could do it.

A special thanks to those who sponsored my book:

Adam Steiner
Adriana y Jacky
Ahuva M
Alberto Buszkaniec
Alfredo Lempert
Andrés Mokobocki
Carlos A. Alarcon
Danny Ascher & Flia.
David Tendler
Egbert Pijfers
Flia. Mitelman
Gad Dishi
GF
Ilan Rosenthal
Ilana & Néstor Gandelman
Jeremy and Rocky Brody
Jorge Lempert
Kirk & Mindy Spencer
Lara & Arel Weisberg and Family
Levi & Miriam Grunhaus
Lior and Drora Arussy
L"N Shlomo ben Itzjak
Marc Lustig and Deborah Geller
Marcos Siennicki
Michael Trachtenberg
Mignone and Ezra Rosenfeld
Mitchell Leifer
Nick Lowenstein
Samy Cañas
Shaia June ben Moshe Zalmen
Simon Lamstein & family
SKM
Tirtza
Vivienne Glaser
Wolf and Betty Gruenberg
Yaron and Michelle Rosenthal
Yehudah Wein

About the Author

Ben-Tzion Spitz is the current Chief Rabbi of Uruguay. He is the author of a blog, Torah Shorts (at ben-tzion.com), where he has published dozens of biblical fiction stories and biblical analysis based on ancient, medieval and contemporary sources. He has been exploring and researching biblical stories and archeological findings for over two decades.

Made in the USA
Charleston, SC
29 August 2014